# It's Never Too Late

*Books by Vernon Coleman*

The Medicine Men (1975)
Paper Doctors (1976)
Everything You Want To Know About Ageing (1976)
Stress Control (1978)
The Home Pharmacy (1980)
Aspirin or Ambulance (1980)
Face Values (1981)
Guilt (1982)
The Good Medicine Guide (1982)
Stress And Your Stomach (1983)
Bodypower (1983)
An A to Z Of Women's Problems (1984)
Bodysense (1984)
Taking Care Of Your Skin (1984)
A Guide to Child Health (1984)
Life Without Tranquillisers (1985)
Diabetes (1985)
Arthritis (1985)
Eczema and Dermatitis (1985)
The Story Of Medicine (1985, 1998)
Natural Pain Control (1986)
Mindpower (1986)
Addicts and Addictions (1986)
Dr Vernon Coleman's Guide To Alternative Medicine (1988)
Stress Management Techniques (1988)
Overcoming Stress (1988)
Know Yourself (1988)
The Health Scandal (1988)
The 20 Minute Health Check (1989)
Sex For Everyone (1989)
Mind Over Body (1989)
Eat Green Lose Weight (1990)
Why Animal Experiments Must Stop (1991)
The Drugs Myth (1992)
How To Overcome Toxic Stress (1991)
Why Doctors Do More Harm Than Good (1993)
Stress and Relaxation (1993)
Complete Guide To Sex (1993)
How to Conquer Backache (1993)
How to Conquer Arthritis (1993)
Betrayal of Trust (1994)
Know Your Drugs (1994, 1997)

Food for Thought (1994)
The Traditional Home Doctor (1994)
I Hope Your Penis Shrivels Up (1994)
People Watching (1995)
Relief from IBS (1995)
The Parent's Handbook (1995)
Oral Sex: Bad Taste And Hard To Swallow? (1995)
Why Is Pubic Hair Curly? (1995)
Men in Dresses (1996)
Power over Cancer (1996)
Crossdressing (1996)
How To Get The Best Out Of Prescription Drugs (1996)
How To Get The Best Out of Alternative Medicine (1996)
How To Conquer Arthritis (1996)
High Blood Pressure (1996)
How To Stop Your Doctor Killing You (1996)
Fighting For Animals (1996)
Alice and Other Friends (1996)
Dr Coleman's Fast Action Health Secrets (1997)
Dr Vernon Coleman's Guide to Vitamins and Minerals (1997)
Spiritpower (1997)
Other People's Problems (1998)
How To Publish Your Own Book (1999)
How To Relax and Overcome Stress (1999)
Animal Rights – Human Wrongs (1999)
Superbody (1999)
The 101 Sexiest, Craziest, Most Outrageous Agony Column
      Questions (and Answers) of All Time (1999)
Strange But True (2000)
Food For Thought [revised edition] (2000)
Daily Inspirations (2000)
Stomach Problems: Relief At Last (2001)
How To Overcome Guilt (2001)


### *reports*

Prostate Trouble (2000)
Vitamins and Minerals (2000)
How To Campaign (2000)
Genetic Engineering (2000)
Osteoporosis (2000)
Vaccines (2000)
Alternative Medicine (2000)

## novels

The Village Cricket Tour (1990)
The Bilbury Chronicles (1992)
Bilbury Grange (1993)
Mrs Caldicot's Cabbage War (1993)
Bilbury Revels (1994)
Deadline (1994)
The Man Who Inherited a Golf Course (1995)
Bilbury Country (1996)
Second Innings (1999)
Around the Wicket (2000)

## short stories

Bilbury Pie (1995)

## on cricket

Thomas Winsden's Cricketing Almanack (1983)
Diary Of A Cricket Lover (1984)

## as Edward Vernon

Practice Makes Perfect (1977)
Practise What You Preach (1978)
Getting Into Practice (1979)
Aphrodisiacs – An Owner's Manual (1983)
Aphrodisiacs – An Owner's Manual (Turbo Edition) (1984)
The Complete Guide To Life (1984)

## as Marc Charbonnier

Tunnel (novel 1980)

## with Alice

Alice's Diary (1989)
Alice's Adventures (1992)

## with Dr Alan C Turin

No More Headaches (1981)

# It's Never
# Too Late

# Vernon Coleman

**Chilton Designs**

Published by Chilton Designs, Publishing House, Trinity Place, Barnstaple, Devon EX32 9HJ, England

ISBN: 1 898146 45 4

A catalogue record for this book is available from the British Library.

Printed by J.W. Arrowsmith Ltd, Bristol

Dedicated to
Donna Antoinette Coleman, my beautiful Welsh Princess

## Note

All characters, organisations, businesses and places in this publication are fictitious, and any resemblance to real persons,
living or dead, is purely coincidental.

# ~ **Chapter One** ~

A podgy man with lank, greasy hair and oily hands picked up the video recorder and examined it closely as though he had never seen anything like it before.

'Does it work?'

'Yes.'

He balanced the video recorder on one hand, as though trying to guess its weight, and looked up at me. He had tiny pale eyes in a large pale face. He was, I felt certain, the neighbour whose car had been sitting on bricks in his driveway for several months. He wore dirty blue jeans and a grubby T-shirt. The faded face of a miserable-looking, long dead rock star stared out at me from the middle of the podgy man's chest.

'How much do you want for it?' He had a shifty, slightly nervous manner. He looked untrustworthy and would have made a poor salesman.

'There's a price on it,' I said, pointing to the sticky label fixed to the top of the recorder.

'£50?' he said, pulling a face.

'Yes.'

'It's not worth that.'

'It's less than six months old. It cost me £300.'

'I'll give you a tenner for it.'

'It's worth more than that.'

'A tenner. That's all I'll pay.' Still holding the video recorder on the palm of one hand he reached into the back
pocket of his oil-stained jeans and pulled out a thin leather
wallet. He flicked open the wallet, put it on top of the video
recorder and, with some considerable difficulty, extracted a
ten pound note. His fingers were podgy and clumsy. At last
he held the note out towards me.

'Sorry,' I said, shaking my head. 'I think it's worth more
than that.'

A woman I'd never seen before rudely pushed in between us. 'How much do you want for these?' she demanded,
thrusting a parcel of gardening books under my nose.

I looked at the label fixed to the uppermost book. '£5.'

The woman pushed the books into my arms, took a
small red plastic purse out of her handbag and counted out
£5 in small change. She poured the coins into my hand. I
put them into my back trouser pocket and handed her the
books. Suddenly, my world seemed to be full of people who
couldn't read price labels.

'Selling up, Tony?' said a voice I recognised. I turned
round and saw Jack Burrows, a man I'd worked with for the
past seven years. Jack was two years younger than me. At five
foot ten he was six inches shorter than me, but what he lacked
in height he more than made up for in weight. He was surprisingly proud of having a waist measurement that matched
and increased with his age. Two months ago we had both
had company medicals and so I knew that at twenty five stones
he weighed exactly twice as much as me. Jack, a friendly,
chatty sort of fellow who had been given early retirement the
same day as I had, was with his wife, Ethel, a slight, short,
rather sour-faced woman who firmly believed that the world
was constantly conspiring against her – she even took bad
weather personally. They lived two streets away and made

an odd couple. She was an Evangelical Christian who regarded her role on this earth as a saviour of sinners and authorised redeemer of souls. Jack was a self-confessed hedonist; left to his own devices he would have devoted as much of
his life as possible to the pursuit of fun. Despite his size and
unromantic appearance he was renowned, within the firm
where we had both worked, as a skirt chaser. In his teens and
early twenties he had been lead singer with a band called
Throbbie Tinsel and the Twinkletones (he had been Throbbie
Tinsel) and although the group had been denied commercial
success (largely, it has to be said, through a lack of natural
talent and musical ability) he had much enjoyed the best-
known peripheral advantage associated with the music business. He still had undimmed vigour in that direction, and
although his notions were now only very rarely converted
into reality, the continued drive he enjoyed meant that he
regarded sexual harassment as an essential part of his job
description. It was once said of him (by a weary typing pool
stalwart) that it was his nature to end every sentence with a
proposition.

'I really don't need any of this stuff,' I replied. 'Selling
the house seems a good opportunity to make a fresh start.'

'Where are you going?' asked Jack.

I shrugged. 'I don't know,' I told him. 'I thought I'd
take a short holiday first and then decide. What about you?'

'I thought I'd get an allotment and join the bowls club,'
said Jack. 'There are two allotments free. Do you want me to
book the other one for you?'

I shook my head. 'No thanks.' I wasn't quite ready for
the Darby and Joan club. I would be 56 on my next birthday.
It felt like people expected me to sit down and wait to die.
But I wasn't ready for that just yet.

'Do you have any kitchen equipment?' asked Ethel.

'I'm afraid most of it's gone,' I told her. 'Whatever's

*13*

left should be over there.' I pointed to a corner of the garage. 'I can see some pots and pans there,' I said. 'And a kettle. Stuff like that. I think my toaster is still there. There doesn't seem to be much of a market for second hand toasters.'

'Thank you, very much,' said Ethel, scurrying off towards the pots and pans. Jack, looking embarrassed, gave me a slight half-hearted smile and then hurried off after his wife. As he caught up with her I heard her comment. 'He'll be back in six months,' she said. 'You mark my words. Wherever he goes, in six months he'll be back with his tail between his legs. It's too late for him to start again.' She didn't even try to make sure I didn't hear her.

My conversation with Jack and Ethel had depressed me and the parting comment which I had overheard had depressed me even more. I decided to ring a travel agency. I had one of those clever telephones that can be used anywhere within a fifty yard radius of the handset. I went into the house, collected the telephone, looked up a number in the telephone directory and went back outside again, dialling as I walked. I had a feeling that if I didn't keep an eye on my customers one of them would probably walk off with the garage.

'Thank you for calling,' said an annoyingly cheerful woman with a mid transatlantic accent and a breezy manner that made me wish I hadn't bothered. She paused for half a second or so, just long enough to fool me into believing that she was a real person. She wasn't. 'If you have a complaint about your hotel or your airline please press one and wait to be connected to one of our highly trained specialist vacation consultants.'

'I'll give you £12 for it,' said the podgy man. He pulled two pound coins out of his trouser pocket and added them to the £10 pound note on top of the video recorder. I shook my head, turned and started to walk away from him. Apart from the clothes and treasured books I had crammed into the two suitcases now standing in my bedroom my remaining worldly possessions lay scattered around on the grass and in the garage. I watched a boy of 17 or 18 slyly slide a silver plated photograph frame inside his leather jacket. If he thought it was valuable he would be disappointed. The silver plating was thinner than the foil they wrap around chocolates. I didn't care enough to say anything.

The woman with the transatlantic voice was just getting into her stride. 'If you are concerned about accidents and illness on holiday and would like to speak to one of our specialist insurance consultants, please press two,' she said. My enthusiasm for travel was beginning to wane.

Having a garage sale had seemed a good idea. I had a house full of possessions I no longer needed. Converting them into cash would be a great help. The house was sold and the buyer's cheque would pay off the mortgage, the estate agents and the lawyers and leave me with a small sum – probably around £5,000. I had arranged for a local junk shop owner to come and clear out my furniture. He had paid me just £100 (in crumpled, used notes) for a double bed and a single bed, two wardrobes, a dining table, a three piece suite (complete with washable covers), gas cooker, fridge and washing machine.

'If you have booked a holiday and your tickets haven't arrived, please press three,' continued the cheery spokeswoman. I had a vision of rows of consultant advisors crouched down in concrete bunkers, hiding away from dissatisfied and anxious customers, all with telephones clamped to their ears.

I looked around the slowly diminishing display of clutter and wondered where it had all come from. I had thought that selling my worldly goods might be painful. But it wasn't. It was one of the most cathartic and liberating experiences

I'd ever had. As I stood there I accepted £2 for my ironing board and iron, £4 for a cardboard box full of pots and pans and £2.50 for two plastic garden chairs. I put the coins in my pockets.

'I'll go to £15,' said the podgy man with the oily hands. 'That's my best offer.'

For a brief moment I was tempted to take the video recorder and smash it onto the driveway. But I didn't. I looked around and felt a great surge of sadness. This had been my world. The accumulated detritus of how many years?

'Take it,' I said, flatly.

'...press four,' said the woman with the transatlantic voice. I'd missed her instruction and I didn't have the enthusiasm to start again.

The podgy man held out a £10 note, four pound coins and a small collection of silver coins.

I held up a hand, palm out, to make it clear that I didn't want his money. 'Just take the damned thing,' I said, shaking my head.

Puzzled, confused, he looked at me. Once again he held out the note and the coins.

I headed for the front door, breaking the connection with the travel agency and taking out my key. I looked back over my shoulder. 'Just take it,' I repeated, 'I don't want the money.' I decided to call in at a travel agency in the High Street. The podgy man stared at me as though I had gone mad. Then, slowly, a new look appeared on his face. It was not happiness, pleasure or gratefulness. And then I realised that what I saw on his face was simple greed. He stuffed his money back into his trouser pocket and waddled away before I could change my mind.

I unlocked the front door and half stepped into the now empty house. And then I paused on the front step and turned. I just wanted to be gone; to be somewhere else. 'You can take the rest,' I said to the small crowd of neighbours collected like vultures around the carcass of my previous existence.

There was a brief pause. Then one or two looked up at me, wondering if what they had heard was truly what I had said. Conscious of their lack of belief I repeated the words. 'There's no need to pay,' I added, in explanation. 'Just take it all away.'

The squabbling began almost immediately. Hands grabbing at small ornaments, mirrors, a radio, a kettle, a couple of old prints in wooden frames, parcels of books, piles of neatly washed and ironed but unwanted clothing. No one said anything to me. No 'thank you's'. I wasn't surprised. They probably felt as little for me as I felt for them. I had lived with them as neighbours for seven years but there is more to togetherness and friendship than merely living in close proximity. Jack and Ethel hurried past, their arms full of kitchen equipment. Jack looked even more embarrassed than before. He actually blushed. As they walked away Jack leant towards his wife. 'He'll regret not taking that allotment,' he whispered.

'Can we take this?' asked a skinny, greasy-haired youth who had followed me to the house.

I looked at him, genuinely puzzled. I didn't know what he was talking about. I shared my bewilderment with him.

'This,' he said, poking a finger at the door jamb.

'You can't have the door!' I warned him.

'No, not the door' replied the youth, as though speaking to an imbecile. 'The bell.' He pressed the door bell to show what he was talking about.

I had heard of this sort of thing happening from friends. One man told me that friends of his who bought a huge house in the country took possession to discover that the previous owners had, when they had left rather more suddenly than had been expected, banked his cheque and then taken all the skirting boards and light fittings with them. Much to my friend's annoyance they had even rolled up, and taken away with them, the entire front lawn. Another friend bought a very expensive house and then, while on a final tour of the property, found himself being coerced into making additional cash payments to pay for the TV aerial and the remaining oil in the tank in the garden.

'The door bell?' He nodded. 'You want to sell the door bell?'

'No.'

I went into the house and fetched my two suitcases. When I came out the squabbling had become more fierce. Half a dozen neighbours were already hurrying home, their new acquisitions clutched to their bosoms like looted gold. They were, I guessed, anxious to stash their gains at home as quickly as possible so that they could return for another armful. Two women were pulling at a small rug which I had inherited from an aunt; one of them was yelling obscenities at the other. A man and a woman were arguing over a pile of bed linen.

Feeling like an alien, I locked the front door, put my key through the letter box. For the first time in my life I didn't know where I was going. I didn't even know where I was going to sleep that night. The only thing I knew for certain was that I wouldn't miss not having the allotment.

Two months earlier I had lost a job I didn't like and hadn't liked for longer than I cared to remember. I had been both in charge of the customer relations department and editor of the company newsletter. The job in the customer relations department might have been worthwhile if anyone else working for the company had given a damn for customers or for the products we made. And the job as editor of the company newsletter might have been rewarding if my sole instructions had not been to produce a quarterly freesheet which included at least one photograph of the chairman and gave offence to absolutely no one – particularly the chairman's wife, a woman whose personal collection of prejudices was so extensive even with a four drawer filing cabinet devoted to them I found it difficult to keep track of them all. There is little point, or pleasure, in producing a publication which is written to give offence to no one but there is no point, and possibly even less pleasure, in producing a publication which is designed to pander to the whims of a woman who believes that being poor should be made a criminal offence.

My boss, for whom I had no respect, had called me into his office one Friday evening, given me my cards and a cheque and told me not to come in the following Monday. There had been no explanation, though the office gossip was that the company had been taken over by a multinational corporation, which had even less need for a customer relations department than we had, and that the chairman (and his fearsome wife) were to be given boats full of money and floated off into a sunset full of luxurious whingeing.

At the age of 55 I knew I had little or no chance of ever getting another job. It took me a while to realise that my career had ended almost before it had begun. At sixteen I had been a cub reporter on a local newspaper. I had rejected school and university for the prospect of making my way in the real world. I dreamt of becoming a feared and fearless investigative reporter – exposing the corrupt, the dishonest and the uncaring. It hadn't quite turned out like that. I had been fired for daring to expose the crooked machinations of a group of local businessmen. It had been a good story and the editor had been delighted. His delight had disappeared when it turned out that the three businessmen concerned were the newspaper's biggest advertisers. The exposé had never appeared in print. The police investigation had been halted before it had really started. And two weeks later I'd been fired. No apology, no explanation, no glowing reference from a guilt ridden editor. I had long since given up wondering what might have been. Instead of a career in journalism I'd spent the best years of my life working in public relations; a stagnant, leech-infested backwater of the profession I had wanted to join since I'd been a teenager.

But, I tried to convince myself that it wasn't all bad. I had no ties and no responsibilities. I had a little money in the bank and so I knew I wouldn't be a candidate for the poor house. In fact after an evening spent with a calculator and a notepad I had come to the conclusion that if I was careful I would be able to get by for a while without working. I had received £40,000 when I had been made redundant and I had around £5,000 due from the sale of the house. I wouldn't have anywhere to live but I certainly wouldn't starve to death for a while.

It had been two years since my wife had left me. She had moved in with a silken-tongued insurance salesman who wore imitation silk suits, tucked his cloven hooves into Italian shoes and drove a small red saloon with a sexy looking but pointless spoiler fitted to the boot lid. There had been no explanation on that occasion either. 'You will remember me if you ever come into a lot of money, won't you?' were my wife's parting words. She always had been a woman who liked to have her own cake and eat someone else's. When the divorce had come through I had made a mental note to send her a postcard if I ever won the lottery. Just to let her know.

We had married after a whirlwind two week romance and regretted the impulse at leisure. She had, by her own admission, been unfaithful to me on our wedding day and at regular intervals thereafter. I have no doubt that she had her good points. The problem was that although we had been married for eighteen years I hadn't been with her long enough to find them. Maybe if she'd stayed with me for another decade or two I'd have spotted the good side to her character. She had constantly changing and always unreachable (and unreasonable) expectations and suffered each new disappointment in pained silence and with unspoken reproval. It wasn't until we had been married three months that I realised that she reminded me of my mother.

I had had just two dates since my divorce. Both had been unmitigated disasters. The first woman had, with commendable and perhaps unwise honesty, bluntly told me, on our first date, that she loathed men but hated her job and wanted to find a man to keep her in the sort of comfort she had often dreamt about but never yet experienced. The second, a plump platinum blonde ten years younger than me, had told me that she liked one night stands and wanted simple, uncomplicated sex rather than a relationship. I was, she told me with some pride, her fourth date of the week. It had been a Wednesday. I felt old-fashioned trying to explain to her that I was looking for something a little more than the opportunity to give her an excuse to carve another notch in her bedpost. I don't think she could really believe it when, in the best tradition of Sunday newspaper reporters, I made my excuses and left her sitting on her faded green velour sofa, blouse unbuttoned and micro skirt mid-thigh.

Both incidents had left me numb for some time afterwards.

I suppose I should have cared about my job and my ex-wife but somehow I didn't. I had been more genuinely upset when the cat had died three weeks ago. She had been fifteen years old and when she died I realised that I had for years felt closer to her than to any other living creature.

My life had become grey and pointless. There was no value and no significance in anything I did. I had started collecting coupons entitling me to purchase decaffeinated coffee and paper handkerchiefs at a small discount to the normal retail price. I actually found myself feeling a frisson of satisfaction when I received a letter from a credit card company telling me how much they would value my custom. I knew there had to be more to life than putting on a clean shirt every day and making sure that the lawn was cut regularly.

I wanted something better.

I didn't know what I wanted or where to find it. I was leaving simply because I knew I had to leave, not because I had somewhere better to go.

# ~ Chapter Two ~

At the travel agency the only assistant who was free looked about sixteen. She had short blonde hair and, in an attempt to make herself look more worldly and sophisticated, she had plastered herself with considerably too much make-up. The irony, which had doubtless escaped her was that she was young enough to have perfect skin and to not need any make-up at all. I doubt if she realised that women only ever started using cosmetics so that they could look as natural and as attractive as she probably would have been had she not been wearing any make-up. She was dressed in a brown jacket and green skirt that matched the clothes worn by the girls sitting either side of her.

'How can I help you?' the young assistant asked, confident and smiling. The overall effect was very slightly spoilt by the fact that she had copious amounts of lipstick on her teeth. She had a white name badge pinned to her jacket lapel and in large printed letters the badge announced to the world that her name was Linda.

I put my suitcases down, unbuttoned my coat and sat down on a chromium plated chair that was every bit as uncomfortable as it looked. 'Do you have any last minute holidays?' I asked.

'When can you go?' asked the girl, brightly. She played with a cheap plastic pen that had the name of an airline printed on the side of it and beamed at me.

'Today,' I replied. I nodded to the suitcases. 'I'm packed and ready to go. I'd like to travel today.'

'Oh,' said Linda, who seemed slightly taken aback by this. 'That's wonderful!' she continued, recovering her composure with commendable speed and greeting my announcement with tremendous enthusiasm. She smiled at me. She increased the speed with which she turned the pen up and down.

'Have you got anywhere in mind?' she asked. Without putting the pen down she started tapping on the keyboard in front of her.

I shook my head.

'You have a passport?'

I patted my jacket pocket.

'Well, let's take a look at what's on offer!' said Linda. She typed with just two fingers and pecked at the keys cautiously, as though anxious not to damage her immaculate, sky blue nail varnish. The nail varnish didn't go terribly well with the uniform. 'Two weeks in Tunisia. Flying from Manchester. A week in Benidorm. Flying from Birmingham. Two weeks in Malta. That's flying from Luton. Five days in Paris, travelling by train from Waterloo. A week in Marbella. Flying from Gatwick...' She was getting into her stride and clearly had more offers to make.

I had thought it would be difficult to choose. It wasn't. 'Paris,' I said, instinctively. I paused and thought for a moment. I'd never been to Paris and I've always liked trains. I have never been particularly fond of the French, who I have always regarded as an untrustworthy lot, but for as long as I can remember I have loved French architecture and French cooking.

'It's a real bargain!' she said. 'Just £75 for train fares and hotel, including half board at your hotel and all taxes. You also get a free map, a complimentary bus trip around Paris at night, a discount voucher for a shop selling perfume and wedding dresses and a voucher for a free lunchtime pizza at a restaurant in Montmartre.'

'What sort of hotel is it?' I asked her, not having any need that I knew of for a voucher entitling me to a discount on a wedding dress.

'It's got two stars and it's on the Left Bank,' Linda replied. 'It's in the student quarter.'

'Oh,' I said, my enthusiasm suddenly melting. 'That sounds a bit worrying. I'm a bit old to be mixing with students.'

'Oh don't worry about that!' said the girl. She smiled at me reassuringly. 'You'll love it. There are plenty of cheap cafés and restaurants. And you're just a short walk away from Notre Dame and the Seine.' She reached forward and turned the computer monitor round so that by leaning across the desk I could read what was written on it. The hotel's name was on the screen together with a small map. The descriptive comment underneath a photograph of a bedroom in the hotel included the very words Linda had used when describing the area to me.

'OK,' I said. 'I'll take it.' I took out my wallet, removed a credit card and handed it across the desk. 'What time does the train leave?'

Linda, looking very serious and professional, checked her computer and looked at her watch. 'You've got plenty of time,' she said. 'What's your name please?'

'Davison,' I replied. 'Tony Davison.'

She smiled and together we filled in a long and complicated form.

When Linda had found out more or less everything

there was to find out about me (I assumed that most of the questions were aimed more at aiding some future marketing campaign rather than providing information required for providing me with a ticket, and I gave my old address with a smile knowing that someone else would have the joy of throwing away the junk mail inspired by my trip) she handed me a bulky cardboard envelope containing return train tickets, a voucher for the hotel, my free map, my ticket for my complimentary bus trip, a discount voucher entitling me to purchase perfume and wedding dresses at a discount, and a voucher offering me a free pizza but warning me that I would have to pay for my drinks and additional toppings myself. The voucher promising me a free pizza was bulkier than anything else. 'Would you like to take out one of our travel insurance policies?' she asked. 'We recommend them to all our clients. It covers illness, accidental damage to yourself or your belongings, loss of luggage or money and covers you for up to £10,000,000 should you be held responsible for accidental damage to a third party or their belongings.'

'No thanks,' I said, embracing recklessness with gusto. I returned my credit card to my wallet, put the bulky cardboard envelope into my coat pocket, picked up my suitcases, thanked her and set off for Paris.

The train to London was surprisingly empty. I put my suitcases into the overhead locker and pulled out a battered P.G. Wodehouse novel – one of the few books I'd kept. I'd read it a couple of times before but it was the sort of book you could read time and time again. And since I'd read it before I found it reassuring and comforting to know in advance that I would enjoy it. Renewing a relationship with a previously loved book has all the advantages and none of the disadvantages of renewing a relationship with a previously loved acquaintance.

At the next stop a middle aged couple got onto the

train. He was short and balding and wore a green sports jacket, brown cavalry twill trousers, a heather mixture tweed shirt and a brown knitted tie. She wore a blue suit and a white blouse and had a double string of pearls around her neck and matching clip on pearl earrings.

I helped the man drag their luggage onto the train and then stow it in various places around the carriage (they had four large suitcases and two canvas bags with them but the woman, who was carrying a small dark blue leather handbag, did absolutely nothing to help) and then the trouble started.

'I thought I told you to book seats facing the engine,' the woman said to her husband, checking their tickets.

I thought it safe to assume that they were married to one another since she spoke to him as an irritable school teacher might address an unruly five year old child and this is something which I have never seen outside marriage.

'I did, dear,' said the husband. He sounded nervous. He peered at the tickets and then at the reservation slips on the backs of their seats. The seats which had been reserved for them were facing away from the engine.

'Well, you can't have done,' snapped the woman. 'The railway people wouldn't have made a mistake.'

I do not normally interfere in other people's arguments. But I decided to make this an exception.

'There's plenty of room,' I pointed out, waving a hand around the deserted carriage. We were the only three people in the carriage. 'Why not just sit in the seats you want?'

'Certainly not,' said the woman, turning her head slightly to address me. 'We paid to reserve our seats. And I want reserved seats.' She had the thinnest lips I'd ever seen in my life. She wasn't my wife but she frightened me. I felt deeply sorry for her husband. I also felt great admiration for him. If she had been my wife I would have either gone mad or killed her years earlier.

'They don't charge to reserve the seats, dear,' said the husband nervously.

'Don't be stupid, Harold,' said the woman. 'Of course they charge.'

I found myself wondering exactly how I would have killed her. Poison? An axe? Maybe, I thought, I would have beaten her over the head with a good, old-fashioned blunt instrument. Poison would have been far too quick and would have provided far too little satisfaction.

'Get the guard,' said the woman. The train jerked a little and to avoid falling down the woman had to hang onto the back of an empty seat. She still wouldn't sit down.

'Why don't you sit down, dear,' suggested Harold. 'While I sort things out.'

'I'm not sitting down until someone sorts out our reservations,' said the woman. 'This is quite unacceptable. I want the seats we booked.'

'Which seats did you want?' I asked.

'Those two there,' said the woman, nodding towards the two seats opposite the two that had been reserved for them.

'That's easy,' I said. I got up, picked out the two reservation slips and put them onto the backs of the two seats she wanted.

'You can't do that!' said the woman, both horrified and indignant.

'I just did.'

'But it's illegal!'

'But now you have the correct seats,' I said. 'Since no one was sitting in them no one will object. And unless you tell them the railway people won't know either.'

'Call the guard!' cried the woman, addressing her husband. 'What this man did was illegal! He could be arrested. And since we witnessed him committing a crime he's made us criminals too.'

'Why don't you sit down, dear?' asked Harold.

'I don't think they send people to prison for sitting in the wrong seats,' I told her. 'Not for a first offence anyway.'

'They aren't the wrong seats!' said the woman. 'Those are the seats we reserved.'

'Then no one can object if you sit in them,' I pointed out.

The woman refused to listen to me. No guard came or ticket collector appeared and she and her husband stood for the two hour trip to Paddington station. It occurred to me that only the English could possibly take such satisfaction from behaving in such a pointlessly self-destructive way.

From Paddington I took a taxi across to Waterloo where I caught the Eurostar train to Paris.

It had been a few years since I'd been abroad. Some things weren't going to be easy. For example, I had forgotten to change any sterling and so had no French currency with me. I thought this might prove to be something of a disadvantage. But not everything was bleak. I rather thought I could probably remember just enough of the French language to enable me to order a cup of coffee. I might not be able to pay for it. But I would probably be able to order it.

## ~ Chapter Three ~

I arrived at the Gare du Nord just as it was getting dark. I took a taxi to my hotel (getting round my inability to speak the language by showing the driver the booking slip from the travel agency) and long before I got there I was in love with the bright lights, the bustle and the exciting looking cafés. Some streets seemed to contain little more than row after row of cafés. Instinctively I knew that Paris was a woman and instinctively I also knew that I was desperately, permanently, irrevocably in love with her.

I really don't know what it was about the place but from the moment I arrived I felt relaxed, at peace and at ease. I was, of course, a stranger. I didn't speak the language and I didn't know my way around the city. But in some inexplicable way I felt happier and more content there than I had ever felt anywhere else. Paris might not be better than anywhere else but it was different to anything I'd ever known before and the difference invigorated me and made me feel younger, more alert and more alive. Maybe all those writers and artists who have lived there have given the place a welcoming soul.

Of course, a cynic would have probably argued that the initial feeling of being relaxed might have been due, in part at least, to the fact that I had left behind all my troubles and I had no horrid job or empty house to go back to. But I was in no mood to listen to such nonsense and I certainly didn't think so. I was happy to give Paris all the credit for the way I felt.

After I had checked in at my hotel (it was much smaller and less imposing than the photograph in the travel agents brochure had suggested but it was also far more romantic and had far more character) I left my suitcases on the small, slightly rickety wooden chair by the side of the double bed, changed some sterling notes into French francs at the hotel and set off to see what Paris could offer me in the way of food and company.

The food I found quickly enough. I had a plateful of excellent chips and a large and tasty salad at a café no more than a hundred yards from the hotel. Before deciding where to eat I had stood on the pavement outside the hotel and counted no less than eight cafés and restaurants. I couldn't help wondering if the French ever ate at home.

The company took a little longer to find.

After eating I studied the small free map which the travel agent had given me with my tickets and decided to head north towards the river Seine. The travel agent had, after all, promised that the river and the hotel were pretty close.

I walked, or rather, strolled, for just over a quarter of an hour. To begin with I tried to count the cafés I passed but when I reached three figures I gave up. I came from a town where there were no more than two or three places where people could eat out. Back in my part of England ordinary people simply didn't eat out unless there was some very special reason – a birthday, an anniversary, a celebration, an apology – but it was clear that the Parisians regarded eating out as a fundamental part of life.

Eventually, I found myself leaning on a stone parapet

staring down into the swirling waters of the world's most romantic river. Just a few hundred yards away I could see the impressive and instantly recognisable spires of Notre Dame Cathedral. There was no sign of Quasimodo but I consoled myself with the thought that he was probably in a café having a bite to eat.

Standing there, as the sun went down, I looked to my left and saw the Eiffel Tower silhouetted against the evening sky.

When M.Eiffel and his team of bridge builders first turned their iron dream into what was intended to be a temporary reality the Parisian aristocracy curled their lips, looked down their noses in disgust and in a fit of English Victorianism couldn't wait for the callus-fingered men with spanners to dismantle the whole thing and turn its composite nuts and bolts into something more useful; a nice bridge, perhaps.

Today, of course, Paris *is* the Eiffel Tower and M.Eiffel is revered for having given the French capital the world's most famous landmark. Anyone who suggested dismantling the Tower would be either locked up as insane or regarded as an excellent excuse for bringing back the guillotine. Age has given M.Eiffel's edifice acceptability and turned those hulking girders into symbols of stylish elegance. The fashionable and the artistic fight each other for the right to shine floodlights at it, perform underneath it, dangle bits of coloured paper from it, or simply have tea at the top of it. Just about every ambitious city in the world has an office building taller than the Eiffel Tower, but that doesn't matter. The Eiffel Tower is such a silly edifice it is exquisitely beautiful.

Today, paradoxically, it is both purposeful and profitable; the most astonishing result of the meeting of modern technology and art. Make something truly exceptional and beautiful and someone will find a use for it. The Eiffel Tower is the best-known man-made erection in the world and probably the most valuable and most beautiful.

I walked on, attracted, like a moth, by the bright lights. The Left Bank seemed ablaze with light. The people who weren't talking were drinking and the ones who weren't drinking were talking.

I wandered about fairly aimlessly for twenty minutes or so and then, picking it out at random, entered a large, friendly looking café, walked up to the zinc-topped bar, squeezed onto a bar stool, and ordered a coffee.

There are times in all our lives when we make seemingly random or insignificant decisions which eventually turn out to shape our future.

For example, I met my former wife in the casualty department of a local hospital. She was working there as a clerk in the reception department. I was a patient. I'd tripped over an uneven piece of pavement and cut open my head. I had been waiting for hours, the blood had long since clotted, and I was bored and so, for the first time in my life, I picked up an abandoned newspaper and decided to do the crossword. Finding this modest ambition thwarted by the lack of a writing implement I asked the clerk if I could borrow one of hers (she had a dozen or more cheap pens rammed into a coffee mug on her desk). Three hours later, when I left I had four stitches in my scalp wound and the reception clerk's telephone number. That was the only crossword puzzle I've ever attempted. I didn't finish that one and I doubt if I will ever try another.

I didn't know it then but walking into that particular café was going to change the rest of my life. It was a random and at the time seemingly insignificant decision. But if I had chosen to go into a café thirty seconds earlier, or thirty seconds later, I would have chosen a different establishment and the rest of my life would have taken a very different path.

Sitting on stools at the bar there were, on my left, two French workmen in blue overalls. One wore a beret. The other had a huge, nicotine-stained moustache. They were both drinking Ricard and both smoking Gauloise cigarettes. They looked like a pair of extras waiting for work in a Hollywood musical set in Paris.

On my right sat a man about my age, wearing a crumpled but well-made and once stylish suit. He was slumped over the bar. He seemed to be at best asleep or at worst unconscious, and he was nursing the empty glass which had once contained what had almost certainly not been his first drink of the day. His top shirt button was undone and his tie, a florid affair consisting of equal quantities of red and yellow, had been pulled down an inch or two into a tight knot.

'What part of England do you come from?' asked the drinker on my right, without raising his head.

I looked at him, surprised. I hadn't realised that he had noticed my arrival. At first I wasn't sure that he was talking to me. He repeated the question.

'How did you know I was English?' I asked him, instead of answering his question.

Very slowly, he turned his head, looked at me and smiled. 'You have a little bit of an accent,' he told me. You could have removed paint with his breath. 'Besides,' he added, 'you're wearing English clothes and no one but the English would ever voluntarily choose to do that.'

I looked down. I was wearing a pair of green corduroy trousers and a scruffy sports coat which had leather patches sewn over the elbows. The leather patches weren't there as a fashion statement but to disguise the fact that my bony elbows had worn holes in both sleeves of the jacket. Underneath the jacket I was wearing a checked shirt and a brown tie. I had an old woollen scarf around my neck.

I told him where I was from.

'Never heard of it,' he said, dismissively. He waved his glass at the barman. 'Do you want a drink?' he asked me, as

34

the barman reached for a bottle of malt whisky and poured a generous slug into his glass.

'No thanks,' I replied.

'So, what are you doing here?'

'In this café ?'

'No. In Paris.'

'I'm just taking a short break.'

'Have you been here before?'

'No.'

The stranger picked up his glass, holding it very carefully so as not to spill any, and emptied it in a single gulp. He pushed the glass back across the bar and the barman immediately refilled it.

'Are you here on holiday?' I asked him. It seemed polite to express some curiosity.

'I live here.'

'What do you do?'

The question went unanswered because with surprising grace and fluidity the man to whom I had been talking slowly slid from his bar stool down onto the floor. Startled, I leapt off my own bar stool, knelt down beside him and tried to move him into what I believed to be some sort of recovery position. Given the fact that the café was fairly busy and the floor rather well-occupied with feet (the owners of which did not seem particularly concerned or interested in helping) this wasn't easy. The stranger seemed to be breathing and his colour, though an objective observer might have perhaps remarked that it was a trifle on the florid side of normal, seemed excellent.

I stood up, my heart racing and called out to attract the barman's attention.

The barman, a portly fellow in a large white apron was a good advertisement for the calorific content of his establishment's produce. He responded with a flurry of something incomprehensible. I assumed it was in French but it all came out so quickly that I couldn't identify any of the words. I began to panic a little. I pointed at the man on the floor, clutched my chest and made a noise like an ambulance. I thought it was a pretty impressive improvisation but the barman looked at me, frowned, rolled his eyes and shrugged his shoulders in one practised and fluid movement. Exhausted by all this activity he turned away and started to do something to a beer glass with a damp and grubby looking tea towel. If the towel had been drier and cleaner I would have assumed that he was drying the glass.

Becoming more desperate by the moment I banged on the zinc counter with my fist and reached across the bar to tug at the barman's apron. He turned round and I could see that his patience was wearing thin.

'A man has collapsed!' I told him. I pretended to sit on the bar stool that the other Englishman had fallen off, and then pretended to fall off it. The barman watched me, thought for a moment and then nodded approvingly.

'Isn't there anyone here who speaks English?' I yelled.

A woman in her late twenties appeared. She was dressed as a waitress, looked rather harassed and was carrying an order pad and a pen. Despite the fact that I was a foreigner in the land I took a wild, reckless guess and assumed that she probably was a waitress.

'What is the matter?' she demanded. 'Why so much noise? What do you want?'

'The man who was sitting next to me has collapsed,' I said. 'Please call an ambulance.'

'An ambulance?' said the waitress, surprised. She laughed. 'Why do you want me to call an ambulance?' She had a throaty forty-a-day voice.

'This man has collapsed!' I said, pointing to the man at our feet. 'He could be very ill. He is unconscious.'

The waitress laughed at me and then told the barman what I had said. The barman laughed. The two men in blue overalls laughed. Soon everyone in the bar was laughing. A stand up comedian would have felt a warm glow if he had managed to inspire so much laughter.

'What is so funny?' I demanded, failing to see the funny side of things. The French don't have much of a reputation for kindness to strangers or foreigners but this seemed to be taking things a little too far.

The waitress shrugged and waved her pad and pen about in a typically Gallic gesture. 'He is drunk! That is all.'

'How do you know?' I demanded.

'For one thing he has been having...' she turned to the barman and asked him something, '...eight whiskies in the last hour and a half. For another thing, he is doing this every evening.' She smiled, reached out and patted me on the arm. 'Do not be a worry to yourself. He has a strong constitution. He will be fine in a few minutes,' she assured me.

I bent down and examined the man on the floor again. He was breathing perfectly well – in fact he was snoring – and his colour seemed good.

I decided that the barman and the waitress were probably right, clambered wearily back onto my bar stool and took a sip from my coffee. It was cold and strong enough to strip paint from wood but I'd bought it so I drank it anyway.

# ~ **Chapter Four** ~

Ten minutes later, I was still sitting at the bar, still sipping my cup of paint stripper, when I realised that I could hear a bird singing.

I looked around the café but no one else seemed to have heard it. If they had they weren't bothered and certainly weren't doing anything about it. The bird was trilling its little heart away as though it had just woken up on a beautiful spring morning and realised just what a wonderful world we all live in.

I sipped a little more coffee and decided to see if more sugar would soften the taste of paint stripper. It helped a little. But the bird was still singing. I opened another packet of sugar and poured the contents into my coffee cup. And then, just for luck, I added another packet of sugar. The bird was still singing its little heart out.

It was at that point that I realised that what I had thought was a singing bird was in fact a ringing telephone. I looked around. No one else seemed to have noticed. I couldn't see a telephone but it was definitely a telephone and not a bird. And it seemed to be chirping and warbling somewhere around my feet.

I looked down.

The telephone was, of course, in the drunken stranger's jacket pocket.

At first I didn't like to answer it. Telephones – particularly mobile ones – are rather private things. Some people get very itchy if a stranger answers their private telephone.

But when the telephone wouldn't stop ringing I eventually decided that I really ought to find out who was calling. Perhaps it was something urgent. Perhaps the drunken man's wife was calling to see what time he would be home. Perhaps a loving girlfriend was worrying herself sick; waiting for him to turn up at a restaurant somewhere. Besides, I was getting fed up with the noise the damned thing was making.

'Hello?' I said, when, after rummaging through several pockets I eventually found the telephone and worked out which button to press.

'What the bloody hell have you been doing?' demanded an angry Scottish voice.

'I've been drinking my coffee,' I replied, rather put out at the rude way in which this question had been phrased. It had not, at this point, occurred to me that the caller would not have expected to find a complete stranger at the other end of the telephone.

'Who is that?'

'Tony Davison.'

'Who?'

Rather wearily, I repeated my name.

'Who the hell are you?'

'I just happened to be here. I heard the phone ringing and thought I'd better answer it in case it was urgent.'

'It is urgent! What the hell has happened to Albert? Have you stolen this telephone?'

'No, of course not!'

'How did you get hold of it?'

'What?'

'The telephone.'

'It was in this chap's pocket. He's lying on the floor a little bit the worse for wear. If Albert is the owner of this phone then the chap on the floor is probably Albert.'

'Pissed again, is he?'

I hesitated. I didn't want to get the stranger into trouble. But, on the other hand, the caller didn't seem too surprised. 'That would probably sum it up fairly well. Who are you?'

'My name's Jack. I'm a sub editor. We're waiting for Albert's copy for tomorrow's paper.'

'He's a journalist?'

'He's a columnist,' replied Jack. He sighed. It was the weary sigh of a weary man. 'Actually, he's our star columnist. His picture is on buses all over London.'

The name suddenly rang a bell. I hadn't seen it on buses (largely because it was a long time since I'd been to London) but I remembered seeing his name and photograph staring out at me on those occasions when I had purchased a copy of the paper he worked for.

Albert, I remembered, wrote a daily column about people he met and whose lives intrigued him and would, he thought, intrigue his readers too. Most of the people he wrote about were the sort usually described, rather patronisingly, as 'ordinary'. Most were either based in Paris or were passing through. They were anything but 'ordinary' but various sections of the media seem to regard anyone who doesn't have a part in a soap opera and regular invitations to social events in London as 'ordinary'.

'I'm afraid he isn't in much of a state to write anything for you at the moment,' I told the fellow at the other end of the phone.

'Shit,' muttered the man. He thought for a moment. 'Would you have a look in his pockets for me?'

'I don't like going through an unconscious bloke's pockets,' I protested.

'You found the telephone didn't you?'

'Yes, I suppose so.'

'Just look and see if you can find a notebook. The rest of us are in the age of technology but Albert always writes his column in an old-fashioned reporter's notebook.'

I slid off my stool, bent down and rather furtively reached into one of Albert's jacket pockets. Less than a minute later I had found the notebook. I passed the good news to the man at the other end of the telephone.

'Look inside and see what you can find.'

'The handwriting is terrible and it's pretty much indecipherable,' I told him.

'Look through and find the start to his latest column...'

I flicked through the notebook.

'How's this,' I said. I started to read.

'That's it! Great. Read a bit more.'

I read a bit more.

'Oh damn. I had a horrible feeling I'd heard that before. That was today's column. Go through and see if you can find the next column – the one for tomorrow's paper.'

I flicked through the notebook. 'How's this?' I said, reading another introduction.

'That sounds great. Does it by any chance have a date at the top of it?'

'Yes.'

'What is it?'

I told him. It was tomorrow's date.

'Fantastic. Look, I hate to have to ask you to do this, but if I put you onto a copy taker would you read over Albert's column for us? If we don't get that copy there'll be a huge hole in tomorrow's paper.'

'OK,' I said.

'Give your name and address to the copy taker. I'll make sure we send you a cheque to cover your time and inconvenience and expenses.'

'I haven't got any expenses. I'm using Albert's telephone and you're paying for the call.'

'OK. Stay on the line and I'll put you through to the copy takers' desk. You've saved our lives. Another five minutes and we'd have had to fill the space with something else.'

A few seconds later a calm voice asked me to start dictating Albert's copy.

The writing was very sharp and funny. Twice I found myself laughing out loud. It was difficult to believe that the comatose drunk on the floor at my feet had written such beautiful, charming prose.

# ~ Chapter Five ~

Albert woke up about half an hour later. He clambered back onto his bar stool and ordered another drink as calmly and unconcernedly as though he'd been to the loo or had just popped out to buy a newspaper. He gave no indication of having been lying unconscious in a drunken stupor on the floor of a French café .

'How are you feeling?' I asked him.

He looked at me. 'I'm fine, thanks,' he said. He looked surprisingly alert and awake. He frowned, as though trying to remember something. 'I'm sorry if I'm being rude...but would you be kind enough to remind me again who you are?'

I re-introduced myself and pushed his telephone and notebook along the counter towards him.

'Mine?' he said. He picked up the notebook and flicked through it.

'Yes.'

'Where did you find them?' Satisfied that the notebook was his he slipped it into the right hand pocket of his suit jacket, where I had found it.

'In your pockets.'

He looked at me and raised an eyebrow. 'You don't look like a pickpocket.' He picked up his mobile telephone and stared at it for a moment, as though making sure that it was his. Then he slipped it into his left hand jacket pocket, again the pocket in which I had found it.

'I'm not,' I told him. 'Your phone was ringing so I answered it for you.'

'Very kind of you,' he said. 'Let me buy you a drink.'

'No, it's OK,' I said, holding up a hand.

'I insist,' said Albert. 'Have a glass of wine? A hot wine?'

'No thanks, really, I'll just have another coffee in a minute or two.'

'Don't you drink?' he asked. There was no judgement in the question. Just surprise.

'Yes, I do...'

'Then try a vin chaud – a hot wine. If you don't like it you can leave it. OK?' He paused and smiled at me. 'Booze is very cheap here you know. Spend two quid on a bottle of wine and you're obviously expecting guests you want to impress. You can buy whisky here at half the price you'd pay in Britain.'

'OK,' I agreed.

Albert drained his whisky glass and ordered two glasses of vin chaud. 'Who was on the phone?'

'Someone from your newspaper,' I said. 'They wanted your column for tomorrow's paper.'

'Oh Gawd,' said Albert. 'I must have forgotten to phone in my copy. What's the time?' He pulled back his left hand coat sleeve and studied an expensive looking watch. He muttered something half under his breath and pulled out his mobile telephone. 'Excuse me,' he said to me. 'I'd better just ring them back.' He looked at his watch again.

'I read your column to one of the copy takers,' I told him. 'If that's what you were ringing about there's no need...'

Albert stopped in mid dial and looked at me. 'You read my column over to a copytaker?'

'Yes.'

The barman put two glasses of steaming red wine down in front of us. Each glass of wine contained a thick slice of orange.

Albert turned off his phone and slipped it back into his pocket. 'Thank you.'

The barman added a bowl full of sugar sachets and something that looked like a pepper-pot.

'My pleasure. I thought it was very funny.'

Albert picked up and tore open a sugar sachet and poured the contents into one of the wine glasses. 'Thanks,' he said. 'You'll probably need sugar in that,' he added, nodding towards my wine glass. He looked at me. 'Thanks a lot,' he said. 'You pretty much saved my life.' He tore the top off another sugar sachet and poured more sugar into his wine. 'If you don't play on the team, you're not allowed to make any mistakes – suck up to the boss and all your mistakes get covered up.'

'I take it you don't suck up to the boss?'

'I've never been a team player.'

I picked up a sugar sachet and followed his example.

'What are you doing here?' he asked me, as he stirred the sugar into his hot wine. He had obviously forgotten that we had already started this conversation.

'Just a few days break,' I said. 'I retired from work a few days ago.'

'You look a bit young to have retired.'

'I took early retirement.'

'How did you come to pick the 'Fag and Ferret'?'

I looked at him, puzzled. 'The 'Fag and Ferret'?'

'That's what I call this place,' he explained. 'The owner doesn't call it that,' he explained, though he said this in such a way as to make it quite clear that he regarded the preferences of the owner as being of little consequence.

'This is your local, then?'

Albert nodded.

'You live here?'

'Round the corner.'

'I suppose Paris is full of writers.'

Albert pulled a face. 'These days most of the ones who call themselves writers are just playing at it. Amateurs kidding themselves they're writers.' He had become very serious. 'You know, it's easy to write something. But there's an art to knowing when and where to start a piece and an art to knowing when and where to finish. Most of those who master the former never master the latter.' Albert picked up the pepper shaker and shook some of the brown powdery contents into his vin chaud.

'What's that?'

'Cannelle.'

I looked at him, blankly.

'Cinnamon.' He handed me the shaker. 'Try some. If you're going to spend time in Paris you have to learn to drink your vin chaud with cannelle.'

I didn't expect to be spending more than a few days in Paris but I did as he suggested.

# ~ Chapter Six ~

Five hours later we were still in the same café . We had moved from the bar and were sitting on more comfortable chairs at one of the window tables.

Two girls had come into the café and were sitting at the table next to us, drinking black coffees. One was wearing a shoulder length blonde wig The other had similar amounts of fake red hair. The girl in the blonde wig was wearing thigh length black patent leather boots, a very short black skirt and a skimpy white blouse. The top three or four buttons were undone, showing a well-filled lacy black bra. The girl in the red wig was wearing red high-heeled shoes, fishnet stockings, a red P.V.C. skirt and a matching bullfighter style jacket. Underneath it she wore a skin-tight pink ribbed sweater which left absolutely nothing to the imagination. When they first sat down I thought they were probably in their mid twenties but, after sneaking a longer look, I realised that they could be in their teens or in their thirties. They both wore so much make-up it was impossible to tell how old they were. Guessing what they did for a living wasn't difficult.

As soon as the waiter had brought them their drinks they wrapped their hands around the cups. They seemed to be using the hot coffee to get warm. It was cold outside and they weren't dressed to keep warm. They both carried tiny black handbags which they had placed on the table in front of them.

'Albert, ça va?' said one of the girls, recognising my companion and smiling at him; she seemed genuinely pleased to see him. Her perfectly applied lipstick framed expensively capped teeth.

The journalist opened his eyes, squinted at the girl and her companion and said something in French which I didn't understand. He then waved a hand in my direction and introduced me.

'The blonde is Nicole, the redhead is Simone,' he told me. 'They're friends of Lucie's,' he added, as though in explanation.

'Who is Lucie?' I asked. But the modest effort had proved too much for him and my companion had drifted off again.

'He is drunk again?' said the blonde, turning what might well have been a statement into a question by raising her voice at the end of the sentence.

'I'm afraid so,' I admitted.

'He is a very good drinker,' said the blonde. She opened her handbag and took out a packet of cigarettes and a cheap plastic lighter. She opened the packet and offered it to her companion who took a cigarette. She took a cigarette herself and then offered the packet to me. I thanked her and declined the offer. I started to tell her that I didn't smoke but stopped myself. Denying vices didn't, somehow, seem the right thing to do.

There was a squeal of brakes in the road outside. I turned and watched as a huge silver Mercedes skidded to an expensive tyre wasting halt outside the café . Two men got out of the car. One, in his early thirties, was tall, slim and olive skinned. He wore faded blue jeans, a white, open necked shirt and a blue blazer with brass buttons and an impressive-looking badge on the breast pocket. The other man, probably no more than a couple of years older, was a foot shorter, totally bald and distinctly chubby. He wore a grey silk suit, a pale blue shirt and an expensive looking silk tie. The two men slammed the car doors, abandoned their expensive vehicle without bothering to lock it, and swaggered into the café . They looked confident and slightly menacing, and although neither of them wore hats they reminded me of Alain Delon and Jean-Paul Belmondo in Borsalino, that classic French gangster movie set in the thirties.

The two girls squealed excitedly and welcomed the men with hugs and kisses. The newcomers, seemingly indifferent to this show of affection, sat down and ordered drinks from an elderly waiter who had gone over to their table even before they had sat down. The waiter, who seemed nervous in their company, scurried away to fetch their drinks.

The small, bald man said something to the girl in the red wig, who was sitting on the other side of the table. She opened her bag, took out a packet of cigarettes and pushed her handbag across towards him. He opened the bag and emptied out the notes it contained. Some were neatly folded, some were rolled and some were crumpled together like bits of waste paper. As he began to sort out the money the woman in the blonde wig pushed her handbag across the table to the tall, slimmer man in the blue blazer. The waiter returned. He put two glasses of Ricard and a jug of water on the table and then put a glass of champagne down in front of each of the girls. There was a rat-a-tat on the café window and to my enormous surprise two policemen, guns, radios and handcuffs attached to broad leather belts around their waists, waved merrily to the two men. The two men both looked, nodded, and resumed sorting the money.

The girls sipped at their champagne while the two men

put the bank notes away into already bulging wallets. I found myself wondering how many other women they had working for them on the overcrowded streets of Paris. I had never been this close to a pimp or a prostitute before. I had only been in Paris for a matter of days and my world had already changed.

'Let's go home,' said Albert waking up suddenly. Without warning he stood up. He swayed for a moment and held on to my shoulder for support. He was clearly unsteady and as I tried to stand up to support him he started to fall. The tall pimp in the blue blazer caught him, apparently effortlessly. 'We'd better help you take him home,' he said, standing up. I was slightly surprised by the fact that he spoke good English but spoke it with a slight American accent.

'I don't know where he lives,' I said, apologetically.

'That's OK,' said the pimp. 'We do.' He smiled at me and shrugged. 'He is a writer,' he said, as though this explained everything. 'We often take him home,' he added.

It was three in the morning but it seemed that most of the cafés were still open. The pavements were almost as busy as they had been five hours earlier but people were walking much more slowly now. It seemed that no one hurried at three o'clock in the morning. Instead of businessmen hurrying to appointments and shoppers scurrying about laden with their purchases the streets were filled with lovers and would-be lovers.

The short, bald fellow drove. His partner sat in the passenger seat and Albert and I sat in the back. I was terrified that Albert would be sick. The Mercedes had beige leather seats and a thick beige carpet. Everything was clean and perfect, as though this was the first trip the car had made since leaving the show room.

'Third floor,' said the tall, thin pimp, when the Mercedes screeched to a halt outside a nondescript hotel in a fairly run down area. 'Room 347.' I got out of the car, walked around and dragged Albert out onto the pavement. The tall pimp, the one in the blazer, had to get out of the car and help me. I thanked them both (neither of them acknowledged my thanks) and, with my arm around Albert's waist, staggered into his hotel. I was relieved to find that there was a lift. A night porter, sleeping at the reception desk, carried on snoring.

Albert didn't regain consciousness until, with him leant against the wall outside his hotel room, I started to look in his pockets for his key. He giggled, as though I was tickling him, and then, when I told him what I was looking for, pushed his hand into his right trouser pocket and, moments later, produced a key which he handed to me.

'Thank you,' he said, as I pushed open his door and helped him into his hotel room. Behind him the room seemed to be filled with books. He stood still, for a moment, seemingly suddenly utterly sober and smiled at me. 'Have I had too much to drink again?' he asked, apparently innocently.

# ~ Chapter Seven ~

Two days after I had met him, I sat in the Fag and Ferret with Albert and drank hot red wine laced with sugar, orange and cinnamon. It was a drink I had already got to know and to love; rather similar to the mulled wine I had once or twice drunk at Christmas time back in England.

This was only the third or fourth time I'd been in the Fag and Ferret but I was already beginning to feel like a regular. French cafés can be forbidding when you visit them for the first time. The proprietor, behind the zinc-topped bar, invariably leans against something, surrounded by a group of suspicious-looking regulars who stare at every newcomer.

I was to learn in due course that while proprietors and waiters tolerate tourists as necessary evils – and tolerating is a long, long way from liking – they are surprisingly quick to accept customers as regulars.

For two hours Albert and I sat together and didn't speak a word. Whenever our glasses were empty Albert simply waved a nicotine-stained finger in the air and the waiter, a sour faced fellow with a droopy grey moustache silently brought replacements. Albert never turned to see if the waiter was looking when he made these signals, but the waiter never missed one.

In the past, whenever I had sat with someone I didn't know very well, the silences had always seemed rather oppressive; demanding to be filled with idle chatter about the weather, the state of the nation or the latest piece of tabloid gossip. But I felt surprisingly comfortable with Albert and to my surprise the silence didn't seem to be a problem at all. As I got to know him better I discovered that sometimes he would talk for hours without stopping, never repeating himself but never being dull. He could be, and often was, outrageous, prejudiced and bigoted but he was always honest, always funny and never, never boring. Not even Albert's worst enemy could describe him as boring.

I was very conscious of the fact that in less than two days time I would be catching the train back to England and for over an hour I had been trying to decide where I was going when I got back. I had originally intended to visit my sister – my only living relative and now my only tie to the country in which I had been born – but that idea was slowly becoming less and less attractive. My sister and I had never been close and over the years our relationship had become more and more strained. She was married to a bank manager who had never made any secret of the fact that he regarded me as a pretty sorry apology for a brother-in-law.

My quandary was made more confusing by the fact that I was not only sure where to go but I was also unsure about why I was going back.

All my belongings (pitiful few that they were) were in my hotel room. The little money I had was in an English bank but could, I felt pretty sure, be transferred to a French financial establishment without too much difficulty. After much deliberation I had come to the pretty sad conclusion that I had lots of acquaintances but no real friends in England. I was beginning to feel sorry for myself, and to slide down into a black orgy of self pity when I suddenly became aware that although I didn't know what he had said Albert had broken the silence.

'Sorry,' I said. 'I was a million miles away. What did you say?'

'Why are you going back to England?' Albert asked.

I looked up and stared at him for a moment. It was as though he had been sharing my most private, innermost thoughts.

Albert, still thinking that I hadn't heard him, repeated his question for the third time. He looked down at the table between us and seemed suddenly to become aware that our glasses were empty. Languidly he raised a hand and waved a finger in the air.

'I don't know,' I said at long last. 'I don't know why I'm going back and I don't know where I'm going.'

'So why not stay here?'

It may seem strange but the thought of staying in Paris had never occurred to me. Rather startled by the idea, I looked at him, frowning, and stared for a moment. 'I don't know,' I said. I racked my brain, desperately searching for reasons which I didn't really want to find. 'I don't know anyone here,' I said, and then quickly added. 'And I don't have anywhere to stay.' I couldn't think of any more reasons for not staying in Paris so I stopped.

'You know me,' said Albert, answering my first excuse. Since this was undeniable I didn't say anything.

The waiter came over, put two more glasses of hot wine down on our table and took away half a dozen empty glasses.

Albert picked up the small bottle of cinnamon which sat in the middle of the table and added a healthy sprinkling to his wine. 'And there are plenty of flats to rent,' he added, answering my second objection to staying in Paris. He tore open a cylindrical paper sachet and added the sugar it contained to his hot wine. 'The big advantage Paris has over every other city I've ever lived in – and over the years I've spent time in most of them,' said Albert, 'is that there are apartments to suit every pocket. You can buy or rent a flat in Paris for less than the price of a terraced house in Liverpool.' He paused. 'Of course it won't have five bedrooms and it won't be overlooking the Eiffel Tower...' he looked around thoughtfully. 'Paris is a wonderful city,' he sighed. 'France is a wonderful country.' There was a long silence. 'Of course, it's a pity about the French,' he said at last. 'You've heard that the French hate the English?'

I nodded.

'This is true,' said Albert. 'But they also hate the Welsh, the Scottish and the Irish. And they loathe the Americans even more than they hate the English. And they hate the Australians. And, of course, the Germans. And the Belgians. And the Italians and the Spanish. And the Algerians. Boy, do they loathe the Algerians. The French are the ultimate racists. They hate everyone who isn't French. And if there aren't any foreigners around to hate they just hate each other.'

I stared at him but for a while said nothing.

'But Paris is the most beautiful city in the whole wide world.'

'Why do you love it so much?

'Well, the weather tends to be much more palatable than the brand we get in Britain, the food is invariably well-presented and tasty and the cheap wine they keep for themselves is usually vastly superior to the expensive stuff they sell us. All these things outbalance the fact that the country is absurdly bureaucratic and if I was trying to describe the French people I would have difficulty in doing so without using the words 'aloof', 'vain', 'pompous', 'smug', 'self-satisfied' and 'humourless'. I love French architecture, French cooking and the French attitude to life – which incidentally enables them to smoke and drink more than the British, and to eat vast quantities of fatty food, while still having a much lower heart attack rate, but I have never been particularly fond of the French.'

'But it isn't the weather, the architecture, the food or the wine that keeps me here,' continued Albert. 'It's the cafés. And the café way of life. I adore French cafés. I love them all: smart fashionable ones where the waiters are all clearly former French aristocrats and small scruffy ones frequented by workmen and run by a couple whose corpulence is an advertisement for the food he cooks and she serves.'

'In winter I love sitting inside, my hands wrapped around a glass of vin chaud, watching soaking wet French businessmen scurrying to and fro in the rain. In the summer I love sitting outside under a striped umbrella, sipping something cold and long and patiently watching the world meander or jiggle by.'

'I love the fact that I can order a glass of Ricard, a beer or a bottle of wine at 10 o'clock in the morning without anyone batting an eyelid. I love the fact that I can order a tomato salad and a plate of frites at midnight without the waiter taking off his watch and winding it up.'

'I love the fact that I can buy a cup of coffee, take out my book and settle down for the day, knowing that the ticket in my saucer isn't for the drink but the rent on my chair.'

'I love the fact that if I go into a café more than once or twice, and acquire my wings as a regular, the waiter and the proprietor will shake my hand and greet me with a smile and offer me the same courtesy when I leave.'

'We used to have good cafés in Britain. Back in the days when Dr Samuel Johnson was struggling with his dictionary, coffee houses were fine meeting places where men could settle down with a cup of good coffee or a pint of best porter and sit in peace and ponder.'

'Today, back in Britain, our cafés are almost all gone.

All that are left are small, mean places in seaside towns where sour faced harridans in dirty aprons serve burnt tea cakes and lukewarm tea that tastes of detergent. We have our pubs, of course. But modern pubs reek of plastic and chemical beer.'

'There are excellent cafés in Austria (two or three of the world's top ten can be found in Vienna), Italy (on the via Veneto in Rome and in St Mark's square in Venice in particular), Holland (Amsterdam, of course) and Germany (Berlin has been a favourite centre for café aficionados for decades) but France is still the undisputed world champion for café lovers.'

My heart was beating slightly faster. Somehow I knew that this was a significant moment in my life and that I would remember everything about it for the rest of my life. Just as I would always remember where I had been and what I had been doing when I had heard that President Kennedy had been assassinated and when I had heard that Princess Diana had been killed in a car crash so I would always remember this conversation with Albert. I looked around at the café in which we were sitting. There wasn't anything special or unusual about it. In a way it was really only notable for the fact that it wasn't notable.

I watched as Albert tore open a second paper sachet and added yet more sugar to his wine. He added a slice of orange and only then, when he had finished, did he look across at me and raise an eyebrow. 'Well?' he asked me. 'Just remember that the future turns into the past, and now into then, in the blink of an eye. Anticipations and expectations become memories at an alarming speed.'

While we had been sitting there it had slowly dawned upon me that for years I had felt like an alien at home. I had felt as though I didn't really belong. In Paris I was, of course, still an alien. But being an alien in a foreign land is far less troubling than being an alien in a land where you think you should feel at home. I puzzled over this for a while and eventually came to the conclusion that being an alien abroad is less of a personal indictment.

And after all, I thought, if you are an alien in your own country you might just as well be an alien in a country where they bake the bread four times a day. Besides, these days, it seems to me that we are all foreigners – wherever we live. So, what does it matter where you live?

Paris wasn't necessarily better than any English towns I could think of. It was simply different – very different – and the difference invigorated me and made me feel younger. I felt more alive and more like living. I felt 'foreign' in Paris but there were good reasons for feeling 'foreign'. I didn't have to feel guilty about it.

'I think I'll stay in Paris for a while,' I said, suddenly, knowing that if I didn't make a decision quickly I would prevaricate until I found so many excuses for not staying that I went back to England by default. I reached inside my jacket pocket and took out my return ticket. I looked at it carefully in an attempt to find out whether the return portion of the ticket was open ended. I couldn't tell. 'Does this have a return date on it?' I asked Albert, handing him the ticket. 'I can't work it out.'

Albert studied the ticket for a moment, hesitated and then slowly tore the ticket in half. 'It was only valid for the day after tomorrow,' he said when he had finished tearing the ticket in two.

He tossed the two halves of the ticket into the ashtray, where they lay on top of the discarded sugar wrappers.

The die was cast. I would not be going back to England.

# ~ Chapter Eight ~

After breakfast the following morning I set out to walk the
streets of Paris in search of accommodation. I couldn't afford to live in a hotel – even a cheap one. I needed to find a
small flat.

In the cold light of a cool morning in Paris I felt rather
less enthusiastic and optimistic about my new adventure than
I had done the night before.

The previous evening, sitting in a warm café with a
glass of hot wine in front of me (and several more of the
same tucked safely away inside my stomach), things had
seemed very different. Inspired by a potent mix of alcohol
and excitement, the terrors of living in a foreign city had
seemed insignificant.

Now, with the street sweepers still trundling through
the city and the gutters awash with rivulets of cleansing water, I felt alone and curiously vulnerable. If Albert had not
burnt my boats for me (or, more accurately, torn up my ticket)
I would have probably changed my mind, hurried to the railway station and gone back to England.

I packed my suitcases and left them in the care of the
hotel receptionist, a stern, efficient woman of indeterminate
years.

'You have a late flight?' asked the receptionist. 'Or a late train?' She spoke good English, but with a slight American accent. I always find this slightly irritating.

I paused, about to tell her the truth, and stopped myself, though I didn't really know why. 'Yes, that's right,' I agreed. 'A late train.' Instantly, I felt guilty, although the lie was quite trivial and didn't really matter, and wondered why I had bothered.

'Have a nice day!' said the receptionist, in that falsely friendly way the Americans have spread around the world. I smiled, thanked her, returned the good wish with matching insincerity, and strode purposefully towards the front door as though I knew exactly where I was heading and what I was going to do when I got there. 'You're going to have beautiful weather today!' called the receptionist.

Twenty five minutes later, as I walked along the Boulevard du Montparnasse, the sky turned grey. Five minutes after that the rain started.

I had neither a raincoat nor an umbrella so I turned up my collar and automatically speeded up the rate at which I was walking. I still didn't know where I was going or what I was going to do when I got there. The rain got heavier. I realised that I hadn't told the hotel receptionist what I was planning to do because I felt embarrassed. Finding a flat in Paris seemed a rather silly and romantic thing to do – especially for a man of my age. I had never been an impulsive person. I decided that I would try to find the travel agent's Paris representative, tell them that I had lost my train ticket and beg them to give me a replacement.

The rain was getting heavier and I stepped into a doorway in between two shops to shelter. It was a quiet street but as soon as I was in there a man appeared in front of me. He looked quite young, considerably younger than myself, and was wearing an anorak which reached down to his knees.

'Do you have money for food?' he asked me in very good English. Like the hotel receptionist he had a strong American accent.

At first I thought he was concerned for my own security. Touched by what I thought was his kindness I thanked him and told him that I had eaten breakfast.

'Do you have money for a drink?' he asked me.

This time I realised that he was asking for money rather than offering it. I rummaged in my pocket, looking for coins. 'You speak good English,' I told him.

'I'm American,' he said. 'I have to get back to visit my sick mother. Do you have money to pay for my airfare?'

I gave him all the coins I had in my pocket. Without thanking me he took the coins and shuffled away.

As he disappeared I watched distractedly as a tall man in a black mackintosh and a blue beret carried on two conversations with two separate mobile telephones. First he shouted into one, then into the other and then into both at once. He didn't seem to spend much time listening to what either of his correspondents had to say; taking as much notice of them as he was of the rain.

'You want to see my apartment?'

I turned away from watching the man in the black mackintosh and found myself looking down at a small, plump woman in her mid forties. She was sheltering underneath a small black umbrella. Better to obtain shelter from the rain I was standing on a doorstep and was, consequently, five or six inches above the woman in front of me. Since I would have been the best part of a foot taller than her if we had both been standing on the pavement I towered above her.

'I beg your pardon?'

The woman repeated her question, speaking English with a heavy French accent. I much preferred it to the American accent favoured by the hotel receptionist. She sounded like a female Maurice Chevalier. She had to hold the umbrella up at arms' length so that we could see each another's faces. She was holding a clipboard and wearing a short black skirt that would have been a tight fit if she had been three or four sizes smaller, a baggy black cardigan and a white blouse that was decorated with little flowers. The top two buttons of the blouse were undone and from my vantage position a foot and a half above her I had a pretty good view of an extremely impressive cleavage. The cleavage might, perhaps, have had a different effect on me if she had not worn a van Dyke beard and had legs well-decorated with varicose veins as thick as hawsers.

I stared at her and genuinely did not know what to say. I thought I was being propositioned and felt embarrassed, flattered and confused all at once. She didn't look much like I expected a prostitute to look like but since my experience in this area was pretty much limited to what I had seen the evening before I didn't count myself as knowledgable in this area. I muttered something which even I didn't understand.

'You are the Englishman?' she asked.

After hesitating I confirmed my nationality with a slightly uncertain nod. The rain was getting heavier and neither the doorway nor the umbrella were providing us with enough protection. I looked up and down and noticed that the street was more or less deserted. The man in the dark raincoat had long ago put away his two telephones and scurried off, perhaps to find somewhere dry, perhaps to recharge his batteries.

'I am the Bertha and I am sorry I am going to be late,' said the woman, in which she clearly regarded as impeccable English. She held out her hand. 'I was delayed be being with the client at another viewing elsewheres.' I took the offered hand and shook it. I had read somewhere that the French shake hands a lot but this was my first experience of it. I had also read that they tended to kiss one another a good deal. I silently hoped that the handshake would suffice. I am always averse to kissing but I did not find myself drawn to this woman's lips. I have no great objection to beards or moustaches but, and I realise that I may be quaintly old-fashioned in this area, but I prefer these items of adornment to be worn by men. The woman raised her eyes to heaven and rolled them around rather dramatically. 'He had a tape measure and insisted on measuring all the chambers.' She shrugged her shoulders as though this sort of behaviour was nothing new to her. 'He even measured from floor to ceiling!' She pulled a face, raised her eyes heavenwards again and tapped her forehead with a forefinger. Her fingernails were painted bright red and this added emphasis to the gesture. 'Shall we go inside and look on the apartment?' She held up a key, levered herself up onto the tips of her toes, reached around my body and poked the key into the keyhole behind me. As the door opened inwards I automatically stepped down onto the pavement to let the woman enter the building. I was confused, and tried to remember if I had made an appointment to see this woman when I had been with Albert. When the woman had lowered her umbrella I obeyed her inviting wave and followed her into a dark passageway.

Like many big people she moved with surprising grace and ease, and for an overweight middle-aged woman she showed a surprising burst of speed as she scurried down the passageway. I had a surprising amount of difficulty keeping up with her. If there was a light she didn't bother to switch it on. At the end of the passageway she darted to the right and although I could no longer see her I could tell from the sounds she made that she was climbing a staircase. I followed.

I later discovered that we had climbed six flights of narrow, tightly twisting stairs, but at the time I would have sworn that we had climbed at least ten times that many. To my shame I found myself having difficulty in keeping up with the plump bottom in front of me. I was puffing and wheezing long before we reached the top.

When we finally stopped climbing stairs the woman, seemingly inexhaustible, launched herself down an exceedingly narrow corridor, unlocked a door and, after pushing at it for quite a while eventually managed to force it open. Once she had separated the door from its frame she flung it open with the sort of flourish usually associated with magicians opening cabinets to show that their assistants have disappeared. She pressed herself against the wall behind her so that I could squeeze past her and go through the door ahead of her. 'The door sticks a little,' explained the woman. 'It needs a little oil.'

This wasn't an empty cabinet but it wasn't all that much bigger and as soon as I entered the room I could see why my plump guide had let me go first. The only light came from a small grubby window a few feet in front of us. The room was about twelve feet square. The walls had been painted purple and the two interior doors which broke up the purple had been painted bright yellow. It was clear from the way the ceiling came down to the floor by the window that we were in an attic space.

The previous tenant had left behind a few pieces of remarkably ugly furniture and a few very grubby rugs. The floor was gritty and dirty and didn't look or feel as though it had been cleaned for a long time. When I looked more closely at the walls I could see that they were covered with stains. By each stain someone had written something in French. I tried to read the graffiti but couldn't understand it.

It wasn't much of a home.

# ~ Chapter Nine ~

'So, Mr Liebermann,' said the woman, following close behind me. 'What are you thinking of the apartment?' She fumbled with something just inside the door and switched on the light. The bulb must have been the smallest available and it added very little to the light in the room. 'The colours may not be entirely to your cup of coffee but if you take the apartment you will be free to be repainting them to your own wishing.'

'Er, I'm afraid that my name isn't Liebermann,' I said. I felt a little guilty and wondered what had happened to Mr Liebermann. I guessed that he must have either been held up or had got fed up of waiting and had gone away. I looked around the apartment. This was not a task which took a great deal of time. 'But it seems very, er...,' I searched for an appropriate word and eventually found something that I thought would seem appropriate and accurate to an estate agent. 'Compact.' The word apartment seemed rather overstated.

As I had already noticed the previous tenant had left behind several pieces of furniture. The more I looked at these the easier it was to see he had left them behind rather than go to the trouble of taking them away with him. I wandered over to the window and looked out. The apartment had a view onto a small courtyard and into a couple of dozen apartments in the building opposite. I realised that I could look straight into a tiny room on the sixth floor of the other building. A well-proportioned woman in skimpy underwear was hanging her washing on a small clothes drier.

'You are not going to be Mr Liebermann?'

'No.' I turned away from the window, feeling rather embarrassed by my inability to be Mr Liebermann.

'Are you sure of this?' asked the woman. The French, I was to learn, are above all else a bureaucratic nation. They invariably prefer to believe things that are typed, rather than to believe their own eyes. For a Frenchman (or woman) once something has been put onto a form it acquires the authority of a papal edict. One in five working Frenchmen (and women) work for the government and the percentage is rising so rapidly that it will not be long before every man in La Belle France is a professional bureaucrat. As a child I grew up with building blocks and matured into a chemistry set. French children of my age probably asked for (and received) bureaucracy sets, filled with rubber stamps, packs of incomprehensible forms and miniature filing cabinets.

'Pretty much,' I assured her.

'Tsk!' said the woman, slapping her hand against her clipboard in disgust; her belief in the infallibility of the typed word temporarily shaken. 'So,' she sighed, 'what are you claiming is your name?'

I told her. She made me spell it and checked it against her clipboard, upon which a list of other names had been typed. She checked again. 'You are not existing!' she declared, at last, in some dismay. 'This is clearly nonsense. Hrmph! You are not there,' she said, stabbing her finger against the clipboard. There was another Gallic shrug. I looked at her. She looked at me. We looked at each other.

'But clearly you are here,' she said, at last. Then, accepting the inevitability of reality, she smiled at me, shrugged her shoulders again and asked me how to spell my name. Using a pen that was attached to her clipboard by a small piece of string she crossed out a name on her list (presumably Mr Liebermann's name) and wrote my name down on her board in its place. She seemed happy when this small piece of administration had been concluded.

The French, I was to discover many times over the coming months, do very much like to have their paperwork in order but when things don't match up they are always perfectly happy to make the necessary amendments. A friend of mine in England kept a shop. He had once spent three days poring over his accounts in an attempt to find a missing two pence. A French businessman would have dealt with the problem by simply changing one of the entries accordingly.

'What does this mean?' I asked her, pointing to what had been written next to a fairly large, angry looking stain about half way up the wall.

The agent leant a little closer and squinted. 'It says that this stain was caused when a bottle of the red wine was being thrown in June 1992. The bottle was being thrown by someone called Francoise at someone called Jean.' The woman shrugged as though this was all quite normal. 'Clearly the bottle missed,' she said. 'Francoise was perhaps not being a very good shot. Or maybe she was with a little too much of the wine.'

'And this one?' I said, pointing to another stain, a little higher up the wall.

'Ah, that was having been caused by a thunderstorm in November 1991,' the agent told me, after studying the graffiti. 'But you must not worry about that,' she assured me. 'The roof was having been repaired in 1996.'

I assured her that I would not worry about the stain caused by the leaky roof.

'Would you like to see the bed chamber?' asked the agent. Without waiting for a reply she pulled open one of the bright yellow doors. The previous tenant had left behind a bed and a mattress which took up three quarters of the room. I edged around the bed and tugged at an ugly mould green plastic curtain and found that behind it there was a shower, a bidet, a wash-basin and a lavatory. Someone had scrawled graffiti on the wall. 'Gertrude Stein was here, here, here' was my favourite. A closer look at the mould green plastic shower curtain showed that the curtain was actually made of colour-less opaque plastic. The curtain was mould green in colour because it was covered in mould. The one window in this room looked out onto the street. There were no curtains at the window but there was a tiny balcony, just big enough to contain a small chair and a table which looked just large enough to accommodate a plate and a cup and saucer.

I opened the window. 'Is it safe?' I asked the agent, who had, given her size and the available amount of space, probably been wise in not following me into the bedroom.

She looked at me, pulled a face and shrugged her shoulders.

Holding onto the window frame, I gingerly stepped out onto the balcony. Nothing terrible happened. I took a big step and put my other foot onto the balcony.

'It seems without danger,' said the agent, from her safe vantage point. 'You are having everything you need here!' she said. 'A completely self-containing apartment. Would you like to meet the kitchen?'

As I retraced my steps around the bedroom she stepped across to the other yellow door (it took her about three fairly short strides) and opened it. The word 'kitchen' was rather grand and 'cupboard' would probably have been more ap-propriate. Whatever it was called it contained a small cooker, a sink and a tiny fridge. Several rather grubby-looking cupboards were attached to the wall. One of the cupboard doors had loose hinges and looked as if it was about to fall off. A work surface, which had been fitted above the fridge, was covered in crumpled up bits of newspaper and empty cardboard cartons. A sheet of discarded newspaper half hid a partly eaten plate of spaghetti. Whoever had occupied the flat had clearly packed in a hurry and not bothered to tidy up when they had finished. The apartment reminded me of a flat I had once shared many years ago. The two companions which whom I had shared the flat had been such messy individuals that you could always walk into the kitchen and find a half-eaten meal or two on plates.

'The person who used to be renting this flat was not a nice person,' said the agent. 'He was a slub.'

'Slob?' I suggested.

'Slob,' agreed the agent. 'He was also making a good lot of noise. The other residents are pleased that he is gone. He once went away for two weeks and left his television set on with the volume turned up very loud as it would go.' She pulled a face and shivered. 'Not a nice person.'

She looked around, as though she was seeing the apartment for the first time and was considering moving into it herself. 'It could be very nice here,' she said. She sounded surprised. 'Of course, it needs some of the cleaning and tidying,' she added. 'Do you have a wife?'

I shook my head.

'A girlfriend?'

I shook my head again.

'A mistress?'

A third shake of the head.

'You are how you say, a 'happy' man?'

For a moment I was slightly puzzled by this but eventually I realised what she meant. 'No,' I assured her. 'I'm not gay. But there just isn't a woman in my life at the moment.'

'Ah,' said the agent, with a broad smile. 'You will soon be finding one.' She winked at me. 'This is Paris and now you have your own apartment and your own bed chamber.'

I walked around for a few moments. I looked at the curtainless windows, the dirty floor, the hideous decorations, the ugly kitchen with its grease covered walls and the cupboard with a door hanging off and the ugly mouldy green plastic curtain hiding the tiny bathroom. It was all so terrible that a loving touch and a few pots of paint could only make it infinitely more attractive.

Across the courtyard the woman who had been hanging up her washing had disappeared but two floors below a couple were arguing soundlessly. I could see them shouting and gesticulating but I couldn't hear anything they were saying. The agent, behind me, was clearly looking out of the window too. 'It is like a big soapy opera!' she said. 'A dozen television channels?'

'Yes,' I agreed. 'I suppose so.'

'No one paints their curtains,' said the agent. 'It is considered rude.'

'Ah,' I said, making a mental note to be rude to my neighbours.

'The building where I live also has a courtyard,' said the agent. 'There are four sides to the courtyard and all the apartments are looking down upon the courtyard. Two of my neighbours were recently having an alliance – how do you call it – an affair of the heart? A romance?'

'An affair,' I said, nodding. 'I understand.'

'The man was a postman, he did not have a wife. The woman was married to a very large Jewish policeman with a bad, bad temper. A very jealous man but as I have heard not a particularly good lover. People say he has a very small...' She placed her hand in front of her and wiggled her little finger and then continued her story. 'So his wife arranged a simple code with her washing so that she could be telling her lover whether or not her husband was on duty and the coast was cleared so that she could safely entertain him in her bed.'

'Very imaginative,' I agreed. The couple across the courtyard were still arguing.

'If she is hanging out two pairs of pink – what is the word – knick-knacks?'

'Ornaments?'

'Ornaments? Can you wear them?'

'No.'

'Then that is not the word.' The agent racked her brain. 'Ah!' she said at last. 'Briefs? No?'

'Panties?'

'Panties? What are these panties?'

'Knickers.'

'Knickers! Ah, yes. That is what I am looking for. Knickers. If she hanged out two pair of her pink knickers then it was a sign to her lover that the coastline was clear and that he could be coming,' said the woman. 'All went well until one day the woman had la grippe...?' she paused.

'The flu, I think.'

'Ah, yes. The flu. And her mother-in-law came over to help with the washing and the cooking for her son the Jewish policeman. She did the washing and not knowing this code that her daughter-in-law had with her lover she hanged out two pairs of the pink knickers!'

'Oh dear,' I said. My neighbours across the courtyard had stopped arguing and were now kissing.

'The postman, seeing the two pairs of the pink knickers was thinking that the coastline was clear. Excited, and full of high expectations he washed his faces and his hairs, put on some of the aftershave, ran down the stairs and bought some flowers and a bottle of the second best wine from the supermarket below. Then he took the lift up to the apartment of his mistress where, much to his surprise and disappointment the door was opened not by the woman of his dreams but by the mother-in-law who was very much not the woman of his dreams.'

'Oh la la,' I offered, thinking this a suitable French interjection.

'Oh la la indeed,' said the agent. 'Bravo! You see, you do speaking French! The mother-in-law immediately guessed what was happened. She threw out the postmen and made the telephone to her son. He run home onto his apartment and insisted that his sick wife tell to him the name of her lover. She did this and then he shot her. And then he shot the postman.'

'Oh dear.'

'But there is the happy ending.'

'Really?'

'After shooting these people he arrested himself.'

'Ah.' This wasn't quite what I would have called a happy ending. 'Did he go to prison?'

'Oh no. It was what we call the crime passionel. You do not go to prison in France for making the crime passionel.'

'Ah,' I said, making a mental note to try to avoid being involved in any crime passionels unless I wanted to shoot someone. 'The apartment is just what I was looking for,' I said. I looked around. 'Although I will need to redecorate. How much is the rent?'

The woman consulted her clipboard. 'The rent is five thousand francs.'

'A month?'

'A month.'

I hesitated. For the centre of Paris it didn't seem unreasonable. And with the proceeds from the sale of my house and contents, and my small pension, I thought I could probably afford it.

The agent misinterpreted my hesitation. 'I am agreed with you,' she murmured, responding to my silence. It was now her turn to look around. She examined the purple, graffiti stained walls carefully, as though weighing up their artistic value, shook her head slightly from side to side, moved her lips in and out a good deal, hummed, sighed and then, having weighed the aesthetic advantages of the flat's current decor and found it slightly underweight, she winked, conspiratorially. 'You are right. It is a little bit too high.' She bent forward and lowered her voice still further. 'Offer to me four thousand.'

'Four thousand,' I suggested. Feeling courageous I winked back at her.

'Done!' said the agent, slapping her hand on her clipboard. She winked again but this time she smiled as well. She handed me her clipboard and her pen and pointed with her finger at the spot where she wanted me to sign. I signed but decided that between us we'd done more than enough winking.

I walked over to the window and looked out into the courtyard. The couple who had been arguing seemed to have settled their argument. They had moved from the living room to the bedroom and were making up. In the flat below a fat man in a pair of brown corduroy trousers and a considerably off-white string vest was playing a soundless accordion.

I had rented a flat in Paris. I didn't have a view of the Eiffel Tower, Notre Dame or Sacré Coeur but I was now a resident in the most glamorous and most romantic city in the world.

The fact that I was alone and unemployed hardly seemed worth bothering about.

In the flat below the accordionist a slender woman in her thirties and her underwear was sitting in front of a mirror making up her face.

'You will be wishing to have had the flat redecorated a little more to your taste?' the agent inquired. 'If so I have the brother-in-law who...' she allowed the rest of the sentence to fade away.

I held up a hand. 'Thank you, but I will do the decorating myself,' I told her. I had discovered some years earlier that the beauty of self reliance – and 'doing it oneself' lies not so much in the money that is saved but in the anguish which is avoided. It is my experience that dealing with workmen is one of life's most consistently, reliably and enduringly painful experiences. I am not good with a paintbrush but I thought I could probably decorate my small apartment myself though I would need to hire outside experts if I needed to have plumbing or electrical work done.

Although I had no justification for this suspicion I felt that it was likely that French workmen, although perhaps more likely to fill the air with garlic, Gauloise and the aroma of cheap red wine than with strong tea and bacon sandwiches, would probably turn out to be every bit as frustrating and enervating as their English counterparts.

I was relieved to see that the agent did not seem to be at all put out by this declaration of independence. Indeed, her nod of acceptance seemed to contain more than a hint of approval and respect.

As she headed for the door, and I followed, it occurred to me that I didn't have the foggiest idea whereabouts in Paris I had chosen to live. I didn't even know the address. I asked the agent for the name of the street we were in.

The agent seemed surprised to hear that I didn't know where I had decided to live. 'This is the rue Napoleon Bonaparte,' she told me. 'It is between the rue Casimir Périer and the rue de Bellechasse in the seventh arrondissement. It is the very fashionable address.'

I tried to look suitably impressed.

'Now we must back to the office go to fill in some forms!'
she said, and it seemed clear from the way she spoke that this
was the part of the job she looked forward to most.

The estate agent's office was about a quarter of a mile
away. Once we had got there I handed over a deposit and a
down payment on the rent. And then we filled in forms. There
were lots of forms to sign. I didn't understand any of them
but the agent assured me that none of them contained anything terribly important.

'The French don't think they're alive unless they've
signed at least a dozen forms every day,' a friend of Albert's
once told me. After I had been living in Paris for a while a
Frenchman I met confided that neither he nor anyone he
knew ever read any of the official or semi official forms they
signed. 'If we are reading all zee forms we have been signed
we would never be having done the anything else,' he told
me, in wonderfully fractured English. (The French are always quick to criticise foreigners who make slight grammati-
cal errors when attempting to speak their language but they
are invariably deeply hurt if anyone has the temerity to correct their errors when speaking English.) At the time, not
knowing any of this, I simply thought that the agent was unusually zealous.

'What is this one for?' I asked the agent when she produced an especially complicated looking form.

'On this you must promise to be sure that when you are
having left the apartment you will be having left it in the condition it was in which you were overtaking.'

'That's a bit worrying,' I said to the agent.

She paused, looking slightly alarmed. 'What is worrying?'

'I want to decorate the apartment,' I told her. 'I was
hoping to make it look a bit more respectable – a little more
homely. To get it back to its present condition I would have

to hold a series of pretty wild parties and invite in a couple of incontinent elephants. Even then I doubt if I could put all the stains back in the right places.'

'Eleph...? What is the eleph...what you say?'

'Elephant,' I replied. I tried to describe one in the air with my hands. I thought I had done quite well.

'Mountains?' asked the agent, clearly very puzzled.

'No, no.'

'Drummers?'

Frustrated I shook my head and wished I had a dictionary with me.

'No. But close. E-l-e-p-h-a-n-t,' I said, spelling out the word. 'Elephant.'

'Ah!' cried the agent, suddenly understanding. 'An elephant!' She pronounced the word in exactly the same way that I had. She looked at me as if I was completely mad.

'That's right,' I said, apologetically. 'It was just a small joke,' I added, rather feebly.

The agent thought about this for a while and then picked up one of the other forms I had already signed. 'You can't have the elephants in the apartment,' she said, very seriously. 'Clause 44 (b) on this form forbids you to have the non-domestic animals in the apartment.' She patted me on the arm, and lowered her voice. 'But do not worry yourself too much about this,' she went on, reassuringly. 'If you have been improving the condition of the apartment I doubt much if the owner will be too upset if you have had the very small elephant.' She nodded sagely. 'He is the very understanding man.'

When the estate agent had finally run out of forms for her to complete and for me to sign she seemed disappointed that the fun had finished. When we parted she hurried off to try to find another client so that she could fill in some more forms.

I went back to the hotel and managed to re-book my room for an additional two nights. I had decided it would take me at least one day to clear out the rubbish (including the disgusting furniture which the previous tenant had sensibly abandoned when he or she had left) and to give the apartment the spring clean it clearly hadn't had since the end of the French Revolution. It would, I reckoned, then take me another day to acquire some furniture.

# ~ Chapter Ten ~

The estate agent had given me the key to the apartment (together with a smaller key to the mailbox in the hallway) and so the next morning I set off to do some basic shopping. Among the other things on my list were a mop and bucket, some soap, and a large bottle of disinfectant. I also needed to purchase the various ingredients I knew I would need in order to redecorate the flat a little more in keeping with my undoubtedly bourgeois tastes.

I was well aware that my shopping expedition was likely to be made slightly more difficult than it might otherwise have been by the fact that the negotiations would all have to be conducted in a language that was foreign to me but not to the shopkeepers with whom I would be doing business.

When I had decided to visit Paris I had more or less brushed aside the idea of there being any problems associated with the fact that my command of the French language is not exactly what could accurately be described as 'masterly'. But there is a significant difference between being a tourist and ordering a cup of coffee and being a resident and trying to buy a mop and bucket.

I already wished I had paid more attention to my French teachers at school.

My most memorable French teacher was female, beautiful, French and in her early twenties. Her name was Nathalie. She wore very short skirts, very high-heels and very tight sweaters. She was the first woman I'd ever seen who wore eyeshadow and artificial eyelashes. She painted her nails bright, fire engine red. We all thought that only prostitutes did that. One warm summer day she came to school wearing open toed sandals and no stockings. Her toenails were painted in the same fire engine red as her fingernails. We were hypnotised, shocked and bewildered. I was fourteen years of age and my classmates and I decided that all French women were probably also prostitutes in their spare time.

What sort of asexual lunatic expects teenage boys to learn anything from a young, beautiful French woman who wears short skirts, high-heels, tight sweaters and artificial eyelashes and paints her finger and toenails fire engine red?

Now that I had decided to stay in Paris it was becoming increasingly clear that my lack of knowledge of the French language was going to add an extra layer of difficulty (and countless extra opportunities for confusion) to problems which already came equipped with their own built in variety of complications.

The first mistake I made was to buy a phrase-book. This seemed a good idea at the time but I quickly found there were two reasons why it wasn't.

First, even though the book was packed with handy looking phrases none of them were of much practical value. The authors of the book had provided copious amounts of help for travellers wishing to purchase gloves or complain about the state of an over-lumpy mattress to the manager of their hotel but it had absolutely nothing of value in it for Englishmen wanting to buy shower curtain hooks or bath plugs. And nowhere in the book could I find out how to explain to a supercilious shop assistant that I needed a can of white emulsion paint that would cover up purple paint and graffiti written in black felt tip pen.

None of the French people I met ever wanted to know that I had just arrived from the railway station or that my uncle's pen was in the bureau of my aunt (even as a schoolboy I had strongly suspected that the ability to impart this particular piece of information to a Frenchman might prove to be overvalued). And I wasn't staying at a hotel where there was much point in asking the receptionist whether my shoes would be cleaned if I left them outside my door at night. I knew darned well what would happen to my shoes if I was reckless enough to leave them outside my bedroom door.

Second, I quickly discovered that the biggest mistake the traveller can make is to attempt to convince the locals that he speaks their language when he doesn't. This is asking for trouble in a big way. And having a phrase book encourages the traveller in a strange land to walk straight into this particular man trap.

For example, before visiting the local post office to purchase a stamp I studied my phrase book carefully and learned the relevant sentence off by heart. I practised it in front of a shop window. Standing outside on the pavement I tried it out half a dozen times in my head and then, much to the astonishment of a couple of passers by, tried it out aloud.

Then I went into the Post Office.

'Quel est le tarif pour une carte postale pour Angleterre?' I said, the words sliding from my tongue like treacle off a spoon.

That bit of the conversation went well. I said what I had wanted to say and I understood – or at least I was pretty confident that I understood – what I had said.

But that part of the conversation went so well that the grizzle headed clerk behind the counter fired a volley of rapid fire French at the ledger in front of him without looking up.

Only when I responded with silence did he look up. He stared at me, skilfully flicked his Gauloise into the other corner of his mouth, and raised an eyebrow slightly in a way that made it perfectly clear that he was asking a question.

Not having understood a single word he had said I stared back at him unblinkingly and opened and shut my mouth as soundlessly as a ventriloquist's dummy.

He responded by repeating whatever it was he had said. Being a caring Frenchman and wanting to make it easier for me to understand what he was trying to tell me he spoke more quickly and increased the volume.

I stared at him, glumly, swallowed hard and wiped the palms of my hands down the side of my trousers. 'Do you speak English?' I asked, in English, utterly defeated.

The clerk looked at me pityingly, sneered and rolled his eyes. 'How is she you are winting?' he asked. He pronounced each word separately and when he had finished stared at me with the arrogance only a multilingual man of the world can command. The French always speak English with great confidence and authority. They believe that no foreigner can speak their language properly but also believe that their command of other languages is always complete.

Not having the faintest idea what the clerk wanted to share with me I tried again. 'I want a stamp for a postcard,' I explained, in English, now feeling very feeble. 'To send to England,' I added. 'A postcard. A stamp. For England. To send to my sister in Northampton.'

The clerk stared at me without comprehension.

I had the postcard in my hand, ready to be stamped and posted, I lifted it up and showed it to him. I then pointed to the address and, finally, to the place where I intended to affix the stamp I wanted to buy. This simple mime proved wonderfully effective and for several years afterwards mime was to be a fundamental form of communication for me.

The phrase book was soon abandoned. I found it useful just once. It proved to be the perfect thickness to jam under the undersized leg of a wobbly table in a café . I left it there as my lasting contribution to the stability of late French furniture design.

In the bread-shop, next door to the post office, I discovered another problem: should I address the woman behind the counter as 'madame' or 'mademoiselle'?

The one thing I remembered from my French lessons at school was that the gravest faux pas any male can make in France is to address a woman as 'madame' when she really wants to be addressed as 'mademoiselle'. The gravity of this error, I had been assured, can only be compared with the gravity of addressing a woman as 'mademoiselle' when it is her heart's desire to be known as 'madame'.

I had learned that while some women in their late twenties or thirties can be roused close to murder by being called 'mademoiselle' (on the grounds that the insult implies that they are unable to find a husband) others, in exactly the same age group, can be equally offended by being called 'madame' on the grounds that, whatever their legal status might be, they want to think of themselves as still appearing to be young and available.

Attempting to deal with the problem by not using either the word 'madame' or the alternative 'mademoiselle' was, I was taught, an even more heinous crime.

And so I stood outside the bakery next to the post office and tried to decide how to address the shop assistant inside. Through the shop window I could see the baker at work in the back of the shop and a large sign in French, fortuitously simple enough for me to understand, confirmed that bread sold in the shop was freshly baked on the premises and that fresh supplies were put on sale at four hourly intervals throughout the day. I wondered if there was a chance that the baker himself might serve me. I even wondered how long I would have to walk about the streets of Paris to find a bread-shop staffed entirely by male employees.

My problem was that there were two women serving in the shop.

Both wore white overalls and sweet little green and white caps and both had their hair tied back in what I believe used to be called (appropriately in view of the establishment in which they were working) buns.

The older woman, who looked to be in her late forties or early fifties, had a friendly smile and was unusually well-endowed in every visible department. She had lots of very white teeth, slightly bulging eyes, plump, red cheeks, vast amounts of blonde hair, huge shoulders, huge arms and a massive chest. Instead of individually defined breasts she had a large single shelf of bosom.

The younger one, slightly taller but much slimmer, was wearing lots of make-up and her hair was perfect. And through her white coat it was clear that she also had two very well-defined breasts. They weren't particularly large but they were separate.

I decided that by any stretch of the imagination the woman with the shelf like bosom had to be a 'madame' whereas her companion with the twin peaks was clearly a 'mademoiselle'.

And it was in this way that I have since then based my decision on how to speak to French women. I address those with two clearly defined breasts as 'mademoiselle'. Those who have a large amorphous bosom, wherein the two separate parts are merged into one and generally speaking indistinguishable, I address as 'madame'. This simple technique has never failed me.

'Avez vous du pain, s'il vous plaît, madame?' I asked the woman with the universal bosom, speaking in my halting, stuttering French. Since I was, at the time, standing in a shop surrounded by several hundred fine examples of the baker's art the question may have sounded a little odd, superfluous even, but it was the best I could do. I had spent several minutes composing the sentence and I was inordinately proud of it.

'Ah, American!' said the woman, presumably coming to this conclusion on the not unreasonable basis that only an American could possibly ask such an inane question.

'No, no!' I cried quickly, anxious not to be mistaken for a citizen of that uncivilised land. 'I'm English!'

'Ah, you are the English!' said the woman, clearly much happier about this than she had been when she had thought I was American. 'I am for speaking the English!'

'Great!' I said. 'That's good.'

'Though my English she is like the weather,' she went on.

I looked at her and frowned slightly, trying to work out why her English was like the weather.

'Why is it like the weather?' I asked.

'Some days she is good,' replied the bosomy madame, smiling broadly. 'And some days she is bad.' She frowned and looked very sad as she said this.

'I would like to buy some bread,' I said, speaking in English but trying to keep the sentence as simple as possible.

'What are you wanting?' she asked me, waving her arms around in that expansive and (if there are delicate ornaments around) slightly dangerous way that continentals favour.

Looking around, without success, for a simple, sliced white loaf, filled to the crust with a variety of homely chemicals and wrapped in a colourful piece of plastic, I chose and purchased a walking stick length baguette.

A few minutes later, clutching my several feet of warm (it was fresh from the oven) and naked baguette (the bread had been handed over to me wrapped only in a tiny square of greaseproof paper which enabled me to hold it without touching it) I called in at a supermarket and picked up a Camembert cheese, a bottle of wine (cheaper than mineral water in England), a bag of apples, a bottle of disinfectant, a packet of highly coloured cleaning cloths, a box of scouring pads and a pair of toilet rolls and headed back towards my new apartment.

On the way back to my new home-to-be, while looking for an ironmonger's where I could purchase a mop and a bucket, I called in at a chemist's shop so that I could pick up those essentials without which no Englishman abroad can possibly ever feel at home – a hot water bottle, a pair of nail scissors and an eye bath.

Not knowing the French words for any of these items turned a theoretically dull few minutes into something of an adventure. The female assistant in the chemist's shop was very nice. She smiled when she asked me if I needed help. I warmed towards her and felt grateful. We are all kings of our domains. We feel at home in our office or our shop and we rarely stop to think how nervous – even terrified – the visitor may be.

'Avez vous une bouteille pour l'eau chaud?' I asked.

The assistant, a shy looking mademoiselle who was prone to giggling, brought me a thermos flask.

Not having the faintest idea how to rephrase my request so as to make my requirement more obvious I abandoned language and reverted to mime. Twenty minutes later I was the proud owner of a bright pink hot water bottle, a pair of gold plated nail scissors and a small porcelain eye bath ('un bains pour les yeux' seemed to me to be an appropriate phrase but resulted in a good deal more giggling so once again I had reverted to mime). As I left I heard the giggling increase in volume. I half turned as I opened the door and saw that the girl who had served me was whispering to a friend (previously unseen). For a moment it occurred to me that they might be trying to work out what illness I had which required clipping nails, bathing eyes and clutching a hot water bottle. But I quickly comforted myself with the thought that since this was Paris she probably thought I was simply practising some form of bizarre English perversion – some private sexual peccadillo undoubtedly picked up at an English boarding school.

# ~ Chapter Eleven ~

After the chemist's shop I managed to find an ironmonger's; a veritable Aladdin's cave of a shop. The owner had crammed half the stock on shelves from floor to ceiling and strewn the other half on the floor in untidy piles. A third half was hanging from the ceiling, suspended by pieces of knotted string from cuphooks. I found it difficult to move without banging either my knees or my head.

A short woman with bright blue hair and a dazzling white overall stood behind the counter with her arms folded across her not inconsiderable chest. Like many French shop assistants she managed to give the impression that she was in reality a member of a major royal family and was merely standing in the shop in order to keep an eye on things for some impoverished acquaintance.

I have for many years been an aficionado of stationery shops. Allow me to wander unhindered amidst racks of brightly coloured notebooks and newly designed pens that can write upside down and under water and I am filled to the brim with that very same sense of well-being that fills the average, healthy small boy let loose in a small copse of conker trees in early autumn.

But I was setting up home, and for anyone setting up

home a good ironmonger's shop is almost as exciting as a good stationery shop. Within moments the lady in the white coat had generously and graciously allowed me to purchase a red plastic bucket, a wooden-handled mop and a lime green plastic dustpan. I was particularly pleased with the plastic dustpan which came complete with a matching lime green brush with pale yellow bristles. An accompanying label, written in five languages, assured me that the bristles were guaranteed to give lasting service and remain fixed in their sockets for a lifetime (though the guarantee did not say to whose lifetime this referred). I also selected a packet of what I guessed (and hoped) from the label was a proprietary stain remover, a very shiny kettle with a removable whistle attached to its spout, two large white breakfast cups with matching saucers and a rather large aluminium stepladder which, according to the multi-lingual brochure, was equipped with patented non-slip treads and a 'unique safety system designed to reduce the risk of accidents'. I also picked up a small bottle of oil for use on the door lock.

If these items had been my first and only purchases of the day then walking back to my new home would have been little more than a difficult challenge.

But, in addition to the bucket, the mop, the dustpan (with matching brush), the oil, the stain removers, the kettle, the cups and saucers and the rather large aluminium stepladder I was already carrying a Camembert cheese, a bottle of wine, a bag of apples, a bottle of disinfectant, a packet of cleaning cloths, a box of scouring pads, a pair of toilet rolls, a hot water bottle, a pair of nail scissors, an eyebath and a rapidly cooling baguette. I was grateful for the fact that the stamp I had purchased had already been stuck onto a postcard and passed on to other hands. A stamp may be small and light but the straw which broke the camel's back didn't weigh a lot either.

The journey back to the flat was not easy. But in the end I managed it, discovering on the way that carrying a ladder may be slightly inconvenient but it is the best way to walk through Paris. Motorists and other pedestrians all give way to a man carrying a ladder, and in a city where the right of way usually goes to the rudest and most selfish that is something worth knowing. While threading my way through rush hour traffic I have often regretted the fact that I did not have a ladder in my hand and I have, on more than one occasion, thought that the inconvenience of carrying a ladder everywhere might well be outweighed by the advantage it brings with it.

Indeed, the journey went remarkably smoothly (and certainly rather better than I had expected) until I got back to the building wherein lay my apartment.

When I had first viewed the apartment I had regarded the absence of a lift as of little consequence. Indeed, I had convinced myself that this could prove to be something of a boon. By forcing me to climb the stairs the apartment would impose upon me the sort of exercise regime I had long intended to impose upon myself.

But when I had first viewed the apartment I had not been carrying anything. I certainly hadn't been carrying a large aluminium stepladder which seemed to defy all rules of science by becoming heavier with every second that I carried it. When I had picked it up in the ironmonger's shop I had been impressed by its lightness. The woman in the white coat had commented upon this very virtue and had taken the ladder from me and shown me, by lifting it with just one hand, that if ever a ladder could be described as light then this was that ladder.

The main problem (apart from the cumbersome nature of my packages and the fact that as the shopping got heavier so my arms seemed to get weaker) was the fact that the stepladder was rather large and the steps up which I was carrying it were rather narrow and twisted upon themselves so much that they could have been almost described as comprising a spiral staircase.

It did not take me long to realise that I was not going to be able to haul all my purchases up the stairs in one trip. And so I left the ladder in the hallway and took everything else upstairs with me. Having dropped my purchases inside the flat I then hurried back downstairs to collect the ladder before someone else decided that it had been abandoned and was fair game for anyone prepared to provide it with a good home.

It was at this point that my problems really began.

Having already decided to defy scientific logic by becoming steadily heavier the ladder now seemed determined to make my life more difficult by also becoming longer and longer. And, of course, as the ladder got longer and longer the staircase responded by becoming steadily narrower and more twisting with every step I took. I lost count of the number of times the ladder banged into the bannisters, the ceiling, the walls and the doors of the apartments we passed.

'Hello!' said someone somewhere behind me. 'What can I do for you?' She spoke in a beautifully elegant accent which had just the faintest Welsh lilt to it. If you could have turned the accent into glass it would have made the sort of container from which one would only dare drink the very finest malt whisky.

I stopped for a moment, rested the ladder and looked behind me. On the small landing below stood a slim woman in a red silk dressing gown and a pair of red slippers. Her hair was wrapped in a towel that had, with a few skilful twists, been turned into a turban. I have never been very good at guessing women's ages but it was impossible even to make a guess at this woman's age other than to hazard a guess that she was probably somewhere in between sixteen and sixty for her face was covered in that white goo that women sometimes smear onto their faces in order to preserve their complexion.

I had by this time lost track of the floors and had no idea whereabouts in the building I was. All I knew was that my apartment was on the top floor.

The woman put one hand on a hip, stared at me rather defiantly and said something in very rapid French. I didn't have the faintest notion what she was saying to me but using information gleaned from her body language and the tone of her voice I felt safe in coming to the conclusion that she wasn't inviting me in for a cup of tea and a sticky bun.

I apologised, in English, and told her, in halting French, that I did not understand her.

'Did you knock?' she asked in English. She spoke rather sharply and then knocked on her own door to illustrate what she had said.

'No.'

'Oh,' she said, looking down the stairs as though looking to see if there was anyone else in sight. 'I thought someone knocked.'

'Maybe it was the stepladder,' I said. 'I'm sorry. It doesn't fit the staircase very well. It might have accidentally banged on your door.'

'Isn't it a trifle large?' asked the woman, after examining the ladder critically.

I looked at her and then at the ladder. 'Is it?'

'The ceilings in these apartments aren't particularly high,' the woman in the red dressing gown pointed out. 'I hope you're going to be able to get that thing to stand up once you manage to get it wherever you are taking it.'

Once again I looked at her and then at the ladder. This time I also allowed my glance to take in the ceiling in the hallway above me. Suddenly, I felt rather uneasy. It had never occurred to me that the ladder might be too big to fit in my room. 'I hadn't thought of that,' I confessed, feeling rather stupid.

The woman frowned, looked me up and down as though preparing to make an offer for the freehold, and then stared at me rather suspiciously. 'Do you work for one of the local decorating firms?' she asked me. 'I haven't seen you around before.'

'I'm not a decorator,' I said. 'I've just rented a flat upstairs – it needs cleaning up a bit.'

'Oh,' said the woman. She did not sound entirely convinced. 'And you're English?'

'Yes.'

'Well do try and be careful with the ladder,' said the woman. 'Try not to make so much noise and try not to do so much damage to the paint work.' She stared rather pointedly at a spot on the wall next to her door where the ladder had damaged the wall. A small shower of fresh paint flakes on the floor below made it difficult for me to deny responsibility. She then went back into her apartment, gave me one last firm look, and closed the door very firmly. If shutting a door can be punctuation in a conversation this was a row of exclamation marks. I got the impression that, generally speaking, she wasn't too delighted to have met me.

Feeling rather chastened after my first experience with a fellow resident I was a little more careful with the ladder for the rest of the journey up the stairs.

Of course, when I finally got the wretched aluminium monstrosity into my new apartment I discovered that the woman in the towelling turban and the face mask had been absolutely right: the ladder, which now weighed considerably more than it had when I had purchased it, was far too big to stand up.

I had to carry it all the way back down the stairs and then retrace my steps to the ironmongers. There I had to wait for twenty minutes while the woman behind the counter finished a vital telephone conversation (presumably dealing with some item of state – possibly the design of a new crown or the amount of ermine to tack onto her next set of royal robes). And it then took me another twenty five minutes to explain that I needed a smaller ladder. Eventually, she allowed me to swap my big ladder for a smaller one that cost considerably less. She didn't offer to refund the difference in the prices of the two ladders and I didn't have the courage to ask.

All things considered it would have been fair to say that my first day as a Parisian had not gone terribly well. At eight that evening, exhausted and dirty, I decided to head back to my hotel to have a shower and to change my shirt. Before I left my apartment, while struggling to close the front door, I remembered the bottle of oil I had purchased earlier that day. I popped back into the apartment, picked up the oil, used the dropper to add a considerable amount of the fluid to the sticking and slightly rusty lock, put the oil back into the rickety kitchen cupboard, closed the front door firmly (with a little oil in it the lock shut with a reassuringly smooth click and when I tried it, as one does, the door seemed convincingly impenetrable) and went to my hotel pleased that the day had not been entirely wasted since I had managed to complete at least one small chore.

The receptionist, busy watching a rerun of Sergeant Bilko on a flickering television set handed me my key without a word.

Forty five minutes later, feeling much fresher, I wandered along to the café Albert had so lovingly described as 'The Fag and Ferret' to do something about refreshing the inside of my body.

# ~ Chapter Twelve ~

In the Fag and Ferret Albert was firmly in residence; sitting on what was clearly his usual bar stool. He had a whisky glass in his left hand and a pen in his right hand. His notebook lay open on the counter in front of him. A couple of lines, written in his distinct handwriting, showed that he had been working.

I sat down on the empty bar stool next to the columnist but said nothing. Since he was working I did not want to disturb him.

'You haven't changed your mind, then?' he said, without looking at me.

'No,' I said. 'I haven't.' I thought for a moment. 'How did you know I hadn't changed my mind?'

'You wouldn't have come back here if you had,' he replied.

I thought for a moment and smiled a little. He was, of course, quite right. If I had changed my mind I would have snuck quietly back to England.

'Now that I'm staying here I'm going to have to learn to speak French,' I said to Albert.

'Why do you want to learn French?' asked Albert. He leant forwards slightly on his stool, concentrating hard.

I thought for a moment. 'So that I can speak to the French,' I answered, rather lamely. 'In shops and so on,' I added, unimaginatively.

'The deaf and dumb get by,' said Albert flatly. 'Besides nearly everyone who matters speaks English. And if they don't then they ought to learn.' He emptied his glass and ordered a refill. I would quickly learn that Albert drank more than anyone I had ever met. If there had been national teams for drinking Albert would have qualified for any team in the world – including a French team – but he somehow managed to remain thoughtful and incisive right up to the moment when he fell off his stool. (This was something he did rather often but always with enormous grace. Albert did everything with grace and style.)

'But I think I ought to make a bit of an effort,' I said. 'When did you learn to speak French?' I asked him. 'Did you speak French before you came to Paris? Did you take lessons? Or did you just, sort of pick it up as you went along?'

'My French is awful,' said Albert.

'It's amazing!' I said. 'You jabber away like a native. Did you go to a language school? Conversation classes?'

'I only know a few words,' said Albert, with a depreciatory shrug.

'Surely we all have some sort of obligation to learn their language,' I argued, rather pompously. 'We're the foreigners here.'

'How can we be foreign?' demanded Albert, indignantly. 'We're English! If we speak English to them it will help make them more international. It'll help them build up their exports. And there will be less need for us to speak French.'

'But you're fluent in French!' I pointed out.

'Only if you ignore the fact that I don't know any grammar and my vocabulary is minuscule,' said Albert.

I didn't say anything. I didn't want to push him into giving me advice if he didn't want to give it. For a while we sat in silence.

'I suppose you're right,' said Albert, after a long delay. He sighed. He was a great sigher. 'You should learn French. You never know when you might need it. Have you heard of Jack Kahane?'

I thought for a moment and then shook my head. 'No.'

'Have you heard of Maurice Girodias?'

Once again I had to shake my head and say 'No'.

'God you are ignorant, aren't you? Maurice Girodias was a publisher who worked in Paris. He published The Story of O. Have you heard of that?'

I said I had.

'Ha!' said Albert knowingly. 'Girodias published many great writers and many great books – most of which had been turned down by other publishers. He published Samuel Beckett, Lawrence Durrell, Jean Genet, Henry Miller, William Burroughs and Vladimir Nabokov.'

I was impressed and said so.

'Maurice Girodias's father was also a publisher. His name was Jack Kahane. I can't for the life of me remember how a Kahane became a Girodias. Kahane was an amazing Englishman who launched the Obelisk Press in Paris and published a book called *The Tropic of Cancer* by an unknown American called Henry Miller.'

'I've heard of that.'

Albert looked at me. 'I'm glad to hear it,' he said wryly. 'Anyway, in 1914, at the outbreak of World War I, Jack Kahane rushed off to join the French Foreign Legion. He was turned down for a position in the Legion – I don't know why but the authorities presumably didn't see him as Beau Geste. Undeterred by this minor setback he got a job as an army interpreter in the French cavalry. There were, however, just two gaps in his CV that might have been considered something of an impediment for a man yearning to make his way as an interpreter in the French cavalry. First he couldn't ride a horse. And second, he didn't speak French.'

'So what happened?'

'I rather think they sent him home,' said Albert thoughtfully. He sipped at his fresh drink.

It seemed to me that the lesson here was that learning French would stand me in good stead if I ever wanted to join the French Army.

'But, on the other hand I remember meeting a woman from Hereford who got herself a job in a large, very bureaucratic French bank,' continued Albert. 'She had lied on her application form and claimed that she could speak French. In fact she spoke only one word – and that was 'Non'.'

'She said it was the most terrifying experience of her life – and not something that she would recommend to anyone else. To begin with she simply said 'Non!' to everyone and everything in the hope that this would keep her out of trouble. Her boss thought her problem was shyness and so she was put on the switchboard. She told me it was a miracle that she didn't ruin the company because she said 'Non' to every caller and shut them off without giving them a chance to say anything. After a week she progressed to adding 'Je suis désolée' and after another week she added 'Il n'est pas ici'.'

'What happened in the end?'

'She was promoted, of course. And eventually she learned enough French to do her job.'

I scratched my head. 'So it might not be a bad idea to start learning a little French now? In case I need to join the French cavalry or get myself a job in a French bank.'

'Exactly,' said Albert. 'I have French conversation lessons with a woman I know,' he added. For some reason it sounded like a confession.

I waited.

'I met her when I first came to Paris,' said Albert. 'There was a notice in the local tobacconist's shop. 'Pretty Young Woman Gives French Lessons.''

I looked at him, not sure whether or not he was being funny.

'I was young and naive,' explained Albert with a shrug. 'I made an appointment and went to her flat.' He looked at me and grinned. 'I genuinely thought she was a French teacher.'

'But she wasn't?'

'Of course she wasn't,' said Albert, with a snort. 'But she was amused by my innocence and, I think, rather taken by the idea of being able to earn money in a relatively honest sort of way. She was twenty-two and she'd been a prostitute for seven years. For her it was a novelty to earn money without having to remove her clothes. So for an hour we just talked and at the end of the hour I booked another appointment. She didn't have the faintest idea what to charge me and so – I found this out much later – she pretended to go to the toilet but instead went out into the hall, looked up a genuine French teacher in the telephone directory, rang her and asked her price. Then she came back and charged me that. That was thirty years ago.'

'Does she take other students?' I asked him.

Albert looked at me and smiled. 'You don't give up, do you?' He thought for a moment. 'I'll take you to her flat and introduce you,' he promised.

I looked at him and started to ask him something.

'Yes,' he answered, guessing my question, and answering it before I had asked it. 'Yes, she still works as a prostitute. Mostly she services her regular clients. Some of them have been going to her for as long as I have.'

I was looking forward to meeting Albert's French teacher.

# ~ Chapter Thirteen ~

I felt rather nervous as I accompanied Albert on the walk to the building where his French teacher had her private apartment.

'Lucie has three homes – all on the right bank,' Albert had explained. 'She has a private apartment near the Palais Royal. That's where she lives and where she gives me my French lessons. The fees I pay are pin money. She couldn't live off her earnings as a teacher – certainly not the way she lives. Her second home – what she calls her working apartment – is just off the Rue St Denis. That is where she entertains the customers whose contributions pay her mortgage and food bills. A small and rather dour Brazilian widow called Marie-Claire lives there. She looks after the apartment and acts as her maid. I'm not sure precisely how a census collector would describe Marie-Claire's job but, among other things, she collects the fees from the customers and makes sure that there are always fresh clean towels in Lucie's shower room and next to the bidet, fresh sheets on the bed and a plentiful supply of condoms in the top drawer of the bedside cabinet. And, finally, Lucie rents a room at a bordello two streets away from her working apartment.'

'What a wonderfully old-fashioned word!'

'Bordello?'

'Round where I lived when I was a kid they were called brothels. Not that there were many of them as far as I know.'

'Paris is full of them. Most of them specialise. But the one where Lucie works is pretty general I think.'

'Specialise? How? What do you mean?'

Albert laughed. 'You'd be surprised! There are houses for men who like to be tied up and beaten. And there are houses where the women all dress in rubber. At one time there was a brothel on the Île St Louis where all the prostitutes were over 70 years old.'

'You're kidding!'

'I'm not,' insisted Albert. 'Prostitution isn't just the oldest profession. It's also always been one of the most popular. At the start of the 20th century there were 100,000 prostitutes in Paris serving a population of under three million. Most of the actresses and nurses in Europe were also prostitutes. Child prostitution was legal and girls of eight toured the cafés at night selling themselves to anyone – male or female – who would pay them.'

It was clear that Albert had done some research. It occurred to me that it probably made it easier for him to accept Lucie's occupation. I was beginning to get the feeling that she was more to him than just a teacher.

'Who owns the bordello where Lucie works?'

'The owners are a Belgian couple – I think they must be in their seventies. He's mean and humourless, has a small toothbrush moustache and looks like a retired tax collector. He looks ten years older than he is. She's still voluptuous, looks at least twenty years younger than she is and looks like everyone's favourite auntie. She still looks after a few of her older clients. They provide room service and the customers and collect the money. They take 75% of whatever Lucie earns and give her the rest – in cash – at the end of every day.

The brothel charges relatively low fees but it's a high through-put establishment – depending more on quantity than qual-ity. Curiously, Lucie once told me that Sunday morning is their busiest time of the week.'

'Lucie doesn't have a pimp?' I asked. I had thought all prostitutes had pimps. It occurred to me that Albert, who had spoken rather lovingly about his friend, was very knowl-edgeable about Lucie's professional habits. He clearly knew a great deal about her domestic and working arrangements.

'I suppose the brothel owners are the nearest she's got to a pimp these days,' said Albert. 'I remember that she used to have an arrangement with a huge West Indian fellow called Eddie. He was coal black, about six and a half feet tall and as skinny as a rake. He looked like the archetypal pimp: huge expensive gold rings, a broad brimmed white Fedora and an ancient Lincoln Continental in powder blue. He was a pas-tiche; absurdly over dressed. He always carried a knife and looked after Lucie and a dozen other girls. If ever they had any trouble with a customer he'd be there and he'd sort things out. She relied on him for years – probably ten or fifteen years altogether – and I never heard her say a bad word about him. But he got arrested for drug dealing about five or six years ago. He was sent to prison and he died after being stabbed in the back with a sharpened spoon. The newspa-pers reported that a teenage drug addict did it because Eddie had beaten him at table tennis. Since then, as far as I know, Lucie has never had a pimp.'

'Does she have any other, er, language students?' I asked Albert as we crossed the Pont Neuf on our way to Lucie's apartment.

'No,' replied the journalist. 'She was charmed and flat-tered when she discovered that people would pay her simply to talk to them – and that she didn't even have to talk dirty. But I don't think she's ever taken any other students.' He stopped for a moment to buy two small conically shaped white paper bags full of hot chestnuts from an Algerian street seller. He handed the vendor a twenty franc note, took the two proffered bags of chestnuts and handed one to me.

'When did you find out that she wasn't just a language teacher?' I asked, picking the top chestnut from the bag and popping it into my mouth. It was hotter than I expected and I bounced the chestnut around in my mouth for a few seconds.

'I don't think it was until about my third or fourth visit,' replied Albert, chewing one of the chestnuts. I had noticed that when he had plucked the chestnut from the bag he had sensibly juggled it in the palm of his hand for a few seconds before putting it into his mouth. 'At the beginning I saw her at her working flat and I had noticed that one or two of the blokes I met on the stairs looked rather furtive,' he said. 'But that didn't give the game away because I knew that most of the men who visit prostitutes in Paris do so pretty openly. They don't much care if their wives find out. It's the French way. So when I noticed that one or two — probably Americans or Germans I suspect — hid their faces with their hands when we passed I just thought they were a bit odd.'

'It was her English vocabulary which eventually gave the game away,' said Albert. 'She had picked her English up from her customers and so, as you can imagine, the words she'd learned were rather...,' unusually he seemed to be struggling for the right word and he left the sentence unfinished.

'Like all professionals she had a rather specialised vocabulary,' I suggested.

'Exactly,' said Albert, gratefully. 'I remember being rather startled when I found myself taking part in a long discussion about the aesthetic and practical advantages and disadvantages associated with circumcision. She seemed to be exceptionally experienced in this area and had clearly had close contact with many examples of both types of penis. When I tentatively expressed some surprise at the fact that a young, unmarried French teacher should know so much about penile architecture she laughed and asked me if I did not know what she really did for a living. When I confessed that I didn't she thought it very funny. She told me the truth without any sense of shame.'

'When I found out I was shocked. I was terribly innocent at the time and even though we hadn't even kissed I rushed out of her apartment at the end of that day's lesson and bought myself a large bottle of antiseptic and some carbolic soap. I then raced home and had a hot bath.'

'When it came time to go back for my next lesson I very nearly didn't go. But in the meantime I'd been to the American library and checked up on venereal diseases. Reassured that it wasn't possible to catch any of the best known diseases simply by sitting on a chair I went back. I even found the courage to accept a cup of coffee and a slice of chocolate cake.'

Albert stopped at a flower stall and started buying flowers. He bought red roses, carnations and irises. When the lady running the stall had wrapped the flowers and Albert had paid her we continued our journey.

'Never visit Lucie without taking her a present,' said Albert. 'Flowers, chocolate, champagne – it doesn't matter which. If you fall in love with her – which you will – you can take her jewellery occasionally.' He looked at me. 'But never take her anything cheap.'

'Are you in love with her?'

Albert looked at me but did not answer the question.

I didn't press him. The answer was obvious.

# ~ Chapter Fourteen ~

The building where Lucie lived was remarkably like the one in which my own apartment was situated, though the entrance was considerably smarter. There was no lift but the narrow, bare wood staircase was obviously waxed and polished regularly by conscientious hands. As we climbed the stairs I noticed that there were fresh flowers on every window sill.

Lucie's apartment was on the third floor and by the time we got there Albert was wheezing and puffing rather badly. He was not in very good shape. A small card carrying Lucie's name and telephone number had been fitted into a tiny metal frame above the door bell.

We stood there for a moment while Albert recovered from the climb.

'Shall I ring the bell?' I asked.

'Not...yet,' wheezed the out of condition journalist.

We waited a little longer while he recovered.

Finally, when his breathing was more normal Albert stepped forward. He ignored the bell and knocked on the door with the knuckles of his right hand.

I felt inexplicably nervous. Although I had no idea what

Lucie looked like I was expecting her to open the door wearing a red PVC micro-skirt, fishnet stockings, red patent shoes with five inch heels, a diaphanous blouse and a cleavage-enhancing black bra. I expected her to be wearing lots of lipstick, half a pound of eye make-up and a shoulder-length strawberry blonde wig. In other words I expected Lucie to open the door looking exactly like the stereotyped Parisian prostitute. When I realised this I felt rather ashamed of myself. She would, I realised, probably be wearing an expensive grey silk Chanel suit and a pair of elegant Christian Dior shoes.

There was a spyhole in the middle of the solid-looking wooden front door to Lucie's flat and I had an uneasy feeling that Albert and I were being spied on by the resident on the other side of the door. Or, rather, that since Albert was well known to the occupier I was being spied on and carefully studied.

Suddenly, there was the sound of a bolt being pulled back. And then the sound of a safety chain being slipped out of its catch. And then the door opened and I met Lucie for the first time.

If I hadn't known that Lucie was much older, I would have guessed that she was about thirty-five. She was surprisingly tall (though several inches of this was down to the heels on her shoes) and distinctly curvaceous rather than plump. She had a mature and memorable figure; she was extremely attractive.

She was wearing a red PVC micro skirt, fishnet stockings, red patent leather shoes with five inch heels, a diaphanous blouse, a cleavage enhancing black bra, a lot of bright red lipstick, half a pound of eye make-up and a shoulder length strawberry blonde wig. In short, when Lucie opened the door she looked exactly like a stereotyped Parisian prostitute.

Of course, sometimes our prejudices and preconceived notions are absolutely spot on.

'My darling!' said Lucie, throwing her arms around the journalist, kissing him and leaving lipstick marks on both cheeks. 'You are so fit!' she said. She turned to me. 'Most of my visitors are out of breath by the time they reach my door, but Albert never is!' Albert turned to me and winked and then gave Lucie the flowers he had bought her. Lucie oohed and aarhed and said how beautiful they were and then Albert introduced me and Lucie gave me the same treatment.

'This man is my very dearest friend,' Lucie said to me with her arms around my neck. 'As Henry Adams once said "One friend in a lifetime is much; two are many; three are hardly possible. Friendship needs a certain parallelism of life, a community of thought, a rivalry of aim".' It seemed odd to hear Henry Adams quoted by a French prostitute but Lucie was, I was to learn, very well read.

She smelt strongly of a subtle and therefore presumably expensive and undoubtedly French perfume. I felt her fingernails dig into my neck and when she eventually released me I instinctively looked down; her nails, which were perfectly manicured and painted bright pink, were the longest I'd ever seen.

'You have to excuse me,' said Lucie, looking down. 'I am still in my working clothes. I got home just two minutes ago and did not have time to change.'

'You've been working hard?' asked Albert.

'Phew!' said Lucie, closing her eyes and shaking her head. 'Oh la la!' she shook her hand as though trying to get rid of droplets of water. 'It has been the world cup,' she sighed, rolling her eyes heavenwards. 'Paris has been full of men full of drink and urges.'

'My friend wants to learn French,' said Albert. 'Would you give him lessons?'

Lucie looked me up and down, as though she were a customer at a slave market and she was trying to decide whether or not to put in a bid at the auction. 'He is a good looking man,' she conceded, seemingly thinking aloud. 'Just coming into the prime of his life.' Feeling rather flattered I felt myself blushing. She nodded and bit her lower lip. 'I will take him,' she said at last. She turned to Albert. 'I would take him anyway because he is your friend, but him I take for him too.' She moved a little closer and took my hand.

'You do not have a wife, do you?'

I admitted that this was an area of my life where there was a job vacancy.

'I can tell,' said Lucie, with a nod. She put her arm around me and gave me an affectionate squeeze.

Albert grinned at me. 'You're falling in love with her already aren't you?'

'I am,' I admitted, without shame or embarrassment.

'Would you like some champagne?' Lucie asked us.

'Splendid idea,' said Albert.

'You drink too much,' Lucie told him. 'You will have one glass only. Or your liver will go poof, like this!' she made a fist and then reached up and threw her fingers wide open. It was obvious from the way she spoke and looked at him that she cared about Albert very much. 'You get the glasses,' she told him. 'I will put these beautiful flowers into water and get the Bolly out of the fridge.'

I looked at Albert as Lucie took her flowers and hurried off, presumably towards her kitchen. 'Bolly?'

'Bollinger,' explained Albert. He walked over to a cupboard, opened it and took out three cut glass champagne glasses.

Lucie returned moments later with the flowers, resplendent in a huge, very expensive-looking vase, in one hand and a bottle of Bollinger champagne in the other.

'There you are,' she said, putting the flower vase down on a small glass-topped table and handing the champagne to Albert. 'You open this, no?'

'Yes, certainly,' said Albert, taking the bottle and quickly and skilfully unwrapping the foil from around the cork, released it without losing a drop of champagne, and carefully filled the three glasses.

Lucie turned to me. 'You have a French girlfriend? You want to make passionate love to her in French?'

'Er, no, I'm afraid not,' I said, shaking my head. 'Unfortunately,' I added.

'Ah,' said Lucie, making a sympathetic moue. 'You want to learn business French? You are a rich businessman?'

'Sadly, no.'

'What then?

'Well, I just thought I would like to know a little grammar,' I explained. 'How to decline a verb, that sort of thing.'

She looked at me and then at Albert. 'How to decline a verb?' she repeated, looking puzzled.

'Verbs are doing words,' explained Albert, now busy with the wire cage which held the cork in place. The foil, screwed up into a ball, had been tossed onto the glass-topped table next to the flowers. 'Like 'to drink'.'

'Drink is a verb?'

'Yes.'

Lucie looked puzzled, and frowned. 'How do you decline a verb?' she asked, looking first at him and then at me. She shrugged her shoulders in the elegant but expressive way that only the French have ever mastered. 'If you are polite you say, "That is very kind of you but no thank you I have already got one". And in French that is "Vous êtes très gentil. Mais non merci. Déjà j'en ai un".' She turned to Albert. 'But why would anyone want to decline a drink – especially a glass of Bollinger?'

And thus began my first French lesson. Learning French with Lucie was clearly going to be lots of fun.

When we left I knew that Albert was in love with Lucie but I found myself wondering if he knew just how much he was in love with her.

# ~ Chapter Fifteen ~

'It's noisy in here,' I said to Albert. We were sitting in the Fag and Ferret and a group of brightly dressed party goers were shouting and drinking very noisily in one corner of the café .

'They're celebrating New Year,' explained Albert.

For a moment I was confused by this remark. I had to look at my watch and check the date. 'But it isn't New Year.'

'It isn't our New Year,' Albert corrected me. 'But it's obviously their New Year. Whoever they are.'

I looked at him, puzzled.

'The ancient Greeks celebrated New Year on 10th June and 20th September,' explained Albert. 'The Phoenicians celebrated on November 21st, the medieval Christians on March 15th. I can't remember when the Chinese celebrate but I'm pretty sure it isn't December 31st or January 1st.'

'Do you often get people in here celebrating New Year?'

'No. It's usually quiet at this time of the evening,' Albert replied. He lifted his glass to his mouth and swallowed a couple of ounces of fluid. 'Under normal circumstances – if you believe there is ever such a thing as normal circumstances – The Fag and Ferret has three types of customer,' he began. (I was to learn that the monologue was Albert's favourite form of conversation. Once switched into action he would talk almost endlessly. But since everything he said was interesting – and the way he said it made it even more so – I never objected in the slightest. My contribution to our conversations was usually confined to tossing in the occasional word of encouragement or, when he seemed temporarily to have run out of steam, tossing another log onto the fire by asking a question or making a comment which would trigger off another stream of consciousness. You didn't have to be with Albert for long to realise that he was not only cynical and sharp but also one of the funniest and one of the wisest men you'd ever known.)

'During the day the Fag and Ferret's clientele consists largely of people who, either permanently or temporarily, work in the area: shop girls, taxi drivers, street cleaners, plumbers, policemen, civil servants and so on.'

'Civil servants?' I said, rather surprised. I had always thought of civil servants as being rather dull individuals; not at all the type of people to patronise a café .

'The French government is by far the biggest employee in France,' explained Albert. 'If you run a business then you inevitably end up with civil servants as customers.' He shrugged and continued. 'The day time clientele patronise the café between about seven and nine in the morning – when they call in for a breakfast coffee, a croissant and, if it's cold, a nip of brandy to keep the chill out of their bones; between twelve and two in the afternoon they call in for lunch, a bottle of wine and half a bottle of mineral water to clean out their livers – and at around six in the evening – when they call in for a Ricard or a brandy before going home for dinner.'

'During the late evening, and throughout the night the clientele consists largely of those who live in the immediate area and of night workers (bar staff, prostitutes, pimps, waitresses, taxi drivers and so on). They don't usually start to patronise the café until about ten at night when the locals call in for a drink, a smoke and a chat before bed and the workers call in for their first interlude of the night.'

'The third type of client, the tourists, are mostly afternoon callers. In the mornings they are usually too busy sightseeing or shopping to sit in a café . In the evenings they are too busy rubbing cream on one another's blistered feet to venture far out of their hotels. They may totter in for a plate of steak and chips – they are always convinced that they are eating a slice of some unfortunate nag which has been retired from the racecourse after a series of disastrous results but although they express some slight disgust at this it never dulls their appetite; in some mysterious way they desperately love the idea of being able to tell their friends back home that they've been to Paris and eaten horse meat but they rarely stay for more than twenty minutes or so. If they are American they like to be in and out even faster.' He shook his head, slowly and clearly with sadness. 'The Americans always think that speed and size are the only things that matter,' he said. I was to learn in time that he loathed Americans more than anyone. 'Their steaks have to be bigger than anyone else's, their women have to have bigger breasts than anyone else's, they have to talk louder, they have to have more money, travel further and go faster,' he shook his head again, and took another sip from his whisky glass. 'They're all size and no substance,' he said. 'They travel more than anyone else but they see far less than anyone.' He emptied his whisky glass and turned to me. 'Sorry,' he said, with a grin. 'Do you want a drink? Will you have a vin chaud?'

'Are you working?' I asked him, nodding towards the notebook. 'I don't want to disturb you.'

'I'd rather talk than write at the moment,' Albert replied. 'It's less tiring on the arm.' He put his pen into his inside jacket pocket, closed his notebook, picked it up and slipped it into his right hand outer jacket pocket. 'Vin chaud?'

I thanked him and said I would. 'By the way, I bought a paper so that I could read your column.'

Albert waved a hand in the barman's direction, told him what he wanted and then looked at me with one eyebrow raised slightly. 'You've already read it,' he reminded me.

'I wanted to read it in the paper,' I told him. I smiled and shrugged, feeling rather embarrassed. 'It seemed odd to see it in print,' I said. 'I know I only read it over the phone but I felt I had a sort of part interest in it.' I looked at him. 'Do you still buy the paper everyday?'

Albert nodded. 'I still get a kick out of seeing my column in print,' he admitted. 'But if you tell anyone I said that I'll deny it.' He paused. 'I pretty much hate newspapers. These days the editors spend their days thinking up new scares so that they can frighten the readers into having to buy tomorrow's paper. It's a twin conspiracy. The advertisers sell products to help people deal with the fears the newspapers have created.'

'Don't you find it difficult – having to think up something new to write about every day?'

Albert shook his head. 'I find it difficult to choose what to write about,' he said. 'Normal people learn to suppress their prejudices so as not to upset others. For years now I've been paid to foster my prejudices and to share them with the good old general public. Most people push their fears and their anger into some deep dark place. I hang mine out in public – and get paid well for it. It's probably the only job in the world that is both cathartic and remunerative.'

The barman delivered two glasses of steaming hot vin chaud. And then brought the slices of orange, the pot of cannelle and the sachets of sugar.

'Of course, all my prejudices are soundly based and

well-founded,' said Albert. 'And one should stick with one's prejudices if they are soundly based and well-founded.' He carefully slid a slice of orange into his hot wine and then added a good sprinkling of cinnamon. 'Fortunately, writing a column is not quite as easy as it looks,' Albert told me.

'I don't think it looks easy at all.'

'A lot of people do,' sighed Albert. 'And it is fairly easy to write one column. Or two. The difficult trick, however, is to manage to keep writing columns week in and week out for a year, two years, three years and so on...' he waved a hand in the air rather airily and then reached out and picked up a sachet of sugar. He tore open the sachet and emptied the contents into his wine. I dropped a slice of orange into mine and as the hot liquid splashed out onto my hand realised instantly why Albert had performed the apparently simple task with such care.

'You have to tell the readers something they already know along with something they don't know,' said Albert. 'You have to give them something to talk about over dinner or in the pub. You have to make them cross, make them laugh or make them cry. You have to make them respond. You have to touch people's hearts from a distance; to make them feel passion where there was no passion and to make them feel joy and delight where there was nothing but sadness and despair. It doesn't matter whether they like you or hate you, agree with you or disagree with you. But it is vital that you force a response out of them. And, when you've been there for a while, if you're any good they end up buying the paper because you write for it. And when that happens you're in a strong position.'

'Which I would imagine you are,' I said.

Albert shrugged. 'If I didn't drink so much I would be,' he admitted. I gathered that the previous evening hadn't been the first time he had ruffled a few editorial feathers. He tore open a second sachet of sugar and added the contents to his red wine. I followed his example.

'Your column reads very easily,' I told him. 'It gives the reader the impression it was easy to write.'

Albert looked at me and smiled. 'Things that look as though they were easy to write are invariably the hardest to write,' he told me. 'The incomprehensible stuff that the broadsheets print, those long, acres of print that look clever and academic, and are nigh on impossible to read, are the sort of stuff that anyone can write. They're easy to write. Pieces that are easy to write are usually full of preconceptions and old, recycled prejudices – they contribute very little that is new.' He paused. 'My prejudices are mostly new and definitely all my own.'

He picked up his glass of vin chaud and sipped at it appreciatively. 'What sort of day have you had?' he asked me, suddenly changing the subject, without any warning. This, I was to learn, was typical behaviour on his part. If he felt bored with the way a conversation was going he would simply stop and start to talk about something else – usually something completely different. 'Are you feeling nervous? Do you think you made the right decision? Have you decided where you are going to live?'

'I'm feeling apprehensive,' I admitted. 'But I think I made the right decision. And rather to my surprise I've already found a flat – sorry an apartment.'

Albert looked at me without disguising his surprise. He raised his glass. 'Congratulations!' he said, and I got the impression that he meant it. 'I've been living in Paris for more years than I can remember and I still live in a hotel. When I first came here I couldn't afford to buy a flat and the banks wouldn't lend me any money because I didn't have any money.' He looked at me. 'Have you noticed that?' he asked me. 'It's one of the great ironies of modern life – banks only want to lend money to people who don't need it.'

I smiled and nodded.

'I didn't have any money because I'd just got divorced. And that's a crazy story. I was working as news editor before I came here. Going home at eleven o'clock one night I realised that I was only going home to sleep. I decided to give in my notice and to try and get a job with more reasonable hours so that I could spend more time with my wife.' He shrugged. 'I was a bit too late,' he said. 'My wife was already having an affair with an assistant golf professional who'd helped her get her handicap down to 18 and her self-esteem up to par. She took me for everything I'd got – and quite a bit more too.'

I thought I ought to say something but I wasn't sure what.

'I thought about finding somewhere to rent,' continued Albert. 'But I was brought up to think of renting as unacceptable and now that I have enough money for the banks to fall over backwards to lend me as much as I need I keep meaning to find a flat but I've never got round to it.' He shrugged. 'Still, there are hot and cold running chambermaids in the hotel.' He grinned. 'How the hell did you manage it?'

'It was more by accident than design,' I admitted. I told him the story of how I had found my apartment. Albert listened attentively.

'I'm impressed,' he said. 'Isn't it an amazing city, though?' Most other big cities are crammed with so many department stores, government buildings, office blocks and theatres that there isn't room for people to live. Paris is full of apartments of all shapes and sizes and prices.'

I agreed with him that Paris did seem to be a wonderful city.

'The real key is the fact that the people who run the city have made sure that they've kept room for the array of little shop keepers who are essential for a decent civilised life.' He sipped from his hot wine. 'How many bakers are there within a quarter of a mile of your new flat?'

I thought for a moment. 'At least three,' I told him. I thought again. 'No, four. At least.'

'How many cobblers?'

'I can think of two within a couple of hundred yards.'

'That's what makes Paris a great and wonderful city,' said Albert, emphatically. 'Not the Eiffel Tower or Notre Dame or the River Seine or the other tourist sights – glorious though they are. It's the fact that it is a real city, with real people living in it. The key is the fact there are plenty of bakers, butchers and candlestick makers around.'

I drank a little of my vin chaud. It tasted very good. Just then another group of revellers who had been celebrating their New Year in a nearby café poured into the Fag and Ferret. They were waving balloons and streamers and bottles of wine and were clearly having a very good time. They made their way over to the corner where the other revellers were sitting drinking and celebrating.

'Goodnight,' I said to Albert, thinking that this was probably a good moment to go back to my hotel and get some sleep. 'Aren't you going to join the party?' asked Albert, who had already acquired a balloon, a paper hat and an opened bottle of wine from the new revellers.

'I'm going to get an early night,' I said. 'I've got a flat to clean out tomorrow...' I looked at my watch and corrected myself...'later today.'

I turned towards the door and waved goodnight.

# ~ **Chapter Sixteen** ~

Cleaning my new apartment was harder work than I had thought it would be and consequently the task took much longer than I had expected.

Things were not helped by the fact that the day began badly.

When I arrived at the flat the next morning I discovered that I couldn't open the door. My key just didn't work; the door seemed to be jammed solid. I was annoyed because, having oiled the lock thoroughly the night before, I thought I had dealt with this particular problem.

Unable to get into the flat I went back down the stairs and walked round to the agents. The woman I had dealt with before was out with a client but a young colleague of hers, called Paulette, came back to the flat with me to see if her key would work where mine had failed. When it didn't we went back to her office and she telephoned for a locksmith. We then went back to the apartment to await his arrival.

'I'm sorry about this,' said Paulette, as we stood together on the landing. Paulette, who was in her twenties, was rather short but generously proportioned. My grandfather, who had never had to confront the concept of political correctness, would have described her as having been built for comfort rather than speed.

'That's OK,' I said. 'It's not your fault.'

'I think it is going to rain later.'

'Do you?'

'I should have brought an umbrella.'

'Umbrellas are brilliant aren't they?' I said. 'Very useful.' I suddenly felt embarrassed at the inanity of the conversation. 'How long have you worked for the agency?' I asked, realising that since it was impossible for two people to stand on a cramped, dark landing and not talk to one another we really needed to find a more convivial and interesting subject than the weather and the usefulness of umbrellas.

'A little over a year,' replied Paulette.

'Do you like it?'

'It is quite an interesting job. I get to meet lots of people. But my real love is antiques.'

'Would you like to work with antiques?'

'Oh yes,' she replied. 'I want to be a dealer. I love old furniture.' Paulette's English was very good. 'My uncle works with antiques.'

'What does he do?'

'He is a dealer. He buys and sells antiques.'

'Ah.' I nodded wisely.

'He has taught me many things about antiques,' said Paulette proudly. 'Have you furnished your apartment yet?'

'Not yet,' I admitted.

'You came from England?'

'Yes.'

'You did not have furniture there? Did you not bring any with you?'

'I sold just about everything I owned,' I said. 'I arrived here with just two suitcases.'

'How romantic!' said Paulette. 'But it doesn't matter. You should find a woman. Women always have lots of stuff.'

119

'It's not that easy,' I told her.

'Then you should buy antiques,' she told me. 'Many people buy cheap furniture as a temporarily measure. They convince themselves that they will get rid of it and replace it with something better. But they don't, of course. They still have it twenty years later. I am furnishing our apartment by buying good furniture one piece at a time. I would rather have two nice pieces of furniture than eight or ten pieces of cheap rubbish.'

'That's good advice.'

'My uncle has taught me a great deal about antiques. He is very creative. He taught me that if you put screws in salt and horse brasses in vinegar you can make them look old. And if you soak a new piece of wood in old sump oil the wood will absorb the oil and look much older than it is.'

'Right,' I said, slightly surprised to receive a lesson in faking antiques from someone I had only just met.

'He makes holes in new furniture and fills the holes with wholemeal flour. This makes it look as though the holes have been made by woodworm which have left their dust behind. When buyers see woodworm holes they believe the furniture to be older than it is.' Paulette smiled at me, obviously proud of her imaginative relative. 'He buys old copies of Le Monde and uses them to line the drawers of cabinets he has had made. The buyer looks at the old newspaper and thinks that this is proof that the cabinet is equally old. That is clever, no?'

'Er, yes. I suppose so,' I agreed.

'He has also taught me how to behave at auctions. When he goes to an auction he takes with him a can of vegetable dye. If he sees a nice piece of lace he sprays the dye onto the lace. This reduces the price. He takes keys and knobs and handles from pieces of valuable furniture and puts them into his pockets. This also reduces the value to other purchasers.

And if he sees a valuable book in a row of books at a house auction he will move it to another row at the last minute. And then buy that row of books instead of the first row.'

I was beginning to get the feeling that Paulette's uncle was more of a confidence trickster than an antique dealer.

Just then the locksmith arrived. Small, gnomish and sporting a long blond pony tail, he wore a smart and surprisingly clean two-piece white suit and carried a huge red plastic box which he quickly opened and which turned out to be full of tools, spare locks and keys – all of them neatly arranged in separate compartments.

I explained the problem, Paulette showed him documentation proving our legal right to enter the apartment, and he knelt down in front of the lock and started to pick away with the tools of his trade.

Paulette and I stood and watched him.

'You are not married?' said Paulette. 'You have no wife?'

'No,' I agreed. 'No wife.'

'You are starting out afresh, yes?'

'Absolutely,' I agreed. 'Naked to the world!'

Paulette giggled.

The locksmith gave up trying to pick the lock. He started to use a screwdriver to remove the screws which kept the lock in place.

'It shouldn't take much longer now,' he assured us.

# ~ Chapter Seventeen ~

'Voilà!' cried the locksmith, removing the lock from the door at last. A few minutes later the door swung open.

'What was the matter?' asked Paulette.

'I don't know,' said the locksmith, studying first the lock and then the door. He frowned, as though unable to believe his eyes. 'It looks to me as though someone has glued the lock together with superglue!'

'That's absurd!' said Paulette.

'Do you have any enemies?' the locksmith asked me.

'I don't think so. Not yet,' I told him. I found his question curiously disturbing. 'I've only been in Paris a few days. I haven't been here long enough to have any enemies.'

The locksmith said something to Paulette. She seemed surprised and sceptical. He insisted that his diagnosis was accurate, showed her the lock and explained how the parts had been very effectively glued together.

'Someone has certainly dropped superglue into your lock,' said Paulette. 'Are you sure you cannot think of a possible suspect?'

I thought for a moment and then shook my head.

'An aggrieved husband? An abandoned mistress?' suggested the locksmith rather knowingly.

'No! Certainly not!' I said, rather indignantly. I had not been in Paris long enough to realise that this was, if anything, intended as a compliment.

The locksmith shrugged his shoulders, fitted a new lock, handed the two keys to Paulette (who gave one to me), packed up his red plastic box and left. Just before he disappeared he handed me the glued together lock.

'A souvenir!' he explained, with a stage wink.

'I am very sorry about all the trouble you have had,' said Paulette.

'That's OK,' I said. 'Perhaps it was done by someone who was angry with the former tenant. I have hardly been here long enough to make any enemies.'

'Perhaps we could have a meal together?' suggested Paulette.

Surprised, I looked at her.

'You are single, are you not?'

'I'm single,' I said.

'Do you find me attractive?'

'Of course,' I agreed.

'Then perhaps we could have a meal together?'

'I would like that,' I said, still rather surprised at the unusual way things were working out. 'You are single too?'

'No,' said Paulette. 'I have been married for six years. But my husband is away a good deal. We do not get on well together.' She shrugged. 'And he has a mistress.'

I didn't know what to say to this and so I didn't say anything.

'When we first got married he said that we should sit down every evening and talk to one another.'

'That sounds a good idea.'

'He said each one of us should tell the other the faults they saw in them.'

I swallowed hard. 'Rather daring I would think.'

'It was perhaps not a very good idea,' admitted Paulette. 'At first I was shy about telling the truth but on the first day of our honeymoon my husband told me that he thought me self-absorbed, intolerant, anti-social and too sensitive. I responded by telling him that I thought him rude, ungracious, boorish and insensitive. I also told him that his organ was too small and that he was not a good lover.'

I flinched.

'Somehow this honesty and openness did not seem to help our relationship or our marriage in quite the way that my husband had expected.'

'Gosh,' I said. 'I am surprised.'

'He also said that we should tell each other a secret every day.'

I stared at her.

'He had read in a magazine that this was a good way to cement a relationship.'

'Did it?'

'No. I found myself making up secrets because I hadn't got anything else to tell him. I felt I knew too much about him and that he knew too much about me. There was no mystery left in our marriage.' She paused, and thought for a moment. 'How about seven o'clock tomorrow outside the St Michel Metro station?'

'Perfect,' I said, unable to think of a way to escape from this proposed assignation without appearing rude.

'I'll see you there then,' said Paulette, giving me a big smile, waving and then skipping down the stairs like a child going out to play. The last thing I wanted was an affair with a married woman – however acquiescent her husband might be. But how, I wondered, was I going to get out of this.

After she had gone I set to work emptying the flat of the rubbish left by the previous tenant. I threw out every piece of furniture, all the carpets and everything else that could be moved – including and, indeed, rather especially, the hideous mould green shower curtains.

The previous tenant had clearly not cleaned the flat for months – possibly years. I didn't fancy sleeping in the bed he had left behind or even sitting on the chairs he had left in the living room. The mattress looked so much like a miniature wild life park that I had to resist the temptation to drag it along to St Germain and donate it to the biology department of the Sorbonne University. I brought in the furniture from the tiny balcony (two small chairs and a tiny table) and found that all three items were so rotten that I could easily break them into small pieces with my bare hands.

I managed to break up the chairs in the living room (they were several decades past their best days and it didn't take a lot of effort) and I took the bed apart with the aid of tools – a rusty spanner and a screwdriver with a broken handle – which I found lurking in the kitchen. When I had dragged all the bits and pieces of debris downstairs I crammed what I could into the two dustbins in the small courtyard and stuffed the mattress and the bed frame into a skip I found nearby. For a few moments, as I walked away, I felt a little guilty about filling up someone else's skip but when I looked back I saw a long haired youth in an army combat jacket dragging the mattress and the bed frame out of the skip and carrying them off down the street. My guilty feeling immediately evaporated.

Once the flat was empty the task ahead seemed a good deal simpler and more straightforward. I scrubbed the floors, the walls and the ceiling. I scraped thick smears of fat from every surface in the kitchen. I repaired the broken cupboard door (this involved another trip to the ironmonger's shop where, once again, the same member of the royal family, was kind enough to allow me to purchase a hinge, a packet of screws and a screwdriver which fitted the screws and had a handle which was not broken) and used up several bottles of disinfectant removing the vast army of microscopic organisms which my predecessor had left behind as souvenirs of his stay. When I had repaired the kitchen cupboard and was about to replace the few items I had stored therein I idly examined the bottle of oil I had used on the lock the night before. I started to read the label but couldn't understand it so I went and fetched my dictionary. To my horror I discovered that the oil wasn't oil at all. It was superglue. Rather embarrassed by this discovery I hid the bottle at the bottom of my rubbish bag.

I then returned yet again to the ironmonger's shop, where I was delighted to find the uncrowned Queen of Ironmongery still reigning over her small but well-stocked kingdom. I purchased several cans of white paint (as much as I could carry) and an assortment of brushes. White may be a rather clinical colour but it does have the advantage of leaving you free to choose your furniture and curtains without wondering whether or not they will fit in with the stuff you've daubed all over the walls. And choosing white means you don't have to waste several hours agonising over the choice between the competing claims of such colours as 'Ripening Autumn Wheat', 'Moroccan Sunlight On Faded Rain Forest Teak' or, simply, but perhaps most curiously, 'Fresh Moldavian Peach'. (Was there, I wondered, a colour known as 'Rotten Moldavian Peach'?)

Cleaning and painting the apartment took me three whole days, during which I slept at the hotel (I had negotiated a deal for an extended stay) and lived on picnics which I consumed while sitting on the floor of my apartment. My two-baguette-a-day habit was helping me build up quite a good relationship with the bosomy matron in the baker's shop. We had progressed to the point where my arrival merited a broad smile and a nod of acknowledgement – as good a sign of residency as a paid up rent book.

Each evening I was so exhausted that after dragging my weary body back to the hotel I just collapsed into the bath, washed away as much of the smell, the stains and the paint as I could and then dragged myself into bed and fell asleep almost instantly; revelling in the crispness and coolness of the hotel's freshly laundered sheets.

So far my life as a Parisian could hardly be described as romantic. When one thinks of impoverished foreigners painting in a French attic one usually thinks of them stylishly daubing oils onto a canvas rather than recklessly slapping two coats of white emulsion onto the walls and the ceiling of a two room sixth floor apartment.

I still hadn't bought anything with which to furnish the apartment.

# ~ Chapter Eighteen ~

I arrived at the Metro station at the bottom of the Boulevard St Michel five minutes early and full of hope. Starting life again was beginning to feel exciting. Beginning afresh, in a new city and a new country, but with some experience of the world, promised much. It was raining slightly and so I sheltered under the awning of a nearby bookshop. It was a long time since I'd dated and dating a married woman wasn't exactly what I'd planned but I was, nevertheless, looking forward to some female companionship.

Every minute or so I looked at my watch, as everyone does when waiting for someone. The Metro station was obviously a popular meeting point for couples on a date and every few moments a man or woman would arrive, wait a few minutes and then go off arm in arm with their companion. After thirty minutes it didn't look as though my first attempt at dating in Paris was going to be a huge success.

But I wasn't the only person who appeared to have been stood up. A tall, slender blonde in a black, ankle length but impractically thin and flimsy coat had been standing with me under the awning for almost as long as I had. Naturally, I found it difficult to judge her age. At first glance I had thought her to be in her early thirties. But after another couple of glances I thought that she was probably a decade or so older than that.

Occasionally we caught one another's eye and smiled or shrugged. The blonde had a fashionable and expensive looking mobile telephone in her hand. The shiny, ostentatious case looked as though it was made of gold – or, at the very least, gold plate. Every few minutes it rang and for a minute or two she chatted brightly and merrily. On several occasions she took out a small notebook and wrote something down. Two or three times she made calls.

'It looks as though we have both been stood up,' she said suddenly.

I had been facing the opposite direction when she spoke but I had heard her speaking on the telephone so much that I recognised her voice instantly. I turned quickly. She smiled and raised an eyebrow slightly. 'I am cold. Would you like to buy me a drink?'

'How did you know I was English?'

'Your clothes,' answered the woman instantly. 'You did not buy those clothes in France.' She looked at me carefully, as though she was shopping and I was in the sales. 'And even if you had no Frenchman would treat a jacket like that.'

I looked down at my jacket and trousers. They were both rather baggy and worn. I realised with some slight shame that the jacket pockets were, as always, bulging. I couldn't even remember what they contained. I tried to compress the mysterious contents a little but it didn't make a great deal of difference. 'Where would you like to go?' I asked her.

'Here will do just fine,' said the woman, indicating the café behind us. She held out her hand. 'My name is Rosemonde.'

I shook her hand, told her my name and then followed her into the café . As we walked in there was an enormous roar and several male voices could be heard shouting out what sounded like approving comments. My companion turned to me and smiled as if to say 'Don't take any notice, this sort of thing happens to me all the time'. I looked around and noticed that there was a large colour television set suspended on a bracket in a corner of the café . A dozen customers were gathered around watching a football match and it was clear from the way the players were behaving that someone had just scored a goal.

'Someone's scored,' I said.

Rosemonde looked at me and raised a perfectly pencilled eyebrow.

'Football,' I explained. I pointed to the television set. 'On the television.'

'Oh,' said Rosemonde.

When I had shaken her hand I had noticed that her skin seemed much older than I had suspected. I was beginning to think that my original estimate of her age might be out by more than a decade. She wore high-heeled black patent leather shoes which had metal plates on the tiny heels; they click-clacked loudly when she walked.

'I don't know why they make so much fuss when one of those little chaps in short trousers scores a goal,' said Rosemonde. 'Isn't that what they are paid for?'

'I suppose it is,' I agreed.

'People don't cheer their accountant when he does their accounts, do they?'

'Er...no, they don't.'

'And they don't jump and down and wave flags when a window cleaner cleans windows?'

'Not that I know of.'

'So why do they get so excited when these little men in the short trousers do what they're paid for?'

'I'm not sure,' I confessed.

We sat in silence for a while.

'I suppose our dates could have been held up in the traffic,' said Rosemonde, while we waited for the waiter to arrive and take our order. She had unbuttoned her coat but not removed it when she had sat down. Underneath it she was wearing a short, simple and probably expensive black dress. Around her waist there was a black patent leather belt with a fancy clasp – although I didn't recognise the design I guessed it was probably done to denote the initials of a fashionable designer. 'There was a demonstration on the Boulevard St Germain and as usual the traffic was held up for hours. I left my taxi and walked here.'

'What was the demonstration about?'

Rosemonde shrugged. 'I don't know,' she said. 'But who cares?' She tossed her head as if to make it quite clear that she certainly didn't. 'The French demonstrate at the drop of a...what is the word?' She flicked her fingers impatiently. I couldn't tell whether she was impatient with herself or with me.

'Hat?' I suggested.

'At the drop of a hat. What a silly expression. Why would anyone demonstrate at the dropping of a hat?' She paused for a moment, trying to answer her own question, and then shrugged. 'There is a demonstration virtually every day on the Boulevard St Germain. They demonstrate for more money, longer holidays, better pensions...,' she waved a hand rather dismissively.

'I take it you don't agree with demonstrations,' I said.

'No, of course not,' she replied. She looked at me, rather sharply. 'Do you?'

I thought for a moment. 'A bit of anarchy can be a counterbalance to an over-regulated society. I'd rather have a bit of chaos and a lot of liberty than be suffocated by conformity and regulation.'

Rosemonde looked at me rather suspiciously. 'If they

spent more time working and less time demonstrating they would probably be better off and not need to demonstrate at all,' she said. She opened her handbag (small, black, patent leather and expensive) and took out a packet of cigarettes (long, purple with gold tips and also obviously expensive). She carefully pulled a cigarette from the pack and put the pack back into her bag. She held the cigarette between her fingers expectantly.

'I'm sorry,' I said, realising what she wanted. 'I'm afraid I don't smoke. I don't have any matches. Perhaps we can get some from the waiter. What would you like to drink?'

'A kir royale,' replied the woman instantly. 'Champagne with blackcurrant,' she explained, rather patronisingly I thought. 'The authorities allow everyone to demonstrate,' she continued, returning to a subject which she obviously felt strongly about. 'The French are stupid. They think that laws are made for those who choose to obey them.'

'You're not French?'

'Certainly not!' she replied, her voice replete with apparently genuine indignation. 'I am Swiss.' She looked at me carefully. 'Why don't you get your hair dyed? You look a little old.'

For a moment I didn't quite know what to say. I have never before met anyone quite so forthright. 'I am a little old,' I replied.

The waitress, a young woman in her late twenties or early thirties, came. I gave her our order and asked her to bring some matches. While I spoke Rosemonde took out her telephone and made a call. I looked around the café , wondering what I would do if I saw Paulette outside, and marvelling at the number of people in Paris who can find the time to sit and sip coffee or pastis for hours at a time. I had not been in Paris long enough to realise that for many Parisians the local café is an extra room in their home. They have business meetings in cafés. They write letters, watch television, have meetings with relatives, do homework and, just occasionally, go there to chill out. Many Parisian apartments are small and cramped. The local corner café provides welcome extra space.

'Do you live in Paris?'

'I've just rented an apartment here.'

'In which arrondissement?'

I told her.

'That is a very good area.' She took out a small green backed diary and a slim, gold pencil. 'What is your address?'

I told her.

She nodded and wrote down my address in the back of her diary. I didn't have the faintest idea why. I wondered if I should ask her for her address in return.

'And your telephone number?'

'I don't have a telephone at the moment,' I confessed.

She looked at me with a mixture of pity and disbelief.

'I've only just moved in,' I said, immediately hating myself for the feeling of weakness which had inspired the unnecessary excuse. The moment to ask her for her address had gone.

The waitress arrived with our drinks and a small book of matches. There was a reproduction of a rather good painting of the café on the cover. Seeing the packet of cigarettes in front of Rosemonde she put the matches on the table alongside the cigarettes. When she had gone Rosemonde put her notebook and pencil back into her handbag, took a sip from her champagne and then pushed the matches across the table towards me. Realising that I was expected to light her cigarette I picked up the matches, tore one out of the book and struck it.

'Jacques – the man I was supposed to meet – is a lawyer,' said Rosemonde, when she had taken a couple of drags at her cigarette. 'He is very rich and has a Porsche but I shall not see him again,' she said. 'Lawyers are always late.' She thought for a moment. 'It is not because they are particularly busy. It is more because they are rude and arrogant. They are also gloomy and pessimistic men.'

She paused and took another long drag at her cigarette. 'Do you know a lot of lawyers?' I asked her, politely trying to keep the conversation going. It had occurred to me to point out that some lawyers are women but I had dismissed the thought almost as quickly as it had occurred to me.

Rosemonde ignored me anyway. 'It makes sound commercial sense for a lawyer to be pessimistic,' she said. 'If he loses his case he can safely say 'I told you so' and leave his client penniless without a qualm. The client may be in prison but he will be content that his lawyer has done all that could possibly be done. And if the case is won then the lawyer can bask in the gratitude and admiration of his client and add another nought to his bill.'

'I take it you don't like lawyers very much?'

'All my husbands have been lawyers,' said Rosemonde. 'Are you a lawyer?'

'Good heavens, no!'

'What do you do for a living?'

'I'm sort of retired,' I told her. 'I sold my house in England and I received a small sum when I was made redundant. I put it all in the bank and I live on the interest from that.'

Her mobile telephone, lying on the table in front of her, rang. The trill tune it played was annoying. Rosemonde picked it up, switched it on and started a conversation in French. Her French was far too good and too fast for me to follow anything she said.

'Did you understand any of that?' she asked me when she had finished her call and switched her phone off again. I had not told her that I did not speak very much French but I assumed that she had drawn this conclusion from the way I had spoken to the waitress.

'No,' I said. 'Even if I spoke French I would not have listened to your private conversation.'

Rosemonde looked at me, seemingly surprised. 'Private conversations are the only ones worth listening to,' she said. 'It was a friend of mine,' she said. 'She is a nice woman, but if she has a fault it is that she always sees the other person's point of view. Today she told me a strange story. You might find it amusing and since it is unlikely that you know her and I will not, in any case, tell you her full name, I will tell you the story.'

'Anita — that is all I will tell you of her name — had a dozen people at her home for lunch yesterday. She was alone in the kitchen making coffee when someone came up behind her and put his hands on her breasts. She assumed that it was her husband. Her husband, whom I know slightly because I once had a brief affair with him, is a remarkably pompous man with no sense of humour. Superficially he earns a living as an art critic on a newspaper and a couple of magazines but he is paid very little for this work. I know that most of his income comes from gallery owners who give him tips — what you would probably call bribes — to give rave reviews to new artists whose work they have bought or contracted to sell in bulk. This helps to build up the value of their work and, therefore, helps the gallery owners to make bigger profits. He is not normally an amorous man but he does have his moments.'

'Anita told me that the man standing behind her lifted her dress and made love to her from where he stood. He seemed to be more skilful than usual and although she found this a little surprising — for in addition to being pompous and humourless he is a very selfish man — she simply assumed that her husband had learned some new tricks from his mistress...'

'Her husband has a mistress?'

'Naturally.'

'And she knows that her husband has a mistress?'

'Of course.'

'And she doesn't mind?'

'Mind?' Rosemonde seemed genuinely surprised. 'Why should she mind? All men have mistresses.'

'Oh,' I said. 'Do they?'

'All French men do,' said Rosemonde. She looked at me hard. 'You have not been in France long?'

I agreed that this was the case and then Rosemonde continued with her story.

'My friend Anita was enjoying the experience when she looked out of the window and to her utter astonishment saw her husband walking across the lawn deep in conversation with another guest – a well-known art dealer.'

'So who was the man making love to her?'

'Anita did not know.'

'Didn't she turn round and look?'

'That would have been embarrassing, don't you think?'

I thought for a moment. 'I suppose so,' I said. 'The man didn't say anything?'

'Nothing. He finished, put his equipment away and left, leaving her more or less as he had found her – a little shaken perhaps, a trifle dishevelled but unharmed.'

'And when she took in the coffee there were no clues from the other guests?'

'None. Isn't that a quite wonderful story?'

I agreed that it was. She extinguished her cigarette, crushing it in the metal ashtray.

'I wish that had happened to me,' said Rosemonde, unexpectedly. She stared straight at me as she said this. I found her stare curiously unnerving.

'You were saying that all your husbands have been lawyers.'

'Yes. All my husbands have been lawyers,' agreed Rosemonde.

'How many have you had?'

'Four.'

'What went wrong with your marriages?' I asked. Normally I would have not asked such a direct question but Rosemonde's bald suggestion that I dye my hair had rather encouraged me to feel that she was not a woman who was likely to be embarrassed easily.

'My first husband was enormously rich but very boring and also quite stupid. He could not do anything. He had to take his shoes into the cobblers when he needed new laces. The second was a cruel man and a bully – he hit me one day and I walked straight out of the house and never went back, not even to fetch my clothes – the third was very handsome but terribly vain an utter fool and the fourth was intolerant.'

'In what way was he intolerant?'

'He found out about an affair I was having.'

'And he objected?'

'He divorced me,' she said. 'It was crazy,' she said indignantly. 'I was, in fact, very faithful to him. I had only two lovers in the three years we had been married and apart from when I slept with those two men I was faithful to him for all of that time.'

I didn't know what to say to this. Having two lovers didn't seem to me to qualify for a certificate as a faithful wife. I had that morning read a news story in Albert's paper claiming that according to some sort of official study one in three people are seriously and probably irretrievably bonkers. I had at first found this news item rather unbelievable. But then I had found it strangely comforting. I was beginning to think that I was sitting with one of the thirty three per cent.

'You obviously haven't been put off lawyers completely,' I said, making a clumsy attempt to revive the conversation.

Rosemonde looked at me. She seemed puzzled.

'You were due to meet one this evening,' I reminded her.

'Oh yes,' said Rosemonde. 'The devil you know, and all that sort of thing. Having been married to four of them I have learned a great deal about lawyers,' said Rosemonde. 'It seems a pity to waste all that knowledge.'

'What sort of things have you learned?'

Rosemonde thought for a moment. 'They all want to be something else,' she said eventually. She nodded, agreeing with herself. 'Lawyers always want to be something else. My friend Anthea, who has been married to a psychiatrist, a surgeon, a paediatrician and two gynaecologists says that doctors are the same.'

'Really?'

'Oh yes. But the thing they really want to be never pays as well as lawyering or doctoring. And so because they like the money they have to carry on as unhappy lawyers or unhappy doctors.' She shrugged, making it clear that this did not concern her in the slightest.

'What did your husbands want to be?'

'Two of them wanted to be businessmen,' replied Rosemonde. 'The first, the boring one, tried to run a travel company in his spare time – arranging specialist trips for groups of people. But he did stupid things.' She took another cigarette out of her pack. I lit it for her.

'And the second husband who wanted to be a businessman?'

'That was the vain one. His father was very, very rich. He had an estate in California, a house in the South of France, an apartment in New York and a skiing lodge in St Moritz. He gave my husband an unlimited budget to organise a wine company,' said Rosemonde. 'But he overspent wildly and the company went bankrupt.'

I resisted the temptation to ask how her husband had

managed to overspend with an unlimited budget.

'He was unbelievably vain and very shallow,' said Rosemonde. 'He used to spend hours getting ready to go out for impromptu meetings. It usually takes me two hours to get ready to go out to lunch but if we started to get ready at the same time I always had to wait for him. I have never in my life known such a vain man.'

I sipped at my Pernod and Rosemonde's telephone rang again.

'Get me another champagne, darling,' whispered Rosemonde, as she picked up her telephone. She started to laugh at something her caller had said. I looked at her but she didn't look at me. She was engrossed in her conversation and didn't even seem aware that I was there.

Eventually Rosemonde finished her call, blowing kisses to the caller. I looked across towards her. She smiled at me, held up a finger to stop me talking and, I suspected, to indicate that I should be patient for a little longer, and dialled yet another number. 'I have to call a friend of mine in Monaco. Could I have another champagne please, darling?' she whispered hurriedly, reminding me of the order she had given a few moments earlier. The person she had called on the telephone answered almost immediately and Rosemonde began to chatter away nineteen to the dozen. This time even if I had wanted to listen to her side of the conversation it would have been impossible. She wasn't speaking French and she certainly wasn't speaking English. It sounded a bit like German but I didn't think it was. She seemed to be fluent in several languages.

I am, I think, a patient fellow but I was beginning to feel a trifle fed up. Rosemonde wasn't much of a date but she was costing me a lot of money. I suddenly wondered if she was simply using me to get free drinks. What if there had been no other man? Was that possible? It occurred to me that perhaps Rosemonde picked men up every evening in the same way that she had picked me up. But what did she get out of it? Lots of free champagne?

I stood up and looked down. Rosemonde hadn't even noticed that I had moved. I walked away from the table and looked back. Rosemonde was still on the telephone. It occurred to me that if I walked to the door and left the café without looking back again Rosemonde would probably not notice.

In time I came to regret not having done just that.

But I am far too polite for my own good.

I visited les toilettes, returned to the table and stayed there. I listened, I paid for the drinks and at the end of the evening I took Rosemonde home in a taxi.

'Thank you,' she said, smiling sweetly and waving goodnight to me. 'I've had a wonderful evening.'

# ~ Chapter Nineteen ~

I spent the next morning buying furniture for my new apartment. I found a store called a 'depo vente' less than a quarter of a mile away from my building. The owner of the store didn't own any of the furniture he had on offer. The tables, beds, chairs, bookcases, mirrors, books and so on had all been put on display by the original owners, who simply paid the proprietor of the store a percentage of their sale price in return for the space he provided. It rather reminded me of an upmarket version of my own garage sale.

I bought a double bed (not through optimism as much as the fact that I like to spread out when sleeping), a single wardrobe (small enough to fit into my tiny bedroom but plenty big enough to contain my modest assortment of clothes), a simple wooden table with four chairs (three of which were in a style that almost matched the table) and a small easy chair which had seen better days but which still had functioning springs and seemed far more comfortable than several more modern and better looking items of furniture which the store owner had for sale.

I decided to carry the easy chair home myself, underestimating both the weight of the chair and the distance I had to carry it. I thought it would be good to have something to sit on while I waited for the removal men to turn up with the rest of the furniture I had bought. However, carrying the chair up six flights of stairs proved to be even more problematical than carrying the ladder had been.

I had managed to manoeuvre the chair up two flights and was sitting down on one of the small landings (not actually in the chair, which was on its side, but on the floor next to it) trying to get my breath back when I heard a woman's voice coming from somewhere below me. I instantly recognised the faint Welsh lilt.

'I know that there are some very small apartments in Paris,' said the unseen woman, 'but if you have already lost your apartment and someone has rented you that landing I hope they had the decency to warn you that you are likely to find yourself being disturbed quite frequently. Since we have no lift and this is quite a large apartment building there is a fair amount of traffic on this staircase.'

I opened my eyes (I had been resting them as well) and looked down through the bannisters. A slim, very attractive woman in a pair of tight black jeans and a pink Angora sweater was standing half a flight below me. Without the towelling turban she had shoulder length brown hair and a figure good enough to illustrate a calendar. Three plastic carrier bags were on the stair next to her. She was not wearing a face mask this time and I could now tell that she was probably somewhere between twenty and forty years old.

'Oh, I'm sorry,' I said, struggling to my feet. 'Do you want to get past?'

'That would be convenient,' said the woman, holding her head slightly to one side and putting her right hand on her right hip. 'I have two large blocks of ice cream in one of these bags and my refrigerator is in my apartment which is a flight above where you seem to be squatting.' She smiled as she spoke.

'I'm sorry,' I said. 'I was just having a bit of a rest. This chair is heavier than I thought.' I started to pull at the chair which now appeared to have got stuck.

'Did your ladder fit your room?' the woman asked.

'No, it didn't,' I admitted. 'I had to take it back and exchange it for a smaller one.' I pulled harder at the chair.

'Do you want a hand with that?' asked the woman. 'It looks as if it's stuck.'

'No, it's OK,' I said, pulling hard but getting nowhere. 'I don't want to trouble you.'

'It's no trouble,' the woman assured me. 'Besides, the quicker you move your chair the better my chances of getting my ice cream into the freezer before it melts.' I thought she had been smiling before. I'd been wrong. Now she smiled. And the sun came out and the band began to play.

'Well, OK. If you're sure. If you could push from below I'll pull from above,' I suggested.

The woman stepped up a step and pushed at the chair as hard as she could. As she did this I pulled from above. The chair still refused to budge.

'I'm very sorry about this,' I said, red-faced and thoroughly embarrassed. 'Look, if you could pass your bags up to me and then somehow squeeze over the chair you could get your ice cream into your freezer before it melts.'

'Thank you,' replied the stranger. 'I think I will do that if you don't mind.' She picked up her bags and passed them over the chair to me. She then clambered over the chair, picked up her bags and continued up to her apartment. She managed all this with a surprising amount of grace.

'I'm sorry,' I called after her.

'Don't mention it,' the stranger replied over her shoulder. 'Perhaps you'd put a note under my door when you decide to try moving a double decker bus up to your apartment?'

Before I could think of a suitable retort she had opened her apartment door and disappeared inside.

Five minutes later I was still fighting to free the chair when the door to the woman's apartment opened.

'I heard you still struggling away and I thought perhaps you might need a drink,' she said. 'Will a beer do?' She held out a bottle of French beer. There was condensation on the side of the bottle and it looked beautifully enticing.

'Thank you,' I said, taking the beer. Her fingernails were painted a beautiful shade of lilac. I glanced at her left hand. There was no ring.

'My pleasure. Do you want a hand with that chair?'

'No, really, thank you. I'm sure I'll manage,' I said. 'But thank you.'

'OK,' she said. 'Just leave the empty bottle outside when you've finished.' And she'd gone.

'And thank you for the beer!' I called, hoping the words would find their way through her closed apartment door. I cursed myself quietly. If I'd accepted her offer I might have got to know her better. I didn't even know her name.

After I had finished the beer it took me another half an hour to free the chair. I was tired and sweating when I finally managed to get it to the top of the stairs and into my apartment. I sat in the chair and cursed myself again for not accepting my neighbour's offer to help.

Apart from the episode with the chair the rest of the delivery went remarkably smoothly. A French delivery driver, assisted by a large and very hairy Algerian, carried my new bed, wardrobe, table and chairs up the stairs to my apartment and installed them in position without any complaints – though both the driver and his corpulent assistant wheezed and sweated a good deal.

And then I discovered that the heating boiler didn't work. This not only meant that the two small radiators in the apartment remained stubbornly cold it also meant that there was no hot water.

I went downstairs and walked round to the estate agents from whom I had rented the apartment and, in my very halting French, asked if they would arrange for a plumber to call round and look at my central heating boiler.

'You want us to have sent a plumber?' said the bespectacled French maiden who was the sole representative of the agency in the office. The other two women whom I had previously met were not there. I had hoped to see Paulette, wondering what excuse she would give for standing me up. The woman I saw had masses of tightly-permed, purple hair and wore spectacles with glass so thick that her eyes were magnified to an unpleasant degree.

'Yes, please,' I said.

The woman looked at me, shrugged her broad shoulders and nodded. 'OK,' she said, in English. 'I will sent you a plumber.'

'When?' I asked. 'When will he come?'

'Today,' said the woman, as though surprised by my question. 'He will come immediately.' I felt impertinent and apologised for my question. 'In England it is sometimes difficult to get a plumber,' I explained, with a diffident and rather embarrassed little laugh.

'In France,' said the woman proudly, 'the workmen always come immediately!'

'Can you ask them to wait an hour?' I asked her. 'I have an errand to run.'

The estate agent assured me that this would not be a problem.

I rushed around to the hotel where I had been staying, collected my luggage, paid my bill, said goodbye to everyone and officially moved into my new home.

As I climbed back up the stairs to my flat, lugging my

suitcases, I confess that I felt quite pleased with myself. I actually whistled a few bars of some half-forgotten tune, innocently convinced that I was coping tolerably well with the complications offered by new life in the French capital.

I made myself a nice cup of tea and sat down to wait for the plumber.

# ~ Chapter Twenty ~

I hadn't had time to drink my tea when there was an urgent knocking on the door.

But it wasn't the plumber.

'Hello, I'm Busty,' said a short, stocky woman dressed in a black leather jacket, a very short black leather skirt and a pair of thigh length black leather boots. 'Lucie says you are to come straight the way.' I had never seen the woman before but she had a firm way with her and it was clear that she was not accustomed to being ignored. The jacket, the skirt and the boots were all generously decorated with silver studs and chains. Black, fish net stockings filled in the gap between the top edge of the boots and the bottom edge of the skirt. A shiny black peaked cap with a huge, ornate badge at the front sat perched at the back of a rather cubic head. Spiky blonde hair stuck out from underneath the cap. The name with which she had introduced herself seemed curiously inappropriate since Busty's chest was as flat as a one egg omelette.

'What's happened?' I asked, anxiously.

'Albert has been having a bit too much to drink,' explained Busty.

'He's not ill, is he?'

'Oh no, he's OK. Or, at least, he will be when he is awoken.'

'Good. Thank heavens for that.'

'But Lucie says to tell you that he has not having written his column for the day after today.'

I winced. I could see instantly that this might be a problem. Albert was an experienced columnist but even he had to be conscious – or something close to it – to put something together to satisfy his editor and his readers.

Struggling to keep up with the woman in black leather (and I could not help noticing that when one took account of the fact that she was wearing a pair of boots with heels which must have added at least six inches to her height Busty made remarkably good speed down the stairs) I hurtled round a corner on my descent down the stairs and found my beautiful neighbour flattened against the wall on the landing outside her apartment. She looked slightly alarmed and had clearly been almost crushed by Lucie's fast moving friend.

'Sorry,' I cried, as I skidded past. Below me I could hear Busty clattering down the stairs at a tremendous pace. It sounded as though the toes and heels of her thigh length boots were tipped with steel plates. I stopped for a moment, a few steps below the landing, and turned. 'I'm sorry,' I repeated. 'Thank you for the beer,' I said.

My beautiful neighbour half smiled and raised a perfectly plucked eyebrow a millimetre or so in carefully modulated surprise. 'Don't mention it,' she said. 'I'm sure you'll catch her eventually,' she assured me. 'But I don't think you should waste any time. Your friend moves very quickly.'

I started to explain, hesitated, halted, mumbled something incomprehensible and then simply thanked her, said 'goodbye' and hurried on down the stairs.

As I was leaving the building I bumped into Paulette, the girl from the rental agency.

'Oh I'm so glad I bumped into you,' she said, grabbing me by the sleeve. 'I'm so sorry about the other evening.'

'Oh don't mention it,' I said.

'The thing is that there has been a change in my circumstances.'

'Ah.' I nodded.

'My husband wants a divorce.'

'Oh I'm sorry.'

'No, no, don't be sorry. It's fine. It's actually a very sensible move for us to make at this stage in our marriage.'

'Oh.'

'So you see the thing is that since we're getting divorced I don't really need a lover at the moment.'

'No?'

'No,' she smiled at me, almost apologetically. 'But I'm sure you would have been wonderful.' She looked at her watch. 'I must fly,' she said. She stood on tip toe and kissed me on the cheek. 'I'm just sorry it didn't work out. And I'm so sorry about standing you up the other night.' She raced into the building, pulling a bunch of keys out of her handbag as she went.

As she disappeared I heard someone calling my name. I looked around. In the back of a taxi, parked by the kerb a couple of yards away, Busty sat waiting for me. She looked impatient and agitated. I got into the taxi and without either of us giving instructions to the driver (or, indeed, saying anything at all to him) we joined the traffic and sped away with a squeal of tyres. Our getaway style departure was accompanied by much tooting of horns as other motorists struggled to get out of the way and got into each other's way instead. The sound of metal arguing with metal, and glass tangling with metal and losing, provided some evidence to support the notion that one or two motorists had not been paying full attention or had been driving too close to one another.

'I am sorry for the rushing,' said Busty.

'That's OK,' I said.

'I'm sorry about to turn up looking like this,' she apologised. She waved a hand, indicating the boots, the micro skirt and the black leather jacket. 'I was at the work when Lucie asked me to come and found you.'

'No problem,' I said, with a smile.

'Lucie would have come herself,' said Busty, 'But she had the appointment upon the client.'

'That's OK,' I said.

'I am afraid I think one of your neighbours may have viewed me,' said Busty.

'You may well be right,' I agreed, remembering my neighbour, spread-eagled against the wall as first Busty and then I had thundered past down the stairs.

'And was that your wife you were speaking at?'

'Good heavens, no!' I said. 'Just someone I know.'

It occurred to me, rather belatedly, that to an uninformed observer it may have appeared that Busty was trying to escape and that I was in hot pursuit. I was not making a good impression with my beautiful new neighbour.

# ~ Chapter Twenty One ~

Lucie was in a terrible state and had clearly been crying. 'Albert is drunk and he hasn't written tomorrow's column.'

'Has he made any notes?' I asked her.

She shook her head. 'No. There is nothing.'

'Then we'll have to do it ourselves. But what on earth are we going to write about? How long have we got?'

Lucie looked at her watch. 'Forty five minuites,' she said and I realised that I had been using the royal 'we'. If anyone was going to write Albert's missing column it would have to be me.

'Before the copy has to be telephoned in?'

'To write it and telephone it.'

I swore quietly and thought for a moment.

'Have you got another story I could use?'

Lucie shook her head and bit her lip. 'I'm sorry,' she said. 'I cannot think of anything.' She started to say something and then stopped. 'Albert often said that he would never run out of things to write about because he simply wrote about the people he met – or the people I met – and the things that had happened to them. He said that his readers loved to read about other people's lives.'

I thought about this for a few moments but I couldn't think of anyone I'd met whose story would fill a column.

'It's no good,' I told Lucie. 'I've met some strange people but most of them have been through Albert. He's probably written about them already.'

'What about you?'

I stared at her, puzzled. 'What do you mean?'

'Your story. How you came to Paris. What's happened to you so far.'

'I couldn't get all this into one column!'

'Then just put down some of it.'

And that was exactly what I did. I pretended I was Albert and I interviewed myself about how I'd come to find myself in the world's most beautiful city. There was no time to write the story before I telephoned it in to the copy-takers so, having made a few notes before I started, I made it up as I went along. I didn't bother too much about punctuation and because I was dictating the copy, rather than writing it down, I didn't have to worry about spelling at all.

When I had finished I collapsed back into the easy chair. Sweat was dripping from my forehead and I was utterly drained. Lucie pushed a large glass of whisky into my hand.

'You were marvellous!' she said, beaming broadly.

'Do you think it was OK?' I asked.

'It was brilliant,' smiled Lucie. She kissed me on the forehead. 'Drink up your whisky,' she said, in the manner of a mother encouraging her child to drink up his milk.

As much as I was encouraged by Lucie's approval I knew I would not rest until the following morning when Albert (still fast asleep and snoring without a care in the world) had woken, read the column I had written and announced himself more or less satisfied.

Lucie, who turned out to be a marvellous cook, prepared a splendid meal for the two of us. We started with wild mushrooms moved on to a vegetable pie, served with three different varieties of potato and finished with an apricot tart which Lucie served together with an exquisite ice cream, the like of which I had never before encountered. We drank champagne before and after the meal and with it a magnificent red Bordeaux which was richer, smoother and more delicious than any wine I had ever drunk before.

'The food is absolutely wonderful and this is splendid wine,' I told her.

'The food I take the credit for,' she told me. 'The claret came from a very rich client of mine who owns one of the very best vineyards in France.'

She spoke about her 'client' in such a matter of fact way that it was not until a few minutes later that I realised exactly what sort of client she meant. She spoke of him with mild regard but no affection, as though she sold him furniture or flowers or exotic motor cars and regarded him simply and solely as a good customer. I had never been friendly with a woman who sold her body and sexual favours for a living and I still found it rather odd and difficult to come to terms with. Back in the part of England from which I had come prostitutes had been generally regarded as though they belonged to some sub-human species.

When I left Lucie's apartment, at about eleven that night, Albert was still snoring and unconscious.

'I hope he likes the piece I wrote,' I said.

'I'm sure he will,' said Lucie.

But I was not so easily reassured.

When I left Lucie's flat I was so worried that I spent the whole night walking the streets of Paris, occasionally calling in at an all night café for a coffee. At dawn I walked to the Gare du Nord where I waited for the English papers to arrive at the station bookstall. I opened the paper with trembling fingers and read Albert's column with great anxiety. It seemed strange to read the story of my recent life in a newspaper. And it seemed stranger still to know that I had written it myself. It didn't seem too bad. Relieved I headed back to my flat.

When I got there Albert was sitting at the top of the stairs. He stood up when he saw me. 'Thanks,' he said. 'You're a real pal.' He put an arm around me and we hugged one another for a moment. 'Thank you,' he said again.

'Was it OK?' I asked him.

'Brilliant,' he said, simply. 'I couldn't have written it better myself.'

I started to ask him if he wanted breakfast but he was gone, already heading down the first flight of stairs. 'I'll see you later,' he called over his shoulder. 'In the Fag and Ferret.' He paused, put his hand in his pocket and pulled out a small card. 'I almost forgot,' he said. 'I found this on the floor outside your front door. I think it's for you.'

I looked at the card. The only word I could read was the word 'Plombier' printed at the top. Underneath an address and a telephone number there was a scribbled note. 'What does it say?'

'It's just to say that the plumber called while you were out,' said Albert. 'Sorry about that.' He shrugged and hurried down the stairs.

I took out my key and entered my apartment. I didn't care two hoots about the plumber. I could not have been more pleased if I had been told that I had won the Nobel Prizes for both Peace and Literature.

I went into the kitchen to put the kettle on but then decided I was simply too tired even to make a cup of tea. I walked into the bedroom, lay down on the bed and fell asleep without even undressing.

# ~ **Chapter Twenty Two** ~

I was lying in bed, dozing, when I was woken by something that sounded like thunder. Alarmed I sat up and listened more carefully. Eventually I realised that someone was knocking on my door. I looked at the clock. It was half past seven.

I staggered out of bed, grabbed a towel, padded across the bedroom and the living room and opened the front door.

A huge man in crisp, clean blue overalls was standing there. The overalls were ironed. I had never seen anyone in ironed overalls before. A name, which I couldn't read, and the title 'plombier' were neatly embroidered in red on the breast pocket.

The caller was holding a smart black plastic briefcase in one hand and a piece of yellow paper in the other. He showed me the piece of paper. It had my name and address typed on it. I confirmed the accuracy of this to him by pointing to my name and nodding. Making a cursory acknowledgement of this he walked past me. Only then did I notice that he had a companion with him. The companion, considerably younger as well as smaller was, presumably, some sort of assistant plumber. He too was wearing a pair of neatly ironed blue overalls. Unlike his mentor he was carrying a large blue metal tool box.

The senior plumber asked me something. I had no idea what he wanted but, not wanting to disappoint such an important looking fellow, and feeling grateful to him for having taken the trouble to climb all the way up to my apartment, I nodded and said 'oui'. After nodding and saying 'oui' several times I began to get worried about what I might be agreeing to. Had I joined the French Foreign Legion? Adopted two children? Had I, perhaps, agreed to buy his unwanted 1958 Citroen, complete with rusty bodywork and a shot gearbox?

Unsettled by these anxieties I took him into the kitchen, showed him the boiler which was suspended above the sink and pulled an unpleasant face. I also held out a hand, with the thumb pointing downwards, hoping that these twin indicators would give the impression that this was the boiler which wasn't working properly. It was the only boiler I had but I couldn't think of a facial expression to make this clear.

The plumber made one of those critical noises which plumbers make, whatever their age, sex, religion or nationality. He then called his assistant over to him. This was difficult because the kitchen was crowded with one thin person in it and the plumber was not a thin person. The assistant, squeezing by, obediently opened the door at the front of the cabinet in which the boiler was ensconced. He then stood back. The senior plumber peered in through the door and poked around at something deep inside. I looked over his shoulder. He sucked air in through his nicotine-stained teeth and shook his head (I was relieved to see that French plumbers worked in a similar way to British ones) and with a single grunt made it clear that he hadn't seen anything quite so bad before, that he could probably find a way round it but that it would undoubtedly cost a great deal of money and take a good deal of time. He stood back and indicated to his assistant that the cover of the boiler could now be closed. The assistant did what was expected of him.

'Salle de bains,' said the senior plumber firmly. He had a very deep voice. After he had repeated the request several times (slowing down the speed on each occasion until the final version consisted of three clearly quite separate words) I eventually worked out that he wanted to see the bathroom. Guessing that there must be some key there that would help him make his diagnosis and, subsequently effect a cure, I took him into the bedroom and proudly displayed the shower, the bidet, the water closet and the handbasin.

The senior plumber regally waved a hand and his assistant, who had followed us like a faithful puppy, obediently stepped forward and turned on the hot and cold taps. He then stepped aside and faded into the background. The senior plumber reached forward, picked up my soap and washed his hands. He did this with as much style and care as a top surgeon might be expected to use when preparing his hands before a heart transplant operation. When he had finished the plumber held out his dripping hands and his assistant, who had opened his blue metal tool box, took out a plastic bag and from it produced a small fluffy white towel. The senior plumber dried his hands. The assistant folded the towel, put it back into its plastic bag and put it away.

Without another word they then left.

I considered making myself a cup of tea but decided against it and went back to bed.

But for half an hour I couldn't sleep for worrying that I might have offended the plumber by not giving him a tip.

For the next half an hour I lay awake wondering how much I should have tipped him.

And I spent the half an hour after that wondering whether I perhaps ought to have tipped the plumber's assistant too.

I then got up and made the cup of tea.

# ~ Chapter Twenty Three ~

'What are you going to do with yourself now that you're a Parisian?' asked Albert, taking a huge bite out of a croissant. Outside the weather was worsening. Paris seemed to have weather which hated to be ignored. It was more dramatic and definite than the weather in England had seemed. When it was warm it was hot. When it was cold it was very cold. When it rained it rained buckets. Crumbs of flaky croissant showered onto the table, Albert's suit jacket and his lap. He ignored them.

'I don't really know,' I stuttered, knowing that this answer was probably unconvincing but feeling far too embarrassed to tell the truth.

'Of course you do,' insisted Albert.

I felt myself going deep red. As a teenager I had blushed easily and often. I had hated it but had assumed that since one didn't see many adults who blushed then blushing was a habit I would grow out of. Other people might grow out of blushing but I hadn't. I still blushed bright red at the slightest provocation and I still hated it. It occurred to me that I was probably the only fifty odd year old in the world who still blushed.

'Let me guess,' said Albert. He took another huge bite

from his croissant and showered himself with crumbs once
again. 'Phhnntrr?' Croissants freshly made in France may look
little different to the croissants sold in Britain but they taste
infinitely superior and they flake and crumble far more spec-
tacularly.

'Pardon?'

'Hnnu hwhannt hnnoo hbee hna phhnntrr.'

'A what?' I laughed.

Albert chewed the remains of the croissant in his mouth,
swallowed, brushed a small collection of crumbs from around
his mouth with the back of his hand and spoke again. 'A
painter? Do you want to be a painter?'

I laughed and shook my head. 'No.'

'Everyone who comes to Paris wants to be a painter,'
insisted Albert.

'I don't.'

Albert frowned. 'Then what do you want to do with
yourself?'

I felt myself blushing an even deeper shade of red and
started to mutter something about now having had time to
think about it.

'A writer! You want to be a writer?' said Albert, grinning at me. There was a mixture of triumph and amusement
on his face.

The blushing got worse.

'I used to be a journalist,' I said, partly as an explanation and partly as an excuse for what seemed, when spoken
out loud, to be an absurd dream. 'I'd like to do some journalism again. Something like that. Work on a magazine perhaps.'

'I didn't know that you used to be a journalist,' said
Albert. 'You never said.'

I shrugged.

'Why did you give it up?'

'It's a long story.'
'Tell me.'
'It was all a long time ago.'
'Does it embarrass you to talk about it?'
'No.'
'So, tell me.'
I told him.

# ~ Chapter Twenty Four ~

'So what did you do after that?' asked Albert, when I'd finished telling him why and how my career as a journalist had ended around forty years prematurely.

'I worked as a corporate public relations officer.'

Albert pulled a face and gave me a sympathetic look.

'I know,' I said, holding up a hand. 'It was absolutely terrible. I had to write press releases and edit the company newsletter. I hated every moment of it.' I paused. 'But I had a wife to keep and she wasn't the sort of woman to put up with living in a garret and starving.'

'Do you still have the wife?'

I shook my head. 'We're divorced.'

'So now you're footloose and fancy free?'

'I suppose I am.'

'And you haven't lost that old dream? The dream of being a writer.'

'I thought I had.'

'What sort of writing would you like to do?'

'I don't know. I don't mind. I don't really care. Articles. Books.' I paused, and thought. 'I'd like to write a book, I guess.'

'Every journalist wants to write a book,' said Albert,

smiling. 'Most start one. Very few of them ever finish one. Walk into the bedroom of a journalist, pull open the bottom drawer of his dressing table and you'll find an unpublishable typescript.'

'Have you got one?'

'Of course. A book about the street people of Paris. The street entertainers, the tramps, the beggars, the vendors – we all see them regularly but we know nothing about their lives, and how they got to be where they are. I'll probably never finish it,' sighed Albert. 'Even if I do the chances are that no one will publish it. And if they do publish it I doubt if anyone will ever read it.' He looked at me, thoughtfully. 'Did you say that when you were working as a corporate whatever it was you edited the company newsletter?'

'Yes. For my sins. I had to interview directors and employees of the month – that sort of thing. We even had a page listing employees who had got married, had babies or done something remarkable.' I felt embarrassed talking to Albert about this. He was, after all, one of Britain's best-known, best loved and most highly paid journalists.

'Full page interviews with a fork lift truck driver who has made a scale model of St Paul's Cathedral with match-sticks interspersed with rather wobbly cartoons drawn by someone in the human resources department who thinks he's got some good ideas and is a bit handy with a pencil.'

'Exactly,' I agreed, laughing. 'I remember interviewing a typist who played hockey for the county second XI and an electrician who had appeared on a television quiz programme and won a teddy bear and a lamp shade. And yes we did have wobbly cartoons but they were drawn by a chap in marketing rather than someone in the human resources department.'

'But you know how to edit a magazine?'

'Oh yes. I guess so.' I thought for a moment. 'I suppose

I could probably try and get a job doing some editing.' I thought still more. 'There must be someone in Paris who needs an over-the-hill Englishman who can't speak French but who knows how to do a bit of editing.'

'You wouldn't mind doing some editing, then?' persisted Albert.

'Not as long as I could do some writing too,' I replied. I hadn't enjoyed interviewing company directors or hockey-playing typists who thought they were doing me a favour by granting me their views on the world, but I had enjoyed the more general aspects of the editing process. It gave me a kick to start with a few blank sheets of paper and end up with something which looked roughly like a magazine.

Albert signalled to the waiter to bring us two more drinks.

'I have a proposal I want to put to you,' said Albert. He hesitated for a while before continuing, as though picking his words carefully and mentally rehearsing what he had to say. This wasn't at all like him. He usually spoke first and worried about the consequences of what he was saying much later, if at all.

I waited. I didn't have the faintest idea what he was going to say to me but if pushed I would, I think, have guessed that he probably knew a publisher somewhere who might be able to find me a job.

'For some time I've been thinking of starting a maga-zine,' said Albert. 'It's something I've always wanted to do. Don't ask me why but I've got this dream of publishing a really good magazine about Paris. There are tens of thou-sands of English speaking ex-patriates living in Paris. Brit-ons. Americans. Irish. Australians. New Zealanders. Some of them live here permanently. Some of them are just pass-ing through – staying here for a couple of years on their way up the corporate or diplomatic ladder.'

'Add to them the umpteen thousands who live some-where else but who regard Paris as their spiritual home and you're talking of a pretty big potential market,' continued Albert.

I nodded. I was trying hard not to get excited.

'There are one or two English speaking magazines around,' said Albert. 'But I don't believe there is anything to compete with what I have in mind.'

'The magazine I'd like to produce – and I'd call it 'Votre Paris' because although that has a sort of French ring to it everyone knows what it means – would be a sort of monthly tribute to the world's most beautiful city.'

'I'd include articles on the history of the city, on the passageways, the hotels, the museums, the shops, the cafés,' Albert waved a hand. 'Plus stories written by people living in Paris or stories with a Parisian flavour to them.'

'And the people,' I suggested.

'Of course,' agreed Albert. 'The people of the city. I already have a mass of material for that feature from the book I'll probably never finish. I think readers would be fascinated to read about those people.'

'I agree,' I nodded. 'It sounds wonderful!'

'Deciding what to put in the magazine is the easy bit,' continued Albert. 'But the clever bit is that I've even worked out a way to make it financially viable.'

'How?'

'What do most people spend most of their time think-ing about?' Albert asked me.

'Sex?'

Albert smiled rather knowingly. 'No!' he said, with sur-prising emphasis. 'That's what everyone thinks. But sex isn't top of the list for most people.'

Puzzled, I shrugged, shook my head and waited to be told what was.

'Money,' replied Albert. He spoke quietly, almost reverently. 'The one thing people worry about more than anything else is money.'

Knowing he was right I smiled and nodded.

'And what is the most valuable thing most people own?'

'Their home, I guess.'

'Absolutely correct. Their home. Their house – or, in Paris, their apartment.'

'So, each month I will include a supplement detailing the prices of apartments throughout the city. We'll include prices for studio apartments, and for apartments with one, two, three, four or five rooms. We'll print little calculations people can do to allow for which floor their apartment is on – and whether or not there is a lift. Readers will be able to go straight to the relevant table and work out exactly what their apartment is worth. To liven things up a bit I'll print one or two special features about how people have made their apartment into something special. They need not be especially expensive apartments. If someone has done something wonderful with a little studio apartment at the back of the Gare du Nord that will be perfect for these pages. Occasionally, we'll have a feature about some celebrity – a film star or a sports star – who has a particularly wonderful apartment overlooking Notre Dame or looking out onto the Eiffel Tower.'

'And it will be the property supplement which will encourage readers to buy the magazine and therefore ensure it is a financial success?'

Albert nodded. 'The magazine will be artistic, literary and valuable but because of the property section it will make a fortune. Everyone who lives in Paris will buy it and so will the tourists.'

'You think the tourists will want to buy a magazine with a property supplement?'

'Of course they will!' cried Albert, enthusiastically. 'Lots of tourists dream of owning their own place in Paris. Most of them will never have one, of course. But they can dream. And 'Votre Paris' will help them dream. They'll buy the magazine for the listings of shows, cinemas, theatres and restaurants. But the property pages will capture their hearts. I reckon a good chunk of them will take out a subscription and have the magazine sent to them in England.' He grinned at me. 'Just think of the advertising and marketing potential!' he said. 'Travel agencies and holiday companies will be falling over themselves to buy advertising space.'

'I can see that the magazine could work,' I agreed. 'But how will it make a fortune?'

'Estate agents in France are at a primitive stage of their development,' explained Albert. 'They charge a fortune for their services but to be frank they haven't got the faintest idea how to sell property. British estate agents, who were, the last time I was over there, a pretty disreputable bunch, do at least make a bit of an effort to sell the properties on their books and to earn their commission. Their French counterparts, however, are useless. They regard themselves as experts in something and don't like to think of themselves as salesmen. Most of the time they can't even be bothered to print out proper details of the properties they've got for sale.'

'So you're going to encourage them to change all that?'

'Any estate agent who wants to offer property to British, American, Irish or Australian buyers will simply have to buy an ad in our magazine,' said Albert. 'We'll have a sophisticated advertising section and encourage them to include photographs and room sizes. Home owners who want to sell their property may even cut out the agents and advertise their home themselves.' He grinned and shrugged. 'In due course we might even start our own estate agency,' he suggested.

'Sounds brilliant,' I agreed. 'Have you got the funding sorted out?'

'No problem,' said Albert. 'Between you and me the newspaper I work for pays me an indecent amount of money. I spoke to a chap in my bank. He said they'll lend me more than enough on the basis of my contract with the paper.'

We both drank some wine.

'And once the magazine is up and running we'll start publishing books,' Albert went on. 'We can sell the books to the magazine readers. We won't need bookshops.'

'What sort of books?'

'Anything and everything to do with Paris,' said Albert. 'The People of Paris. The Parks of Paris. The Restaurants of Paris. The Cemeteries of Paris...'

'The Cemeteries of Paris?'

'Oh, absolutely,' insisted Albert, his enthusiasm growing as he spoke. 'Have you seen how many people visit Père Lachaise cemetery every year? Thousands and thousands. They go to see the graves of Oscar Wilde and Jim Morrison and Colette and Chopin and whoever else is buried there.'

'And we'll do individual books on the various arrondissements, and a book about walking in Paris, a book for people staying here for a weekend and a book for people who are here for a week. We'll do a book about literary Paris – detailing the houses where famous writers lived and the cafés where they drank. And we'll do a book about French cafés! There's a book for you. Full of amazing photographs and anecdotes. The Dôme, Brasserie Lipp, Deux Magots, Café de Paris, la Rotonde, Café de la Paix. Some of the most famous cafés in the world are in Paris.'

We both drank some of our hot wine.

'Up until now there's been just one snag,' said Albert, with a sigh.

I looked at him. 'What's that?'

'I'm a great ideas man but I need an editor and I couldn't find an editor I wanted to work with,' he said. 'I talked to a few people. But the ones who were interested didn't have any experience of editing. And the ones who had experience of editing didn't want to leave their good, safe jobs to work with a brand new company full of promises but guaranteeing absolutely nothing.'

I nodded. 'I can see the problem.'

Albert raised his glass and looked straight at me. 'Now, at last, I think I might have found the solution,' he said with a smile.

I looked at him. I had begun to have hopes of my own. Now I admit that I felt a little disappointed. It seemed that my hopes were about to be dashed.

'The fellow I'm thinking of is absolutely perfect for the job,' said Albert.

My heart fell still further. I felt rather bitter about this Mr Perfect.

'Do you want the job?' Albert asked me.

# ~ Chapter Twenty Five ~

I took a towel from the rail beside the washbasin, wrapped it, as best I could, around my waist and padded to the door. The tapping on the door had been so light that I wasn't even sure I would find anyone there.

'Hello,' said Rosemonde, the woman I'd met outside the Metro. Her eyes were red and her cheeks were streaked with mascara. You didn't need a medical degree and a decade of work in psychiatry to work out that she'd been crying. I recognised the perfume she had used when we had met the first time. I still didn't know what it was but I was still pretty confident it was expensive and not the sort of stuff they sell by the gallon in chain stores.

We stared at one another for a few brief moments. I was surprised to see her and didn't know what to say. I got the impression she didn't know what to say either. But it was Rosemonde who eventually broke the lengthy silence. 'I'm sorry to bother you,' she said. There was a long pause. 'I didn't know where else to turn.'

'What's the matter?' I asked her. 'What's happened?' I didn't understand why Rosemonde had chosen to turn to me but I was, I suppose, rather flattered that she had done so.

'It's...er...rather personal,' said Rosemonde, lowering

her voice and looking first to the right and then to the left in the deserted hall-way.

'I'm sorry,' I said, stepping back so that Rosemonde could enter. 'It's all a bit cramped,' I apologised as she swept past me.

Rosemonde said nothing but hurried past me and I followed her into the living room.

'Please,' I said, 'sit down.'

She sat down on the easy chair. I sat on one of the four upright chairs which had come with the dining table.

'I'm so sorry to bother you,' she said. She got up. 'I should go.'

'No, no!' I said, getting up and holding out a hand. 'You must stay. Please. Perhaps I can help. If I can I will.' I wasn't captivated by her and I wasn't even sure that I liked her very much. I felt sorry for her.

She sat down. I sat down.

'Would you like a cup of tea?' I asked her. 'Coffee? Can I make you a sandwich? A bowl of cornflakes?'

'No thank you,' she said. 'I am too upset to drink or to eat.'

'I don't have any champagne,' I said.

'It doesn't matter. Do you mind if I smoke?' Before I could answer she took out a packet of French cigarettes and a small gold lighter. She took out a cigarette and put it into her mouth then she handed me the lighter. Although I hate the smell of cigarette smoke, which always seems to hang around on carpets and curtains for weeks afterwards, I found myself lighting the cigarette for her. She inhaled, exhaled and then sat back, slightly more relaxed.

'I had nowhere else to go,' she said.

I didn't know what to say and so I said nothing.

'When we met you struck me as a very kind and sensitive man,' she said. 'A man who would understand.'

I still didn't know what to say and so I still said nothing.

'You are my knight in shining armour,' she said. She smiled at me. 'Rescuing me from the depths of my despair.' She turned up the voltage on the smile. She was very beautiful and she had, as I suspect she well knew, a captivating smile.

'What's happened?' I asked her. 'If I can help then I will, of course,' I added, anxious not to let down my new found image as Robin Hood.

'I just need somewhere to stay for a few hours,' she said. She looked at her watch. 'Two hours. Two and a half at the most.' She opened her handbag and took out the small notebook in which she had written my details. 'I wrote down your address when we met.' She opened the notebook and showed me the page with my name and address written on it.

'You can stay here,' I told her.

'You are very kind.'

'Not at all. It's nothing. You can stay as long as you like. Are you sure you wouldn't like a cup of tea? Coffee? I have some bread. I could make you a sandwich. I haven't got any butter but I've got strawberry jam or Marmite.'

She held up a hand. 'No thank you,' she said. She spoke very quietly, as though exhausted. 'I really couldn't eat anything.' She tried to smile. It seemed an effort. 'But you are very kind,' she said. 'I knew you were a kind man.'

We sat in silence for a while. I refastened the towel.

'Do you want to talk about it?' I asked her, at last. I hesitated for a moment. 'Is there anything else I can do for you?' I paused. 'There must be something.'

'There isn't anything anyone can do,' she replied. Now it was her turn to hesitate before continuing. 'I have been let down very badly,' she said.

'By whom?' I asked her. 'Your lawyer friend? I'm sorry, I've forgotten his name.'

'Jacques is the name of my lawyer friend,' she said.

'But it was not by him that I have been let down. It was by my last husband, Hugo.'

'In what way?' I paused. 'I'm sorry, I shouldn't intrude.'

Rosemonde waved her cigarette around. Ash fluttered onto the carpet. She did not seem concerned. 'No, you are not intruding. Not at all. I have no secrets from you. When my husband and I were divorced it was agreed that he would pay me a sum of money – not a large sum but enough to help me find somewhere to live until I could get back onto my feet. He is a very rich man and the amount of the settlement was not large enough to embarrass him.' She waved the cigarette around again. 'I have very modest tastes,' she insisted. She smiled at me. I thought about the champagne.

'On the basis of our agreement I purchased a small apartment in the sixth arrondissement, near to the Church of St Germain du Prés. A tiny apartment. Just three rooms.'

I nodded.

'Are you not cold?' she asked suddenly.

I looked down. 'No,' I said. 'I'm fine.' I gestured to the towel. 'I'm sorry,' I said. 'I should perhaps put on some clothes. This is not a very good way to entertain a guest.'

'Please! No! Stay as you are!' she insisted, holding up a hand. 'I was just worried in case you are feeling the cold.'

'I don't know the sixth arrondissement very well but it is a part of Paris I want to explore when I have the time.'

'I wish I could be here to show you around,' said Rosemonde. She began to cry.

'What on earth has happened?' I asked. I started to get up, intending to move across to put my arm around her shoulder, but the towel became unfastened and I sat down again quickly, fumbling with my towel and feeling rather embarrassed.

'Hugo agreed to pay me the settlement we had agreed in two halves – one half when our divorce was first certified

by the courts and the other half one year later. He had – I'm
sorry I don't know the correct phrase – a problem with raising the money.'

'A cash flow problem?' I suggested.

'Exactly,' said Rosemonde. 'He said he had a cash flow
problem.' She wagged the cigarette at me. 'But he had the
money. Of that I am sure. He is a very rich man.'

'And he hasn't paid the second instalment?'

'It has been on the way for over a month,' said
Rosemonde. 'And yesterday I learned that it will arrive here
tomorrow.' She took out a small lace handkerchief and
dabbed at her eyes. 'But tomorrow will be too late.'

'Too late for what?'

'The people from whom I purchased my apartment
also agreed to accept the money in two halves,' said
Rosemonde. 'I explained to them my arrangement with my
ex-husband and they agreed to it. But because it is a little
unusual their lawyer put in a clause saying that if I did not
give the second half of the money on time then I would lose
the apartment and all the money I had already paid for it.'

'Of course I did not worry about this,' said Rosemonde.
'I knew the money from my ex-husband would arrive a month
before I needed to hand it over to the people from whom I
was buying my apartment. I did not worry about it at all.'

'But your husband's money has not arrived?'

She shook her head.

'The bank has the money,' she said. 'The cheque arrived yesterday. But he is in America and because the cheque
was drawn on a foreign bank it will take another forty eight
hours for the funds to be put into my account. And by then it
will be too late.'

'And you will lose your apartment?'

She nodded. 'I love the apartment very much but knowing that I cannot stay there breaks my heart. I have to return

*173*

to my parents' home. I am going to catch a train.'

'You are on the way to the station now?'

'Yes. I put my luggage in a locker there. But I could not bear to be alone at the railway station. I remembered you and...' she waved a hand.

'Why on earth did your ex-husband leave it until the very last moment to send you the money?' I asked her. 'Didn't he know what would happen?'

'Of course he knew!' said Rosemonde. 'I told him exactly what would happen.' She took out a lace-edged handkerchief and dabbed at her eyes.

'At first I thought it was simple laziness,' she told me. 'Or perhaps the fact that he is very busy.' She puffed at her cigarette. 'I must look very much of a mess,' she said. 'I have been crying. I should deal with my make-up.' She took out a make-up bag and a tiny gold-backed mirror and did things to her face.

'You look wonderful,' I lied to her. 'But was it not laziness? Nor simply the fact that he is very busy?'

She shook her head. 'Then I thought that he was being malicious. But yesterday I discovered that it was none of these things. A girlfriend of mine in New York telephoned and told me that Hugo had been boasting at a party that he has done the dirty on me.'

'How? What has he done?'

'He found out the names of the people from whom I bought the apartment...'

'...how on earth did he do that?'

'He is a lawyer. I had told him the address of the apartment. It would not have been difficult.'

'No, I suppose not.'

'...and then he made a deal with them.'

'What sort of deal?'

'If I do not pay them the rest of the money for the

apartment they agreed to give back my ex-husband a large portion – I think it is half – of the sum I have paid over. So he gets back a big chunk of that which he has already paid.'

'What a crook!' I cried.

Rosemonde shrugged. 'He is a lawyer,' she said. 'I should have expected this from him. He doesn't need the money. But he is a very mean man.'

'And there is no way you can do anything to stop this happening?'

'No,' she said. 'Nothing.' A tear started its journey down her cheek.

We sat in silence. She started to say something and then stopped herself.

'What were you about to say?' I asked her, gently. I felt very sorry for her.

'It's nothing,' she said, shaking her head.

'There is something you can do to stop him?'

She hesitated for a moment. 'Well there is a way...but only in theory.'

'Tell me about it.'

'Well, I know that his money will be in my account tomorrow. If I could borrow the money I need for just twenty four hours then I could save my apartment and his little game would fail.' She started to cry again. 'But where on earth could I borrow so much money – even though it is only for 24 hours?'

'Perhaps I could help,' I said. 'I have a little money in a bank in England – around £45,000. Would that help? How much do you need?'

At first, Rosemonde insisted that she couldn't possibly borrow so much money from me. 'You hardly know me,' she said. 'It would be an imposition.'

But I insisted and in the end she relented. It was, she said, a miracle. It was just enough to help her keep the apartment. She was very grateful. Since I did not have a telephone in the apartment we went downstairs and walked around to a local café. While Rosemonde sipped her customary glass of champagne I telephoned my bank in England and told them to transfer the money to Rosemonde's account in Monaco. 'I have an account there because the manager is a good friend,' she explained. 'I met him through one of my husbands.' She promised to send me a cheque within three days and she gave me her telephone number and her address. She even offered to pay me interest on the loan. Naturally, I refused.

We celebrated the saving of her flat with a bottle of champagne. Naturally, she didn't have any money and so I paid the bill. Being a knight in shining armour can sometimes be an expensive business.

# ~ Chapter Twenty Six ~

I was beginning to feel at home in the city. My first French lesson with Lucie seemed to have gone well and I was getting accustomed to the fact that one never knew what one was going to see next. Paris was never, ever dull; never, ever boring.

Nevertheless, when I walked into the Fag and Ferret a few days later I blinked involuntarily. For a brief moment I wondered if I had perhaps been working too hard.

It was late afternoon and Albert, who was sitting on his usual bar stool had one arm around Lucie and with his other hand he was holding his mobile telephone. He was dictating copy, presumably to his newspaper in London. As I approached I could hear him talking. '...couldn't pronounce his 's's properly,' said Albert. 'And naturally a speech impediment of this type, associated with a confidence trickster, was known as a swindler's lisp.'

Lucie was wearing a skin-tight red dress and Albert was wearing the rumpled suit that he always wore. For some reason which was never explained they were both wearing slightly crumpled paper hats. Two rather deflated balloons were tied to their bar stools.

Next to them sat two other women. One, wearing a short green skirt and a white blouse, I immediately recognised, although I did not know her name. It was the beautiful woman I had seen several times on the stairs in the building where I was renting an apartment. I did not think I had ever seen the other woman before. She was wearing a dark blue dress with a slit which travelled almost to her thigh.

I said a quiet 'hello' to the woman in the white blouse. She smiled and mouthed 'hello' back. Albert seemed to be near the end of his column.

Lucie got up, found a spare stool and squeezed it into position against the bar so that I could sit next to Albert. I whispered 'thank you' to her and smiled and mouthed a silent hello to the two women whose names I did not know. The woman from my apartment building, the woman I had recognised, seemed surprised to see me. I thought she seemed rather embarrassed too. As I sat down Albert, who had finished dictating his column, slipped his telephone back into his jacket pocket.

'How are the celebrations going?' I asked him.

He looked at me and frowned.

'Party hats, balloons...'

'Oh, very well, thanks,' said Albert. 'Glad you could make it back before the party ended. This is Busty,' he said, introducing me to the woman in the blue dress. 'And this is Felicity,' he added, introducing the woman in the short green skirt. 'She's Welsh but don't let that put you off her. She's the only reason I can think of for not declaring war on Wales.'

He told the two women my name and while we all kissed one another on the cheek in the affectionate and theatrical style which I now understood to be the Parisian way, he ordered five glasses of hot wine and asked the waiter for a bowl of olives and a bowl of peanuts. 'Do you know the trick of successful drinking?' he asked me. I shook my head and confessed that this was one of the many things I did not know. 'Make sure you eat while you drink,' he said, prodding the bar counter with his forefinger to give extra emphasis to each word. The waiter put a bowl of olives and a bowl of peanuts on the counter top. 'Peanuts, olives, crisps – it doesn't matter what you eat as long as you eat a good balanced diet while you're drinking,' said Albert. Taking his own advice he took a large handful of peanuts, popped them all into his mouth and started chewing.

I had by now remembered where I had seen Busty before. She had fetched me when Albert had been too drunk to write his column. She looked completely different in a dress.

'I didn't know you two knew each other,' I said to Busty, waving a hand in Felicity's direction.

'We only met this evening,' said Felicity.

'You nearly met a few days ago,' I told her. 'On the stairs of our apartment building.'

'Really?' said Felicity, frowning and searching through her memory.

Busty was the first to remember. She screamed with laughter. And then explained to Felicity what she had been wearing at the time.

'Busty is celebrating leaving her husband,' said Albert.

'He was a bastard,' Busty said. She spoke with a very broad French accent which made her sound very sexy. 'I was a lightly buttered wife. I am living in a home for buttered wives.'

I turned and looked at Albert for help.

'Battered,' he whispered, spluttering bits of peanut onto his tie.

'Oh,' I said. I turned to Busty. 'I'm sorry to hear that,' I told her. I looked at her in some surprise. She was a big woman. I would have not liked to have tried to batter her.

'He is a pig, my husband,' said Busty. She pulled a face. 'All his life he has been a judge of gays but now he goes off with a woman who turns out to be a transcendental female.'

I stared at her and looked at Albert again. This time he shrugged and made it clear that he didn't understand either.

'Transsexual,' whispered Felicity.

'I'm sorry,' I said.

'He has been having carnival knowledge of her for months,' complained the woman, full of indignation and, under the circumstances, justifiably upset.

'Carnal,' translated Albert, though I had worked that one out for myself.

The woman in blue turned to me, stared at me and raised a querulous eyebrow. 'Are you gay?' This was the second time a Frenchwoman had asked the same question. I was to discover that Frenchwomen living in Paris are obsessed with male homosexuality. This is, I was later told, because such a high proportion of Parisian men are gay.

'No!'

'I thought all the English were gay. Did you not go to school?'

I heard Felicity giggling and looked across at her. She grinned at me. She had a beautiful smile which quite lit up the cafe.

I told Busty that I had gone to school but explained that there wasn't an essential link between education and homosexuality and assured her that not all Englishmen were gay. She had had far too much to drink to be interested in this revelation or, I suspected, in anything else I had to say. She grabbed the hot wine the barman had put in front of her and took a large gulp. She didn't bother to add cannelle, orange or sugar.

'I got his own front,' she said, defiantly, licking her lips.

'She got her own back,' translated Albert, *sotte voce*, though I was, by now, beginning to get the hang of Busty's strange way with the English language. It seemed that the more she drank the worse her English became.

'I did workings for him in his office,' she said. 'So I deliberately mixered the xerox machine and the ...er...how you say?' She made a whirring noise and made rapid chopping movements with her hands.

'Food mixer?' suggested Albert.

'Toaster?' was my first suggestion.

'No, no!' cried the woman, frustrated by our inability to understand her mime. She moved her hands faster and made a louder whirring noise.

'Fax machine?' suggested Lucie.

'No.'

I looked at Lucie. 'A fax machine doesn't make a noise like that.'

'It might do,' said Albert indignantly. 'If it wasn't working properly.'

Busty turned to the nearest table and repeated her mime. 'What is this?' she demanded.

'A shredder,' said a white faced, black haired man without hesitation. He was wearing a black suit, black shirt and black tie and spoke in an American accent. He looked like a role model for movie bad guys.

'Shredder!' screamed Busty with delight. She got up, went over to the man in black, threw her arms around him and burst into tears. The man in black seemed surprised at her response which could, it is only fair to admit, have been regarded as slightly more enthusiastic than might have been considered appropriate. The man's wife, a large woman with mauve hair, did not seem pleased.

'It was a shredder,' Albert assured us all, when Busty had disentangled herself from the man in black.

'I put all the papers he wanted to be photocopies into the shredder,' Busty said, sitting down again and miming the action of putting papers into a shredder. 'And the papers he had put aside for the shreddings I photocopied.' She mimed the actions of putting papers into a photocopier. 'When I the copies had made I handed them around the office.'

I nodded. I could see that this would probably provide pretty good revenge.

Exhausted by these revelations Busty, now smiling broadly, slid gracefully forwards onto the bar counter. Albert peered at her and lifted one of her eyelids. 'She is unconscious,' he reported.

'I think that she may be drunk,' said Lucie. 'Lord Byron said that, 'Man, being reasonable, must get drunk' and I daresay that what he said was as true of women as of men.'

Albert sipped at his wine. 'How is the apartment coming along?' he asked me.

'Pretty well,' I said.

Albert turned towards Felicity. 'You should talk to Felicity about doing up apartments,' he said. 'She's got an apartment somewhere. She's bound to be able to give you all sorts of tips about decorating and stuff like that.' I looked across at Felicity. We smiled at one another. I really wanted a chance to get to know her better. Albert climbed off his stool. 'We'd better carry Busty home,' he said to Lucie. He eyed Busty up and down. 'I think she'll need the two of us,' he said.

'Let us get a taxi first,' said Lucie, sensibly. She climbed off her stool and tottered off towards the door. 'Wait here!' she called over her shoulder. I had never before seen anyone walk in such high-heeled shoes. The heels must have been six inches long, and for most of that height no thicker than a pencil. Within less than half a minute a taxi had screeched to a halt outside the café. Lucie, looking justifiably pleased with herself, turned and waved to us through the open door. 'You see,' she called, 'as Rudyard Kipling said 'He travels the fastest who travels alone.' Seconds after the first taxi had stopped another taxi skidded to a halt. Then a third did the same thing. In a city where finding a taxi is notably difficult Lucie didn't seem to have many problems. This may, of course, have had something to do with the dress she was almost wearing but I suspect that it had more to do with the way she wore it.

'Busty and Lucie live in the same building,' explained Albert, indicating that I should take Busty's top half while he took her legs. 'They're in the same line of business and they've been friends for years.'

I helped Albert carry Busty out onto the pavement. She was not a light woman and this was not an easy task. Felicity walked behind us carrying Busty's handbag.

Somehow Albert and I managed to squeeze the still unconscious Busty into the backseat of the taxi. Lucie kissed both Felicity and I and then climbed in beside her. Albert opened the front door.

'Are you going to be OK?' I asked him.

He looked at me, puzzled.

'Will you be able to get her out of the taxi by yourselves?'

'Oh, don't worry,' said Albert, with a nonchalant wave of a hand. 'We'll manage.' He peered into the taxi. 'The driver will help,' he said with a grin. The taxi driver half turned, looked at the recumbent Busty, tight skirt pulled high up her thighs, nodded, and grinned.

'Oh, don't forget this!' said Felicity, remembering Busty's handbag. She gave it to Albert who climbed into the taxi and put the bag on his lap. The taxi driver put the car, an almost new Mercedes, into gear and sped off into the night. Through the back window we could see Lucie waving to us.

Felicity and I stood on the pavement for a while. It was a strange moment. In a way we knew each other but we were still strangers. And there we were standing together on the pavement waving off our friends like an old married couple.

# ~ Chapter Twenty Seven ~

'I hope they're going to be all right,' I said.

'I'm sure they'll be fine,' said Felicity, confidently. 'Albert and Lucie are both very competent people.'

We stood there for a few moments more.

'It's becoming quite chilly,' I said, looking up at the sky, as though it was in some way to blame.

'It is late,' said Felicity, in explanation.

'Would you like another drink?' I asked her. Although our first meetings had been hardly romantic, I found her extremely attractive and really wanted to get to know her better.

'Oh, I don't think so, thank you,' Felicity said, slightly embarrassed, though I felt sure that she must have expected the invitation.

She looked at her watch. 'It's late,' she said again. But she didn't move and she made no attempt to leave. We were standing near a set of traffic lights and another free taxi was waiting for the lights to change. She could easily have got into it if she had wanted to leave. She half turned and smiled at me. I was blushing and sweating and my heart was beating so hard that I felt sure she must have been able to hear it. I hadn't felt so nervous with a woman since I'd been sixteen. I wondered if I was sounding too eager but I felt encouraged by the smile and the still vacant taxi and, emboldened, I tried again.

'I'm going to have something to eat before I go home,' I said. 'Would you like to eat? Then we could share a cab back?'

'Actually I am rather hungry,' Felicity admitted.

'Do you want to eat here?' I asked, indicating the Fag and Ferret. 'Or would you prefer to go somewhere else?'

'No, here is fine.'

We walked back into the café and sat down at a window table for two. In halting French I asked the waiter for two menus.

'Have you managed to finish decorating your apartment?' Felicity asked me.

'Pretty much,' I said. 'It's very small so there really isn't all that much to do.'

The waiter came with two menus.

'How do you know Albert?' she asked me.

'I met him here,' I said. 'In this café. On my first day in Paris.'

'And Lucie?'

'I met her through Albert,' I explained. Remembering what Lucie did for a living I blushed.

'Sorry,' said Felicity, suddenly giggling. 'I've just thought,' she said. 'That was a slightly tactless question.'

'Er...well...no...not really,' I said, conscious that I was blushing. 'Though I suppose it might have been.'

'They make an odd couple,' she said.

'They seem very loving,' I said. 'And Albert doesn't seem to mind what she does for a living.' The waiter came back and we ordered our food. Felicity asked for a chicken salad. I said I would have egg and chips. I realised, rather to my surprise, that I really was hungry. Inviting Felicity for a meal had been a ploy.

'Shall I order a bottle of wine?'

'No thanks. Not for me. I've drunk enough for one evening. I can hardly keep up with Albert. He just keeps buying drinks. You go to the loo and by the time you get back there are two or three drinks stacked up waiting for you!'

I ordered a bottle of water.

'And she doesn't mind him being a journalist,' Felicity responded, when the waiter had gone.

Puzzled, I frowned. 'I beg your pardon?'

'You said that Albert didn't mind what Lucie does for a living. I said that she doesn't mind him being a journalist.' I looked across the table. Felicity was smiling and her eyes were twinkling. It suddenly occurred to me that I didn't know what she did for a living, or how she and Lucie had met. I found myself wondering if she could possibly be in the same line of business as Lucie. Or was she Albert's friend? Was she, perhaps, an old girlfriend of his? This was all very complicated. I would, I thought, have to tread very carefully.

'Have you been living in Paris for long?' I asked her, deciding that this was probably a fairly safe question.

'Two years.'

'Do you like Paris?'

'Of course. But I was brought up in Port Talbot. After Port Talbot everywhere is beautiful.'

The waiter brought paper place mats, cutlery, a small metal holder containing olive oil, vinegar and mustard, a pot of pepper and a pot of salt. He spread the place mats on the table with smooth efficiency and then arranged the rest of the items to his satisfaction.

'What made you come to Paris?' I asked. I found myself wondering if it would make any difference if I discovered that she worked as a prostitute. Would I still fancy her? Would I mind?

'I'd never been here before,' I replied. 'I just came for

the weekend. I wanted to see the river Seine and the Eiffel Tower I suppose.'

'And you stayed.'

'And I stayed.'

'Have you seen the Eiffel Tower?'

'Only from a distance.'

'And the river?'

'I've walked along it and across it but I haven't been on it yet.'

'You should. At night. It's very beautiful at night.'

'I should imagine it's very romantic.'

She blushed. 'I suppose so.'

The waiter brought a paper lined metal basket filled with slices of baguette. Felicity took one of the pieces of bread and bit off a piece. 'Do you mind?' she said. 'I really am starving.'

I took a piece of bread too. 'It's warm,' I said, in surprise. 'They must have put it into the oven to heat it up.'

'It's fresh from the bakery,' said Felicity. 'There is a bakery round the corner which bakes bread eight times a day.'

'How do you know that?'

'In Paris there is always a bakery around the corner which bakes bread several times a day. I just happen to know this one bakes fresh bread eight times a day.'

The waiter brought Felicity's chicken salad and my egg and chips. The table was too small and so he dragged another table alongside ours and moved the bread basket, the cruet and the vinegar and mustard pots onto it. I decided that I didn't care what she did for a living. What did it matter?

'Would you like coffee?' I asked her when we had both finished eating.

'No thanks. I really ought to be getting back.' She looked at her watch. 'Gosh is that the time!' She took a black leather wallet out of her pocket. 'We'll share the bill,' she said.

'No, no!' I said. 'Please.'

'Oh I can't let you pay.'

'Why not? I'm old enough to regard it as a pleasure to buy a meal for a beautiful young woman.'

Felicity laughed. 'You're not that old!'

'Sadly,' I sighed. 'I'm afraid I am.'

'Well, I like older men anyway,' she said. And then went bright red.

I picked up the bill that the waiter had left when he'd brought the food. 'It's not that much anyway. This isn't exactly the Ritz.'

I pulled some notes out of my pocket and left them, together with the bill, on the table. Then I pushed my chair back, got to my feet and held out my hand to help Felicity to her feet.

We left the café hand in hand and I felt as though I was walking on air.

## ~ **Chapter Twenty Eight** ~

Fifteen minutes later I helped Felicity out of a taxi in front of
our apartment building. We then walked up the stairs together.
The moment of intimacy we had shared as we had left the
Fag and Ferret had gone. We were, I suspect, simply both
rather nervous and unsure of where our very young relationship was going or, indeed, whether it was going anywhere.

'I'm glad we met properly at last,' Felicity said, suddenly rather formal, when we reached the door to her apartment. She held out her hand, which I took and shook.

I suddenly realised that I still knew virtually nothing
about her. I didn't know whether or not she was married. I
still didn't know what she did for living. I didn't know whether
she liked me. But I desperately wanted to see her again.

'It was lovely to meet you,' I said, blushing and even
stuttering a little. I wanted to kiss her goodnight but wasn't
quite sure whether or not she wanted me to. Instead I found
myself holding out a hand again. I felt gauche and foolish as
I did it. The Parisians kiss everyone when they say goodbye.
But it was too late to withdraw my hand so I left it where it
was. When Felicity reached out across the void and took my
hand for a second time I held onto her for a little too long. I
didn't want to let her go. To my delight and relief she made

no effort to free her fingers from mine.

'Can I see you again?' I asked her.

'We're bound to bump into one another,' she said. 'On the stairs.'

'No,' I said. 'I meant, for dinner, the cinema, a drink. That sort of thing...'

'You mean a date?'

'Yes.' Besieged by uncertainties I hesitated, cleared my throat and spoke again. 'Of course if you'd rather not I'd quite understand.'

'I like older men. Remember?'

I blushed, then reached across and took her other hand.

'You don't know anything about me,' she said.

'I don't need to know anything else about you.'

'You don't even know if I'm married.'

'Are you?'

'No.'

'Good. I'm not either.'

'I know.'

'How do know?'

'If you were married you would be more confident. And you wouldn't be so nervous.'

I didn't think it was possible but somehow I managed to blush an even deeper shade of red.

'I'm sorry.'

'What for?'

'For being so nervous.'

'Don't be. It's rather charming. And very flattering.'

We stood there in silence for a moment or two, just gazing into one another's eyes. I was still holding both her hands. Gently, very gently, I pulled her towards me.

'Haven't you wondered how I met Lucie,' she said.

'No.' My arm was getting tired and I suppose hers must have been tired too but I had no intention of letting go of her fingers. 'Well, actually, yes. But it doesn't matter.'

'I know. That's sweet too. For the last two hours you've been wondering if I'm in the same line of work as Lucie. And you haven't said a word about it.'

'It really doesn't matter.'

'Doesn't it?'

'No.'

'Are you sure?'

'Absolutely sure. The only thing I'm sure of is the fact that I want to see you again.'

Felicity smiled. 'When?'

My heart missed a beat and I looked at my watch. 'Tonight.'

'You don't waste any time, do you? OK. Where?'

'I'll pick you up and we'll sort something out.'

'What time?'

'Seven?'

'That's a little early.'

'Five past seven.'

'Make it half past.'

'OK. Half past seven.'

We stood for a little longer, staring at one another. I couldn't take my eyes off her. She had eyes like stars and a smile that could have brought a statue to life. We were still holding hands and she was standing about six inches away from me. I was intoxicated by the smell of her hair and her perfume.

'I'm afraid you'll have to let go of my hands.'

I looked down. 'I suppose so.' I wondered again if I should kiss her.

Slowly she untangled her fingers from mine and stepped backwards.

'Goodnight,' she said. She smiled at me.

'Goodnight.'

She turned, opened her door, turned back, blew me a kiss and disappeared.

I stood on the stairs for another five minutes or so, staring at her closed door. I was happier at that moment than I could ever remember being. I don't even remember climbing the stairs up to my own apartment.

There was a note on the mat telling me that the plumber had called while I was out.

# ~ Chapter Twenty Nine ~

I thought of little but Felicity the following day. I could not remember ever having been so captivated by a woman. I thought back to when I had first met my wife, trying to discount the disastrously souring effect of a loveless marriage and a bitter divorce, and realised that nothing I had felt then had matched what I felt now. I wondered if, perhaps, I was fooling myself. Maybe I was simply captivated, temporarily flattered by Felicity's beauty and youth. I didn't think so. I wondered if it was maybe nothing more than a simple infatuation. I decided that I didn't care if it was.

And through it all I wondered whether Felicity really was in the same profession as Lucie. She hadn't said she wasn't. And yet when I thought about it – which I did often – it seemed so unlikely as to be impossible. She seemed so pure, so innocent, so delicate. She almost seemed too unworldly. But then, who said hookers had to be brash and worldly? Lucie and Busty were the only hookers I had ever really spoken to. Was there any rule which said that all hookers had to be like her? Or, indeed, like anyone? Surely hookers, like shopgirls or bank clerks or doctors or nurses or airline pilots, were entitled to be individuals.

Naturally, I also tried to decide if I cared. I had, of

course, insisted to Felicity that I didn't care what she did. Did I? Did it really matter more than I had said it did? Was I fooling her and myself?

By lunchtime my mind was buzzing. I needed some air. I rang the plumber, left a message for him to come back again and then headed off to have a drink at the Fag and Ferret.

# ~ Chapter Thirty ~

'I've had a pretty exciting morning,' said Albert, who was, as usual, sitting at the bar. 'I went to see an accountant and set up a company to publish our new magazine.'

I looked at him, surprised.

'I had a set of the company papers copied out for you,' said Albert, pulling an envelope out of his pocket and handing it to me.

I opened the envelope. Most of the papers were boring and pretty incomprehensible.

'It looks very impressive,' I said. 'But I'm afraid I don't understand very much of it.'

'That's the important page,' said Albert, rifling through the papers and pulling one out.

'The accountant suggested that we started off with 1,000,000 shares,' said Albert. 'I gave him 10,000 francs so the shares aren't worth much at the moment.'

'That's brilliant,' I said. I looked at the page Albert had handed me and suddenly spotted my name.

'We have 500,000 shares each,' said Albert, pointing to a relevant line on the page. 'Is that OK?'

Stunned, I stared at him. 'Oh no!' I said. 'I can't let you do that!'

'I thought you'd complain,' said Albert. 'That's why I didn't tell you beforehand what I was doing.' He grinned. 'It's too late now. You own half the company.'

I opened my mouth several times before I managed to get anything out. 'Thank you,' was all I could manage. I was amazed but also proud and excited.

'That isn't all that happened today,' Albert continued. 'I also resigned from the newspaper. My last column appears at the end of the month. I'd leave today if I could but I seem to have some sort of contract.'

'Is that good news?'

'It's wonderful news,' insisted Albert. 'I've been writing that column for longer than I can remember. It's about time I had a change. Anyway, this will give me more time to concentrate on the magazine.'

'Great,' I said. There was something niggling at the back of my mind but I couldn't quite work out what it was.

'A new editor was appointed two days ago,' said Albert. 'Miserable little bug of a fellow whom I remember bumping into once the last time I was in London. He was twelve years old and an assistant on the gossip column at the time. Miraculously, the directors seem to think he has metamorphosed into an editor.'

'Didn't you get on with him?'

'Don't know him enough to know whether or not I get on with him,' said Albert. 'The last time I spoke to him was to tell him to get me a cup of coffee. Now he's too busy to ring me himself. He got some minion to ring and tell me that his lordship wanted me working in the office in London.'

'London?'

'Every day. Nine to five. Or whatever the hours are these days.' Albert shuddered. 'There's no way I was going to agree to go back to work in a newspaper office. What the hell difference does it make to him where I work?'

'So you resigned?'

'Matter of principle,' insisted Albert. 'A spotty teenager wants me to work in London and I won't go.' He ordered another round of drinks. 'It's going to give me far more time to work on the magazine,' he said. 'I'm looking forward to it.' He rubbed his hands. 'Who knows?' he said. 'I might even finish my book.' He ordered more drinks. 'So, what sort of a day have you had? I didn't see you last night.'

'I had a date.'

'Aha! Tell me more. Who was it? Do I know her?'

'You do, actually,' I told him. 'I had a date with Felicity.'

'Felicity! Congratulations!' said Albert. 'She's a smashing girl. I expect to be asked to be best man if there's a wedding.' 'It was only one date,' I protested.

'But you're obviously taken with her,' said Albert. 'You're blushing.'

'No, I'm not!'

'You are.'

'I'm very fond of her,' I admitted. I hesitated for a second but Albert spotted that I had been about to say something else.

'What?' he asked.

'What what?'

'You were going to ask me something?'

'How do you know?'

'You were, weren't you?'

'Yes.'

'Well ask away.'

'Do you know what she does for a living?'

'She works at Le Lapin Fou,' replied Albert.

I frowned. 'What on earth is Le Lapin Fou?' I asked him.

'You haven't heard of it?'

'No.'

'Oh. I thought everyone had heard of Le Lapin Fou.'

'What is it?'

'It's a sort of, well it's...,' Albert seemed unusually embarrassed. 'It's a sort of clubby sort of place.'

'What is it?' I asked him.

'It's a tourist place,' he said. 'For tourists,' he added lamely. 'Lots of tourists go there.'

'What sort of tourists?' I asked him.

'Oh, you know. Touristy type tourists.'

'Fat American women with noisy children or fat American businessmen in badly fitting suits?' I was beginning to feel like a contestant on a quiz programme.

'Er, probably more of the latter than the former. I should imagine.'

'In the daytime or at night?'

'Oh probably the evening. By and large.'

'Do they serve food?'

'I think they do, as a matter of fact,' said Albert. He seemed relieved. 'Yes, I'm pretty sure that they do serve food.'

'But it's not primarily a restaurant?'

Albert pursed his lips and thought for a moment. 'Not what you would primarily call a restaurant.'

'How many have I had?'

'How many what?'

'Questions.'

'I don't know,' said Albert. 'Eight or nine I should think. Call it nine.'

'Call it eight.'

'OK. Twelve more.'

'Do the people working there take their clothes off?'

'That's a leading question,' protested Albert.

'I'm allowed to ask leading questions.'

'Some of them do,' sighed Albert.

'It's a strip club.'

'It's a strip club,' agreed Albert, wearily.

'Ah.'

'I don't know what Felicity does there,' said Albert. 'But it's a very upper class place. Lots of English girls work there. I used to go there when I first came to Paris.' He paused and thought for a moment. 'But I haven't been to one of those places for years,' he added. 'We should go sometime.'

'But it's definitely still a strip club?'

'Oh yes. Strip acts. Singers. Lap dancers. Hostesses. The usual sort of thing. It's in Montmartre.'

'I suppose she could be a singer,' I said.

Albert said nothing.

'Do you think she could be a singer?'

'Er, well, as a matter of fact I know she isn't a singer,' said Albert. 'We were both at some sort of party about nine months ago. They had one of those sing-along machines – what are they called?'

'Karaoke machines, I believe.'

'That's it. Karaoke. She's a terrible singer. No one would pay her to sing. But she's got a terrific body...' He allowed the sentence to tail away, realising that he had made a mistake. 'She sometimes wears rather revealing dresses,' he said. 'Tight. You know the sort of thing.'

'She's probably a dancer then,' I said.

'No,' said Albert. He sighed. 'She's not a dancer.'

I looked at him.

'Same party,' he sighed. 'I tried to get her to dance with me. She claimed she had two left feet.'

'Perhaps she just didn't want to dance with you,' I suggested.

'Maybe,' said Albert. 'Probably.'

We sat in silence for a while. 'It doesn't matter anyway,' I said. 'There must be thousands of girls in Paris doing that sort of thing.' We sat in silence for a few minutes longer.

The trivial, niggling thought at the back of my mind got up and tottered to the front. I tried to send it away again but it wasn't having any of it. I wondered whether to mention it or not. I was still coming to terms with the fact that Felicity worked as a stripper. I had never been out with a stripper before.

'Do the girls there go home with the customers?' I asked.

'The girls where?'

'The girls at Le Lapin Fou. Do they go home with the customers?'

'Do they sleep with them?'

'Do they sleep with them?'

'I don't have the foggiest,' said Albert. 'I should imagine that some of them do and some of them don't.' He looked at me and raised an eyebrow. 'Does it matter?'

I thought for a while before replying. 'No,' I said at last. 'I don't suppose it does.'

We both sipped our drinks for a while.

'Are you sad to be leaving the paper?' I asked.

'Not in the slightest,' said Albert. He seemed very happy and I really didn't like to mention the thought I'd had.

'I'm too old to work for a daily newspaper,' he said. 'I'm going to spend the rest of my days working on our new magazine.'

I had to tell him.

'I hate to mention it,' I said. I paused, searching for the right words. 'But something occurred to me...'

'What's that?' asked Albert.

'The financing for the magazine,' I said.

'What about it?'

'Well, it's just that I remember you saying that the bank had agreed to loan the money for the magazine because you had a contract with the newspaper.'

Albert went a sickly looking off white and I felt terribly

guilty. I hated myself for having mentioned it and for a long moment wished I had said nothing. 'I'm sorry,' I said. 'I shouldn't have mentioned it. I'm sure it won't make any difference to the bank.'

'No,' said Albert. 'You were right to mention it. It is important.' He rubbed his fingers through his thinning hair and looked at me. The joy, the excitement that had been there a few minutes earlier had disappeared.

'I think maybe we could have a bit of a problem,' he said.

# ~ Chapter Thirty One ~

'What's the matter?' I asked Felicity. 'What's wrong?' She seemed upset.

My day had not gone well. I was still worried about how Albert and I would finance the magazine. And I'd wasted the afternoon waiting in vain for the plumber to call. The one bright spot had been the knowledge that I was having dinner with Felicity that evening.

Felicity sighed and moved her glass around on the table, as though playing a game of chess with no other pieces and no other player. 'My parents are coming to France,' she said at last.

There was another long silence. Felicity took a sugar packet from the bowl in the middle of the table.

'Don't you get on with them?'

'We get on pretty well, actually,' said Felicity, after a pause. She put the sugar down and moved her glass forwards two spaces and one space to the side. She laughed. 'I wouldn't want to live with them, but we get on fine.' She picked up her glass and sipped at her wine. 'They fuss a lot but then that's what parents are supposed to do, isn't it?'

'Do they, er, know what you do?' I asked her. 'For a living?'

Felicity looked at me. She seemed surprised at the question. 'Yes, of course,' she said at last.

'They don't mind?'

'No. I don't think so. Not that I know of.'

'So what's the problem?' I asked her, surprised but impressed that she had such broad-minded parents. I had assumed, obviously quite wrongly, that her parents were rather respectable people who might take a dim view of their daughter taking off her clothes in public in order to pay the electricity bill. 'Take them out to dinner, buy them a glass of wine in a café...'

'It's not that simple,' said Felicity, with another sigh. She put her glass back down and it turned from a knight into a bishop, moving diagonally across the table. 'Ever since I got divorced my mum and dad have been nagging me about finding a new boyfriend.' She paused and looked across at me, rather guiltily. 'And to keep them happy I told them that I had a boyfriend.'

'So surely that's good,' I said. 'What's the problem?' I felt surprised and disappointed that Felicity had a boyfriend. More than surprised. And much more than disappointed.

'I haven't got a boyfriend,' said Felicity.

'Oh.' I now felt enormously relieved. I resisted an almost overwhelming urge to burst into song.

'They want me to take him over to their hotel to meet him.'

'The boyfriend you don't have?'

'Yes.'

'Ah,' I said. I waved a hand, caught the waiter's eye and, when he came over, ordered two more glasses of wine. 'I see the problem.'

'To stop them worrying about me I've written and told them all about him.' Felicity finished her wine. 'And so now they want to meet him.'

'This is the parental interview?'

'Yes.'

'The "Are your intentions to my daughter honourable?" sort of thing?'

'That sort of thing.'

'Ah.' I paused. 'I see your problem.' I finished what was left of my wine. 'Can't you just tell them that he's had to go away for a few days? Can't he be out of the country?'

Felicity shook her head. 'I wish it was that easy. But I know them too well to try that. They'll just replan their visit for a time when he is here.'

I nodded and thought about all this for a few moments. The waiter came with two fresh glasses of wine. 'You've got no choice,' I said at last.

Felicity frowned. 'What do you mean? I have to tell them I've been lying? That there is no boyfriend?' She picked up her wine and took a large sip. If she hadn't been a lady it would have been a gulp. 'I can't do that,' she said, shaking her head.

'No! No! You have to find a ringer.'

'A ringer?'

'A stand in.' I waved a hand around, hoping that I might catch hold of a suitable phrase. 'An ersatz boyfriend.'

Felicity drank some more of her wine and thought about this for a moment. 'It could work, I suppose,' she agreed at last. 'But where am I going to rent a boyfriend? I can hardly ring up Galeries Lafayette can I?' She paused and looked at me quizzically. 'Or do you think they might provide escorts? Hey! I could ring an escort agency!' She thought for a moment and then shuddered. 'Oh, I couldn't,' she said. 'It would be too awful. He'd think I was desperate for sex and just wanted a man to take me to bed.'

'How old is this imaginary boyfriend of yours?'

Felicity thought for a moment. 'I don't think I ever said.'

She thought for a while. 'They know I like older men and they would expect him to be older than me. Probably in his early forties.'

'Maybe a bit older than that?'

'Maybe.'

'Hair colour? Build?'

Felicity thought again. 'I haven't ever described him. I just wrote about what sort of person he was.'

'What sort of person did you say he was?'

'Kind, gentle, funny, generous, good with children, that sort of thing.'

There was a silence. This was much longer than a pause. When this one had lasted long enough for a short European war I spoke again.

'Good. It's easy then.' I plucked a packet of sugar from the bowl in the centre of the table and started to undo the wrapping. My fingernails weren't long enough and I couldn't get started.

There was a silence. This one was long enough for seeds to germinate.

'You?' cried Felicity.

'Me.'

'Would you really do this for me?'

'I'd be delighted.'

Felicity leant across the table, put her hand behind my neck, pulled my head towards her and kissed me on the cheek. I just managed to put my glass down in time to avoid spilling my wine.

'You'll have to tell me everything you've told them – or everything you can remember.'

'OK.'

'What does your imaginary boyfriend do for a living?'

'He's a professional golfer.'

'A golfer?'

'I'm sorry. It seemed a good idea at the time,' apologised Felicity. 'It explained why he was away so often. Besides, my dad's keen on golf...it seemed a good idea,' she finished rather lamely.

'A professional golfer?'

'He's on the senior European circuit.'

'Does he have a name?'

'Omar.'

'Omar?' I picked up my glass and drank some more wine.

'Omar.'

'Great. My name is Omar and I'm a golfer. I have an identity crisis already.'

'Forget about it,' said Felicity, leaning back in her chair and waving a hand from side to side. 'You don't have to do it.' She picked up her glass and half emptied it in a single gulp.

'I'll do it! I said I'll do it and I'll do it. But why couldn't you fall in love with a clerk called Bert?'

'My mum has been in love with Omar Sharif for years. I made him a golfer because my dad is keen on golf and called him Omar to please my mum. The only reason for inventing him was to make them happy so I tried to make them really happy.'

'Haven't they noticed that Omar doesn't win any tournaments? The senior tour is sometimes on TV these days. And the results are often printed in the papers.'

'I told them he isn't very good.'

'Oh thanks.'

'I've read that you can make quite a good living on the golf circuit even if you aren't very good.'

'Great. That's even better. Now I'm a not very good golfer called Omar.' I groaned. 'I don't know anything about golf. And your dad is keen on it. He's bound to ask questions about mashie niblicks, bogies and sand pits.'

'Bunkers.'

'Pardon?'

'The sand pits are called bunkers.'

'There you are. What I know about golf you could write on a golf ball with a four inch paintbrush. This is going to be disastrous.'

'Aren't you supposed to be a bit more positive?'

'OK.' I paused. 'I'm positive this is going to be disastrous.'

Felicity laughed. There was another silence.

'You don't have to do it.'

'No, no! I'll do it,' I said. I found myself smiling too. I liked her laugh. I liked her. 'I like a challenge.' I finished my wine and looked around for the waiter. I liked her a lot. 'When are they coming?'

'In three days' time.'

I looked back at her. 'I should have started on whisky,' I said. 'It's going to take far too long to get drunk on wine.'

# ~ Chapter Thirty Two ~

Albert was right. We did have a problem with the bank. When they found out that Albert had resigned from the newspaper for which he had worked for so long the offer of a loan was withdrawn.

We were sitting in the café, nursing glasses of hot wine and trying to work out what to do.

'I should have saved some money,' said Albert, cursing his profligacy for the umpteenth time. 'How can a fellow like me not have any savings? I've been earning a fortune for years. Where's it all gone?' He paused, picked up his glass and examined it carefully as though looking for the answer in the wine. 'I suppose I drank quite a lot of it,' he said, though there wasn't much, if any, regret in his voice. 'Who was that chap who once commented that he'd spent most of his money on booze and women but had wasted the rest?'

'I think it was a footballer.'

Albert shook his head. 'It was a gangster. No, not a gangster. Movie star. Movie star who played gangsters. Give me the name of a movie star who played gangsters?'

'Bogart?'

'No.'

'Jimmy Cagney?'

'No.'

'George Raft?'

'That's the one!'

'He went bust and explained that part of it went on gambling, part of it went on horses and part of it on women. He then added that he had spent the rest of it foolishly.' Albert sighed. 'I just paid a hell of a lot of mine to the government,' he moaned. He thought for a moment. 'Since I gave them money when I had plenty of the stuff perhaps they'll give me some now.... They don't do that, do they?'

'Do what?'

'Well, when you make a profit they want their cut. But if you make a loss they don't chip in, do they? They don't take the risk, do they? They just want the profit if you make a bit. Not fair is it?'

'Whoever said governments were fair?'

'True,' nodded Albert.

'Maybe I could help,' I said suddenly.

Surprised, Albert looked at me.

'I don't have a great deal but I do have some savings,' I told him. 'I sold my house before I came over here,' I explained. 'And I got some redundancy money too,' I added.

'How much is there?' asked Albert.

I told him. A few hours before it had seemed a massive amount of money. Suddenly it seemed a pitifully inadequate sum with which to start a magazine.

Albert whistled softly. 'That's a lot of money,' he said, looking surprisingly impressed. He took a sip from his glass and then, very slowly, shook his head. 'You should keep it where it is,' said Albert. 'This is far too risky.'

'But you said yourself that the magazine will make a fortune,' I reminded him.

'Ah, that is quite true,' he agreed. 'But there's always a risk when you start something new,' he added after a moment's pause. He looked defeated. Suddenly, he looked tired and rather old. He produced a weary looking smile, reached across the table and patted my hand. 'But thanks,' he said.

'You don't understand,' I told him. 'This is something I want to do.' I paused and thought for a moment. I smiled at him. 'Besides,' I said, 'we'll make a fortune when the magazine is a great success.'

'You're just a filthy capitalist at heart, aren't you?' said Albert.

'Absolutely,' I agreed enthusiastically. 'It's been hiding in there waiting to come out.'

When I got back to my apartment that evening there was a card on the mat telling me that the plumber had called while I had been out.

# ~ Chapter Thirty Three ~

'So, Omar, you're a professional golfer,' said Gilbert, Felicity's father. He took his pipe out of his mouth and stuffed it stem first into the breast pocket of his tweed sports jacket.

He had given me this piece of information as though it was something of which I might not have previously been aware. As he spoke he peered over the top of half-moon spectacles which were perched precariously on the end of a rather large nose. I wondered if the spectacles ever slid off and if so whether I would be expected to try and catch them before they crashed onto the floor.

We were standing in the tiny lobby of the hotel at which Felicity's parents were staying. I was still recovering from discovering that Felicity's parents were about my own age. On reflection I suppose that I should not have been surprised at this but up until that moment I had not realised that Felicity was at least twenty years younger than myself. Finding that I was going out with someone young enough to be my daughter was something of a shock. I couldn't help wondering whether Felicity had noticed. I was pretty sure that the age difference would not have escaped her parents' notice.

'We've heard a lot about you,' said Gilbert, looking me up and down.

'Nothing too bad, I hope,' I said, wondering exactly what Felicity's father thought he knew about me.

'We've been staying here for twenty three years,' Felicity's mother said. 'We always have the same room.' She leant towards me confidentially and spoke with some pride. 'It's one of only two rooms in the hotel with its own bathroom.'

'We've been here so often that the receptionist knows us by name,' Gilbert added, also with obvious pride. 'We like Paris and we love this hotel. It's peaceful and quiet. We love the place.'

'I'm afraid we can't have dinner here,' Marion explained, almost apologetically. 'They only do breakfasts.'

'But we booked a table at a very nice little French restaurant just along the street,' Gilbert told us. 'We found it years ago and we eat there once or twice every time we come here. It's very French. Not one of these tourist traps you find in the guide books.'

'Well it would be French, dear, wouldn't it?' said Marion. 'Considering where it is.'

'Not necessarily,' said Gilbert. 'There are Italian, Greek and Japanese restaurants in Paris...'

'But they're all French restaurants, aren't they?'

Gilbert looked puzzled.

'They're restaurants in France,' Marion explained. 'So, even if they serve Japanese food that must make them French restaurants, mustn't it?'

'Have you noticed that no one in France ever opens an English restaurant?' I interrupted.

Gilbert and Marion looked at me. Felicity, who was standing next to me, took my hand and gave it a squeeze.

'You can find French, Italian, Greek, Chinese restaurants everywhere,' I explained. 'But you never see anyone advertising an English restaurant...' I gave up in mid sentence, rather regretting having started the interruption. I had only spoken to try to halt what appeared to be developing into an argument between Felicity's parents.

'Very good point,' said Gilbert, taking his pipe out of his mouth, and stabbing a podgy and presumably fireproof forefinger into the bowl. 'And a good opportunity for an entrepreneur with a bit of flair. Open an English restaurant serving roast beef, Yorkshire pudding, toad-in-the-hole, spotted dick – all that sort of thing.' He looked at me over his spectacles. 'Maybe it's something you might consider trying when you give up the golf circuit?'

'It's certainly an idea,' I agreed.

'Felicity could help with the cooking and the waitressing,' continued Gilbert.

'She doesn't want to be a waitress, dear,' Gilbert's wife pointed out.

'You could always serve the food topless,' I suggested to Felicity and instantly regretted the remark. 'It would be good for business...' I added, rather lamely.

Felicity's mother looked puzzled. 'I'm afraid I'm very provincial, dear,' she said to me. 'But what's topless food?'

Felicity and her father both laughed.

Blushing wildly I looked around for help.

'Omar doesn't mean the food,' said Felicity. 'He means that I should be topless.'

'You, topless?' said Felicity's mother. 'You mean serve the food without any clothes on above the waist?'

'That's right,' said Felicity, looking in my direction and clearly enjoying my embarrassment.

'But why on earth would you do that, dear?' asked her mother.

'Men seem to like eating in places like that,' said Felicity. 'Personally I've never seen the appeal.'

'How very strange!' said her mother. 'It sounds frightfully unhygienic.'

Gilbert had ignored all this. 'But then again I suppose most of you chaps end up working as club professionals? Giving lessons to old duffers like me, selling clubs, that sort of thing?'

'Oh absolutely,' I agreed.

'Shall we go and eat dear?' suggested Felicity's mother. She looked at her watch. 'Our table is booked for eight. They'll be expecting us.'

I could have kissed her.

Felicity's father checked his watch. 'Five to eight, you're right dear, we should be making a move.' He turned to face the reception desk and removed the pipe from his mouth. 'Bonsoir Yvette,' he said to the smartly dressed Frenchwoman standing behind the reception desk.

'Bonsoir Monsieur Dingle,' responded the receptionist, looking up from her calculator.

'This is our daughter, Felicity,' said Gilbert proudly. 'You remember her, of course? She used to stay here when she was little.' He spoke in English, but spoke very slowly and rather loudly, as many people tend to do when talking to foreigners.

'This is Felicity?' said the receptionist, who spoke perfect English, albeit with the ubiquitous American accent. She smiled and showed two rows of expensively capped teeth. 'It is some time since she stayed here, no?'

'Five or six years, don't you think, dear?' said Gilbert, turning to his wife for confirmation.

'It's longer than that,' replied Marion.

'It must be more than ten years,' said Felicity. 'We haven't been on holiday together since I was at school.' She looked around. 'Though I recognise everything. Nothing much has changed.'

'Our daughter lives in Paris now,' Gilbert proudly told the receptionist. 'She has her own apartment.'

Yvette, the receptionist, started to say something but the telephone rang and saved her from having to make any more polite conversation.

'Have you got your hat and scarf, dear?' asked Marion, as the two of them led the way out of the hotel lobby and into the street.

'Don't fuss,' said Gilbert. 'It's not as cold over here as it is at home.'

'Thank you for trying to change the subject when they started arguing,' whispered Felicity as we followed a few paces behind her parents. 'But don't worry. They argue all the time. It's harmless.'

'It didn't seem very harmless.'

'It is. They've always argued.'

'Here it is!' said Felicity's father. He was proudly standing in front of a small restaurant, the door and window of which were festooned with sticky labels informing passers by that the restaurant was approved by a number of English, American, German and Japanese tourist guides and accepted credit and charge cards belonging to around a dozen different banks and financial organisations.

Felicity and I looked at one another. 'Very typically French,' she whispered.

'They do a wonderful cheese soufflé,' said Marion.

'And their puddings are exquisite,' added Gilbert. He pushed open the front door and we followed in line behind him. I brought up the rear.

Inside, the restaurant bore more resemblance to the sort of restaurant English people put together when they are trying to create something that they think looks like a French restaurant, than it did to anywhere I had eaten since I'd been in Paris. The tables were covered in red and white check tablecloths and each one was lit by a single red candle stuck into the top of a wax encrusted wine bottle. A red paper serviette, folded into a cone, stood guard at each place setting. Highly polished farm implements were fixed to the walls and a huge fishing net, decorated with green and blue glass floats, hung from the ceiling like a tent roof.

'Wonderful, isn't it?' said Felicity's mother. She chuckled with pure delight. It was not a laugh, it was a chuckle. When she chuckled her chins vibrated.

A waiter rushed up and started flicking a white linen napkin over the perfectly clean looking chairs. He beamed with delight when Marion thanked him and he pulled her chair out so that she could sit down.

'This meal is on us,' said Gilbert, speaking to me. 'Let's get that straight before we start.'

I started to protest, in a polite sort of way, but Felicity's father would have none of it.

'This is a big day for us,' he said, sitting down next to his wife. 'We've been waiting for Felicity to find Mr Right for some years now. Her mother was beginning to despair and we'd almost begun to accept the idea that she would simply become an old maid – like her Aunt Rebecca.'

'Don't be silly, dear,' said Felicity's mother, who seemed to regard contradicting her husband as an essential responsibility. 'We always knew that Felicity would find the right man in the end.' She spoke to him as a weary mother might speak to – or rather over – a slightly precious child.

Felicity sat down next to her mother. I took the only remaining chair, between her and her father.

'So this evening is on us,' said Gilbert, looking first at me and then at his daughter. 'Eat and drink as much as you like. And as a treat we've booked you a room in our hotel.'

I looked across at Felicity. She looked across at me. I felt startled. She looked shocked.

'Oh no don't worry, dad,' she said, recovering her composure. 'There's no need for you to go to that expense.'

'Not another word about it,' insisted Gilbert. 'The room is booked and that's where you'll be staying tonight.' He looked at us both in turn and winked. 'I'm sure you two modern young people are long past the point where you're likely to be embarrassed by having to share a room.'

'We got them to book you a room with a double bed,' whispered Felicity's mother. 'Your father and I have slept in separate beds for twenty years and I may be old but I can still remember what it was like to be young.' She smiled, first at Felicity and then at me. I got the distinct impression that if she had known how to wink she would have done so.

Felicity and I looked at each other again but this time although we both opened our mouths with the obvious intention of saying something neither of us spoke.

# ~ Chapter Thirty Four ~

'Do you have any other interests?' asked Gilbert, as the waiter removed our empty soup bowls. 'Other than golf, of course.'

The restaurant was slowly filling up. As far as I could tell everyone in there, apart from the solitary waiter, was English or American. I wasn't sure whether the waiter was Italian or Spanish. I was pretty sure he wasn't French.

I looked across at Felicity, desperate for some sort of hint. We had spent several hours going over everything she had told her parents about Omar. I had made copious notes. Now, my nerves were in such a state that I could hardly remember who I was or why I was there; I certainly couldn't remember whether Omar had any interests outside golf. I had my notes, folded neatly, in my jacket pocket but I could hardly keep slipping out to the loo to rebrief myself every time Felicity's father or mother asked me a question.

Felicity was trying to tell me something but I couldn't make out what it was. I stared hard at her lips as she continued to repeat whatever it was she was silently saying.

'The violin,' I blurted.

Felicity shook her head violently and tried again.

'I used to play the violin,' I said, correcting myself. 'But

I gave it up.' I shuddered and pulled a face. 'I hate the violin.' I stared at Felicity. 'You have beautiful hair,' I whispered.

She blushed. 'Don't be silly,' she said.

'Don't stop him,' said her mother, who had clearly overheard my *sotto voce* remark. She gently placed a hand on her daughter's arm. 'Take the compliments now, while you can still get them. I haven't had an unsolicited compliment off your father for a quarter of a century.'

'Yes you have!' insisted an indignant Gilbert.

'When?' demanded his wife.

'Last week,' said Gilbert. 'I told you that the rash on your leg was looking a little less fierce.'

'That wasn't a compliment!' complained Marion.

'Of course it was!' insisted Gilbert.

While Gilbert and Marion were arguing Felicity was still soundlessly trying hard to tell me what my interests were. And I was still unsuccessfully trying to lip read.

'What sort of car do you drive, Omar?' asked Gilbert.

'I, er, I don't have one at the moment,' I answered, feeling that this was not perhaps the best answer even though it was the truth and, as the truth always is, probably the wisest reply. With some relief I realised that I had unintentionally managed to change the direction of the conversation.

'No car?' Gilbert seemed surprised, not to mention horrified, that his daughter was going out with a man who didn't own a car.

'With all the intermittent travelling he has to do there isn't any point in Omar having a car,' said Felicity, coming to my rescue.

'That's it,' I said, gratefully. 'With all the travelling...,' I waved a hand around to give the impression of someone who is constantly flitting from continent to continent. 'Of course, if it wasn't for the travelling I'd have a car,' I said. 'Probably two,' I added. 'What sort of car do you have?' I asked Felicity's father, hoping that the question didn't seem to be too obvious a change in direction. I was anxious to change the subject as quickly as I could. I didn't want Gilbert asking me which tour I played or when I last had a win. I guessed, rightly as it turned out, that asking him about his choice of car would help send the conversation in a new and less dangerous direction. Most men welcome the chance to talk about cars.

'A BMW 5 series,' replied Gilbert. 'I've always had BMWs.'

'Ah,' I said, nodding as though I knew what I was talking about. 'Very sound motor cars.'

'Very sound,' agreed Gilbert.

I nodded, hopefully as though knowledgeably.

'Talking of cars, a pal of mine is in tyres,' said Gilbert. 'Nice fellow. I play golf with him. I expect you chaps just talk about golf. He just talks about tyres.'

'Hmm,' I said.

'Tyres and rubber,' he said. 'Amazing the way they still get the rubber from trees, isn't it? Just like those pictures in the geography books we had at school.' He paused and frowned. 'At least I think they do.'

'Oh yes,' I agreed, though I didn't have the foggiest.

'Funny story about why I drive BMWs,' said Gilbert.

'Oh you're not going to tell Omar that silly story are you, dear,' said Marion. I looked across at her, surprised. I wasn't aware that she was listening to her husband. She looked slightly embarrassed.

'Why not?' asked Gilbert. 'It's an interesting story. One of my best.' He cleared his throat, and sat up straight, preparing himself to tell his story. 'When I was courting Felicity's mother...'

'Try to catch the waiter's eye, dear,' interrupted Felicity's mother. 'We need another bottle of wine.'

Gilbert dutifully spent a few minutes catching the waiter's eye and persuading him to let us have another bottle of wine.

'Where was I?' he asked, when the new bottle was, at last, sitting on our table and everyone's glass had been replenished.

'You were talking about cars,' I reminded him.

'Of course I was,' said Gilbert. 'When I was courting Felicity's mother – we were both students at the time – we went back to see her parents one Easter and because we were both broke we decided to hitch-hike.'

'It was a long time ago,' said Felicity's mother.

'You wouldn't believe it now,' said Gilbert, 'but back in those days Marion was a bit of a snob.'

'Don't be silly, Gilbert,' said Marion, sharply. 'I was never a snob.'

'Sorry dear,' said Gilbert. 'But I think you were.'

'You're exaggerating as usual,' she said. She reached across the table and touched my hand. She was a keen toucher. 'You have to learn to take everything my husband says with a pinch of salt.'

'So, anyway, we were standing there by the side of the road. I was hidden behind a tree with our bags while Marion was getting ready to stick out her chest and her thumb to get someone to stop and give us a lift.' Gilbert paused and added what was clearly intended to be an aside. 'In those days hitch-hiking wasn't as dangerous as it is these days,' he explained, as though he was much older than I. 'Everyone did it,' he added.

'I never stuck out my chest,' complained Marion, blushing enough to make me suspect that her husband's version of what happened was probably pretty accurate. 'You make me sound like some sort of cheap floozy.'

'You were no cheap floozy,' agreed Gilbert. 'But you used to stick out your chest when we were hitch-hiking. You used to stick old tights in your bra to give yourself more, you know,' he used his hands to illustrate the anecdote and searched around for a few moments for an appropriate word. 'Oomph' was the word he finally deemed appropriate.

'Well, I did that maybe just once or twice,' admitted Marion, blushing bright red. 'I wasn't terribly well-endowed in those days.'

'Mother, you didn't!' said Felicity, laughing. She instinctively looked down at her own chest. The scallop-shaped neckline of the dress she was wearing revealed a perfectly ample natural cleavage

'Well if it had been left to your father we would have never got a lift anywhere,' said Marion to her daughter. 'One of us had to use a little ingenuity. You were always nicely developed in that department but I only blossomed when I had you. Before that I looked like a boy when I wore a jumper and jeans.'

'You *never* looked like a boy,' said Gilbert gallantly.

'Anyway, the tights were just a marketing ploy,' explained Marion. 'And I seem to remember that they worked,' she added, with a glance at her husband.

'They certainly did. My wife has always been a genius at marketing,' said Gilbert proudly. 'When we opened our first shop it was Marion who had all the best ideas.'

'Don't be silly, dear,' said Marion, blushing again.

The waiter came to collect our plates. No one spoke while he skilfully used one hand to pile used crockery and cutlery onto the other hand and arm. When he had disappeared Gilbert lowered his voice and leant in towards the centre of the table. 'That waiter reminds me of someone,' he said, furrowing his brow. 'Can't remember who but the name begins with a B.'

There was a silence while Gilbert tried to remember the name of the person the waiter reminded him of.

'What did your first shop sell?' I asked, when it seemed

that the silence had gone on for long enough.

'Stamps,' said Gilbert bluntly. 'We started a stall at the local market and it sort of, well grew from there.'

'Gosh!' I said. 'How fascinating.'

'Three shops and a thriving mail order business now,' said Gilbert. 'Collectibles,' he said. 'There's lots of money in collectibles.'

'I had never really thought about it,' I confessed. 'But I suppose there probably is.'

'Bulpit,' said Gilbert.

We all looked at him.

'The name of the bloke the waiter reminds me of.' He thought for a moment and then shook his head; his disappointment undisguised. 'No, it's not Bulpit,' he said, sadly. 'But it's definitely a B.'

'I gather you are something of a collector, Mr...er...,' stuttered Felicity's mother. 'I'm so sorry, Felicity told us so much about you but never told us your surname.'

'Sheriff,' I said, without thinking. 'But call me Omar. Please.'

'Omar Sharif?' said Marion, clearly astonished.

'Sheriff,' I said, quickly. 'S-H-E-R-I-F-F,' I said. 'It sounds the same but it's spelt differently.'

I felt a pain in my ankle, looked to my right and saw Felicity staring at me with a raised eyebrow.

'What an astonishing coincidence!' said Marion.

'I think my mother was probably a fan,' I said. 'And with our surnames being similar...'

'Really?' said Mrs Dingle. She frowned and seemed puzzled by something. It was probably the same flaw that had occurred to me.

'Of course I don't think Omar Sharif was a big star when I was born,' I said. 'But she had me re-christened when I was a teenager.'

'Really?' said Gilbert. 'Can you do that?'

'We were talking about your collection,' said Marion, sensing my discomfort.

'Oh yes,' I said. 'Fascinating. Absolutely fascinating. My collection is the most important thing in my life.' I rambled on. 'After Felicity, of course.' I turned to Felicity and smiled.

'Of course,' smiled Marion.

I looked at Felicity, desperate for help. 'Omar has been collecting all his life,' she said. 'Haven't you, darling?'

'All my life,' I agreed. I looked into her eyes, begging her to help.

'My father collects all sorts of things,' said Felicity. 'Stamps, cigarette cards, match boxes, souvenir ashtrays, beermats.' She looked at her father. 'Are you still collecting beermats, father?'

'Oh yes,' he said, with undisguised enthusiasm. 'I picked up five rare German ones last week.'

'So what's your speciality, Mr Sh...Omar?' asked Marion.

'Norton!' said Gilbert suddenly. He spoke so loudly that half the other diners in the restaurants stopped talking and looked in our direction.

'Sshhh!' said Marion. 'Everyone's looking!'

'Who is Norton?' asked Felicity.

'The chap that waiter reminds me of,' said Gilbert. 'Edward Norton. He's a salesman at the BMW garage.' He smiled and looked very relieved. 'It was driving me mad!' he said. He looked across at me. 'Does that ever happen to you?'

'All the time,' I agreed.

'I thought you said his name began with a B,' said Marion.

'An N,' said Gilbert. 'It starts with an N.' He paused, thinking again. 'Maybe his first name starts with a B.'

'Oh, don't start all that again!' said Felicity.

'That reminds me, I was saying something about BMWs

before,' said Gilbert. 'What on earth was I about to say?'

'How do you expect us to know what you were about to say?' demanded Marion, perfectly reasonably.

'You told me that you had a BMW,' I reminded him.

'I know what I was going to tell you,' said Gilbert, once again greatly relieved. 'I was telling you about the first time that Marion and I went hitch-hiking.'

'Oh dear,' muttered Marion, only half under her breath. 'I thought you'd forgotten all about that.'

'We had been standing on the grass verge for a quarter of an hour and hundreds of lorries, vans and cars had gone screaming past,' continued Gilbert, bravely ignoring his wife. 'Marion still hadn't put her thumb up...'

'...or stuck her chest out!' added Felicity.

'...or stuck her chest out,' agreed Gilbert. 'So I popped out from behind my tree to ask her why she wasn't trying to get us a lift. And do you know what she said?'

Neither Felicity nor I could guess.

'She said she was waiting for a BMW,' said Gilbert.

Felicity laughed out loud. I smiled.

'Well, you'd have accepted a lift in anything,' complained Marion.

'Of course I would,' said Gilbert. 'I just wanted to get where we were going as quickly as possible.'

'He'd have had me laid out in the back of some dirty old van,' complained Marion.

'Oh, mother!' said Felicity, laughing again.

'I didn't mean that!' insisted Marion, going bright red. 'You know what I meant.'

'What happened in the end?' I asked. 'Did a BMW come along?'

'No,' said Gilbert. 'But I eventually managed to persuade her to accept a lift in a Mercedes.' He sighed at the memory of it.

'So, that's why you always buy BMWs,' I said.

'That's why I always buy BMWs,' agreed Gilbert.

'So, what do you collect?' asked Marion. She was clearly not a woman who gave up easily.

'Napkins,' I blurted out, holding up the red paper square which had been crumpled on my lap, allegedly protecting my clothes from stray bits of food and wine. 'And serviettes,' I said.

'Good heavens,' said Gilbert. 'I've met all sorts of unusual collectors. I know a man who has the biggest collection of coloured pencils in the world. I heard of a fellow who collects airline sick bags. And a friend of mine knows a chap in New Zealand who collects plastic tea spoons. But you are the first person I've ever met who collects napkins.'

'And serviettes,' I reminded him.

'How big is your collection?' asked Gilbert.

'I'm not sure,' I said. 'I'm reorganising things at the moment,' I said, twisting the red paper napkin on my lap so hard that a piece came off.

'You didn't tell us that Mr Sh...', began Mrs Dingle.

'Omar,' I reminded her.

'Omar,' said Mrs Dingle, with a smile and a nod in my direction. 'You didn't tell us that Omar collected napkins,' she said to Felicity. 'You said he collected golf tees.'

'I'd forgotten about the serviettes,' said Felicity. 'But it's nice to have a man who has two interests,' she said, glancing in my direction. 'It makes it so much easier to find presents for birthdays and Christmas.'

'You've spoilt the surprise now,' I protested. 'I'll know what I'm getting when I find my parcel under the Christmas tree!'

'Of course you won't,' said Felicity, putting her hand on my arm. She seemed to have inherited her mother's habit of touching people. I liked it. I liked it very much. I looked at her. 'You won't know whether you're getting a packet of Japanese golf tees or a rare old Italian serviette.' I suddenly realised that I wanted very much to spend next Christmas with Felicity. And I didn't want her putting her hand on anyone else's arm.

# ~ Chapter Thirty Five ~

'I hope you don't mind my asking you,' said Gilbert, leaning a little closer and lowering his voice, 'but since you're a golf professional I simply can't resist the temptation to ask you just one question.'

If Gilbert had asked me a question about golf at the beginning of the evening, when I had been stone cold sober, I would have panicked. But having consumed the best part of a bottle of wine I had acquired more confidence. The confidence may have come out of a bottle but the beauty of confidence which comes out of a bottle is that it is, to the consumer, indistinguishable from the real thing. (To the sober observer, of course, there are startling differences between these two types of confidence. But, fortunately, Gilbert had drunk as much wine as I had.)

'Oh daddy, you really shouldn't ask Omar for advice,' said Felicity. There was panic in her voice. She knew that I had never picked up a golf club in my life. 'It's like being at a cocktail party and asking a doctor about your bad back.'

Gilbert looked puzzled. 'We aren't at a cocktail party and I haven't got a bad back,' he protested, not entirely unreasonably. He looked at me. 'And you're not a doctor, are you?'

I shook my head. 'I'm definitely not a doctor,' I told him.

'There you are!' said Gilbert, genuinely puzzled. 'Why is my asking your boyfriend for advice about my hook like being at a cocktail party, which we're not, asking a doctor, which he isn't, about a bad back which I'm glad to say I haven't got?'

'Because I expect Omar wants to get away from golf for the evening,' said Felicity, not in the slightest bit put off by the complexity of this protest. Her voice was full of finality. Only a brave man – or someone emboldened by alcohol – would have ignored her.

Marion added her voice to Felicity's. 'Don't listen to him Omar, dear,' she said.

'Why not?' demanded Gilbert, whose alcohol enhanced confidence was great enough to enable him to withstand this twin approach. He slapped me on the back. 'Chap is about to become my son-in-law!' he reminded his wife and daughter, though this was of course almost as much of a surprise to them as it was to me. 'It's a poor show if I can't ask my son-in-law about my golf swing.' He turned to me, his face about six inches from mine. 'Do you?' he asked suddenly.

I stared at Gilbert, completely confused and with no idea what he was talking about. 'Do I what?'

'We're not engaged, daddy,' said Felicity, clearly keen to put the record straight. 'No one has said anything about marriage or about Omar becoming your son-in-law.'

'Do you want to get away from golf?' Gilbert asked me.

'No, no, not at all,' I said, full of alcohol inspired irrational confidence. I waved a hand around magnanimously. 'Ask away!'

Beside me Felicity put her hand on my thigh and squeezed. Emboldened by circumstances and alcohol, I misinterpreted this restraining gesture as a sign of affection and responded by boldly placing my own hand on her thigh.

'There you are, you see!' said Gilbert to his wife and daughter. There was unmistakeable triumph in his voice. I suspect that it was not often that he enjoyed such a noticeable victory over the women in his family.

'Ouch!' I said, as Felicity removed her hand from my thigh and immediately used the liberated fingers to remove my hand from her thigh.

Alarmed by my cry Felicity's mother, clearly a caring and solicitous woman, leant forward. 'Oh dear, what's the matter?' she asked. 'Are you all right?'

'I've talked to the pro about it, of course,' said Gilbert, unmoved by my pain and blissfully ignoring the drama unfolding beside him. 'It's a problem I've had for years.' He sighed. 'I thought I'd got it licked but in recent months it's got worse.'

'Are you all right, Omar?' repeated Mrs Dingle.

'Just a touch of cramp, I expect,' I said, rubbing my wrist.

'The pro says my grip is one of the best he's ever seen,' said Gilbert, who had picked up a coffee spoon and was attempting to use it to illustrate his grip. Since a coffee spoon is considerably smaller than the average golf club he was having some difficulty with this. 'And he tells me I keep my head as steady as a rock,' he said, using the coffee spoon to hit a stray piece of bread off the table cloth. The bread headed off in the direction of his wife. 'But he thinks I drop my left shoulder an inch too much. Do you think that could be the problem?' Displaying excellent reflexes Mrs Dingle ducked and the piece of bread flew through the air and landed in the bouffant hair of a blonde woman at the next table. Fortunately, neither she nor her companions noticed the arrival of this unsolicited addition to her coiffure.

'How strange,' said Mrs Dingle, ignoring her husband's

display of indoor golfing prowess. She leant towards me, her face full of care and concern. 'Are you all right, dear? Do you want to lie down? Shall we get you a glass of water? An aspirin tablet?'

'And so if the problem is that I'm dropping my shoulder – and I'm not saying it is – what should I do about it?' finished Gilbert.

'I'm sure he'll be fine,' said Felicity, putting her hand on my arm. Feeling her fingers touch me I looked at her in alarm but she smiled sweetly and I relaxed a little.

'Are you closing your eyes through the swing?' I asked.

Gilbert looked at me and frowned. He seemed puzzled and slightly sceptical. 'Closing my eyes?'

'Closing your eyes helps your mind and body concentrate on the ball,' I explained, looking around as though to check that no one at any of the other tables was listening. 'It cuts out distractions from the outside world.'

'I've never heard that one before,' whispered Gilbert, óbviously impressed.

'And scrunch your toes up in your shoes.'

'Scrunch my toes up?'

'Scrunch your toes up.'

'What does that do?'

'Improves accuracy off the tee,' I told him. 'It liberates inappropriate muscle tension.' I leant across the table. 'These are secret tips we professionals use,' I told him. 'Don't whatever you do tell anyone I told you about them.' He stared at me, open-eyed. 'You must have noticed that professionals hit the ball further than amateurs?'

'Of course.'

'These are the tricks we professionals use to enable us to hit the ball further and straighter than the amateurs,' I told him.

'Really?' said Gilbert, leaning closer to me. If I was

drunk enough to think these things up he was certainly drunk enough to believe them.

'Really,' I said.

Gilbert leant even closer and looked from side to side before speaking. 'Can I tell my chum Bernard?' he asked, in a whisper. 'We've played together for fifteen years. I trust him with my life. He's a tyre salesman. I know he wouldn't tell a soul.'

'Sorry,' I said, putting a finger to my lips and shaking my head.

'Enough said!' said Gilbert, nodding to show that he understood. 'The secret stops here,' he said, tapping his lips with his right forefinger. 'Sealed,' he said. He winked at me.

# ~ Chapter Thirty Six ~

We were standing on the pavement outside the restaurant.

'So,' said Mrs Dingle, looking first at me, then at her daughter and then at me again. 'Put us out of our misery. Have you two set the date yet?'

Felicity looked at me. I looked at her. Neither of us said anything.

'For the wedding,' explained Gilbert, in case we hadn't understood what his wife had been talking about. 'When are you two getting married?' Both he and Mrs Dingle stared at us. Their eyes were full of both hope and expectation.

I looked at Felicity. She looked at me. I put my arm around her. She stiffened for a moment and then to my surprise (and delight) I felt her relax. I felt her arm slide around my waist.

'We haven't got a date yet,' I said.

'What on earth are you waiting for?' demanded Gilbert, with clearly faked gruffness. 'You're both obviously madly in love with one another.'

'Well,' I began, and shrugged.

'If you were worried about the little...you know...between the two of you then you can forget it,' said Gilbert. 'Isn't that right, mother?'

'It doesn't bother us at all,' said Felicity's mother. She reached out and put a hand on her daughter's arm. 'We're both just pleased to see you happy, dear,' she said.

I looked at Felicity who clearly didn't have any more idea about what her parents were talking about than I did.

'The, you know, the difference,' said Gilbert. He seemed embarrassed.

'The difference?'

'The fact that you're, well, you know, and she's, er...' Gilbert continued. 'The difference...er vive it, that's what I say. Vive la difference, isn't that what the French say?'

'The age thing,' said Felicity's mother, bluntly, spotting our confusion. She shook her head. 'Gilbert and I talked about it. It doesn't bother us a bit.'

Felicity looked at them and then at me and then back at her parents. Then she burst out laughing.

'What's the matter, dear?' asked her mother, solicitously.

'There's nothing the matter,' said Felicity. We all looked at her, waiting to hear why nothing was the matter. 'It's just, well, just that I hadn't thought about it. To be honest, I hadn't even noticed the difference!'

'There you are then,' said Felicity's mother, patting her daughter on the arm. 'It's of no consequence. Your Aunt Giselda will probably have a thing or two to say about it. As you know she has always been a little old-fashioned about these things, but you just leave her to me. You let us know the date when you're ready.'

'There's no hurry,' said Gilbert, with a smile. He looked up at the sky. 'Nice night,' he said. 'But a bit chilly.' He started to walk slowly towards the hotel. His wife followed him.

Felicity and I followed along behind them, still with our arms around one another. It was a moment which I wished could go on for ever.

'Would you like to go for a walk by the river?' I asked

Felicity. It had occurred to me that if Felicity and I went upstairs with her parents I would either have to creep back down again afterwards or else climb out of the window and slide down a drainpipe. Neither of these possibilities appealed to me. I had a vision of falling, hurting my back and turning up at breakfast the following morning with a bad back. Gilbert would derive a good deal of amusement from that.

'That would be nice,' she said. 'I'd like that.'

'Ah, how romantic!' said Felicity's mother, who had overheard. 'Your father was just the same when he was younger.' She paused and leant a little closer. 'Before he got his arthritis,' she whispered. 'He doesn't like to be out too long in the night air these days. He's not as young as he used to be.'

We both smiled at her as though we understood. I didn't draw attention to the fact that Gilbert was quite probably a year or two younger than I was.

'You two are in room 220,' called Gilbert, now a few yards ahead, on the steps to the hotel. 'We'll see you at breakfast in the morning.'

'Don't forget,' I said to Gilbert as we left them for the night. 'Close up your toes and scrunch your eyes!'

'Close your toes and scrunch your eyes!' said Gilbert. And he gave me another conspiratorial wink to confirm that my secret was safe with him.

'Goodnight, dears,' said Felicity's mother. She gave her daughter a kiss and then surprised me by giving me one too. 'We specially asked for a room with a double bed,' she told us for the second time.. 'I know what it's like to be in love. Your father and I once changed hotels four times because all they had to offer were twin beds.'

'You already told us that, mother,' said Felicity.

I thanked Mrs Dingle for her thoughtfulness, hoping that she could not see my blushing cheeks, and then they were gone and Felicity and I were standing alone on the pavement.

'Do you really want to go for a walk by the river?' I asked her. I still had my arm around her waist and she still had her arm around mine.

'Yes,' she said. She turned, slid her other hand and arm inside my jacket and looked up at me. 'As long as your arthritis won't be too badly affected by the damp air down by the river.'

I smacked her bottom lightly. She wriggled and giggled. And then, for the first time since we had met, I kissed her. To my immense surprise and delight she kissed me back.

# ~ Chapter Thirty Seven ~

The most beautiful river in the world divides Paris into two exquisite halves. One half is bejewelled, commercial and extravagant. Listen carefully and you can hear the jewellery clanking together. The other half, replete with intellectuals, administrators and bureaucrats, is quieter and much less flamboyant. There you can hear the brains clinking and churning. It is on the left bank that people have ideas and design things. It is on the right bank that they sell the things which are thought up and designed on the left bank.

In the daytime the Seine is something of a working conduit. Barges full of coal and other essentials glide gently up and down the middle of the river. By and large the tourists stay on the banks, having picnics, watching the boats, basking in the sunshine.

At night the Seine changes its nature. It becomes a conduit for romance. The boats which glide up and down from the Eiffel Tower and the Trocadéro to the Pont Neuf and the cathedral of Notre Dame are full of rich tourists, eating five course meals and enjoying the spectacle as the Seine's adjacent skyline is floodlit by lamps fixed on the decks of the boats. On the banks stroll lovers, arm in arm. The benches which, just a few hours earlier, were packed with eager picnickers eating sandwiches and drinking wine from plastic beakers are now full of lovers kissing and cuddling and whispering sweet nothings into one another's ears.

Felicity and I strolled arm in arm along the river bank. It was one of those warm evenings which France in general, and Paris in particular, does so well. France is an outdoor country. The weather is frequently perfect for eating outside, strolling through the fields or by a river.

'I hope you didn't find my parents too intimidating,' she said.

'Not at all,' I assured her. 'I enjoyed their company.'

She looked up at me.

'No, really,' I said. 'I admit I didn't expect to get on with them. But I did.'

'My father can be a trifle intimidating at times,' she said. 'But he liked you.'

'I just hope he forgets those golf tips I gave him,' I sighed.

'He was certainly impressed. I was too. I thought you didn't know anything about golf.'

'I don't.'

'Well, you must have done some very quick research then!'

'I didn't.'

'So, where did you get those tips from?'

'I made them up.'

'You didn't!'

'I'm afraid I did.'

Felicity started giggling. 'Oh dear. But you sounded so very convincing.'

We walked on for another hundred yards or so. I had one big worry lingering at the back of my mind – whether or not to tell her that I knew what she did for a living. As we walked it had occurred to me that it might make it easier for her if I told her that I knew, that I didn't mind and that I would love her whatever she did for a living. There were several difficulties in the way of this confession. Not the least of these was the fact that I still wasn't entirely sure what she did do for a living. I knew she worked at Le Lapin Fou but just what else her work entailed I had no idea. Albert had told me that the club employed hostesses and lap dancers but I wasn't sure whether Felicity was a lap dancer or a hostess. And I didn't know what obligations went with these occupations. Were they expected to sleep with the clients? Did Felicity? She didn't look like the sort of woman who earned her living having sex with strangers but I'd been around long enough to know that it isn't always possible to guess someone's occupation simply by their appearance. I had once met a man who looked like a bishop. He had turned out to be an arms salesman specialising in the nastier forms of anti-personnel mines.

Three jazz musicians were playing on a wooden footbridge above the Seine. We stopped, stood and listened to them for a while.

'By the way, I'm sorry about all that 'when are you getting married' stuff,' Felicity said, as we started walking again. 'I hope you weren't too embarrassed by it.'

'I wasn't embarrassed by it in the slightest,' I told her. I stopped walking again, though we had only travelled a few yards, took her free hand in mine and pulled her to me. 'In fact it seemed a good idea to me.'

'Now you're being silly,' she said, looking away. 'Just look at that,' she said, nodding towards a *bateau mouche*, gliding along the river beside us.

The boat's searchlight lit us up. I pulled Felicity to me and kissed her. The beam of the light was astonishingly powerful. It was like standing there in broad daylight. When the boat had passed by we slowly parted, but stayed close together.

Felicity laughed. 'OK. So what do you do for a living?'

'At the moment I don't do anything. I used to have a terrible job in public relations but I gave that up a few months ago. I took early retirement. A sort of voluntary redundancy.'

'Why did you stick with the job if it was so terrible?'

'I don't know. I needed the job when I was married. My wife got through money as if it was bad for our health to hang on to it. And afterwards I suppose I was too frightened to give it up. I didn't have any hobbies. I didn't have any friends. It was the only thing I had. Sad, eh?'

'What are you going to do now?'

'Albert's starting a magazine. He's asked me to edit it.'

'That's wonderful! Are you excited?'

'Very.'

'Is this Albert's magazine about Paris?'

'Yes. You knew about it?'

'He's been talking about it for years. He's got it all worked out. It sounds as if it could work. I really hope it does. Is the bank going to lend him the money?'

'No. I don't think so. Albert is leaving the paper. But the magazine is going ahead.'

'How? Who's putting up the money?'

I felt rather embarrassed. 'I am.'

'You are?'

'Yes.'

Felicity looked at me, clearly surprised.

I laughed and raised a hand. 'Don't get the wrong idea,' I said. 'I haven't won the lottery. I'm not rich. But I've got a few thousand pounds in the bank. Some of it is my redundancy money and some of it from the sale of my house in England. And to be honest I can't think of a better use for it.'

'Are you sure?' asked Felicity, concerned. 'Starting any new business is always risky. But a new magazine...'

'I know,' I said. I shrugged and smiled. 'But what the

hell. Albert has been a real friend to me since I came to Paris. It'll be a pleasure to work with him. Besides, I rather think it will be fun. What about you?'

'Me what? Of course I think it's exciting.'

'No. Your work. Your job. I've told you my dark secret. Now it's your turn.' I was dreading this moment. Not because I was bothered. I had come to terms with what Felicity did for a living. I really didn't care whether she worked as a heart surgeon, sold real estate or acted in pornographic movies. It didn't make any difference to how I felt about her. And I had already decided that I wouldn't object if she wanted to carry on doing whatever it was she did after we were married. But I did fear that she might be embarrassed about telling me.

'I work at a club in Montmartre,' she told me, as though telling me she worked in a store on the Boulevard Haussmann.

'How fascinating!' I managed to cry, anxious to feign surprise but also delighted that she had chosen to tell me the truth.

'How long have you worked there?' I asked her.

'Since I first came to Paris,' she replied. 'Seven – no, eight – years ago.'

'Do you enjoy it?' I asked.

'Very much. It's very interesting work,' she said. 'The people are very nice.'

'Do you have to work very late?' I asked.

'No, not really. We start a little later than offices, banks and shops – and finish a little later too. But that suits me because I like to sleep late. And the traffic is always quieter when I am going to work and when I am coming home. Sometimes I have to stay later in the evenings but my boss, who is very kind and thoughtful, always gets me a taxi to take me home.'

'It must be very exciting,' I said. 'Being in show business.'

'Oh, I don't know that I would call it show business,' she said, rather shyly. 'It's just a job.'

I still hadn't found out exactly what she did for a living. But I strongly suspected that I had been right.

'I've never been to Montmartre,' I admitted. 'Let alone been to a club.'

'Then you must come there very soon,' she said.

'Tomorrow?' I suggested. Then, suspecting how late it was, I looked at my watch. 'Today?' I corrected myself, realising that tomorrow was already today.

Felicity laughed. 'OK.'

'Can we have dinner together afterwards?'

'Thank you. I'd like that. Very much.'

'You're shivering,' I said.

'It is a bit chilly.'

I took off my jacket and draped it around her shoulders and then we walked slowly back to her parent's hotel where the double room had been booked for us.

'I'll go back to my apartment,' I said, as we stood on the doorstep outside the hotel. It was the last thing in the world I wanted to do at that moment. The words of Felicity's mother rang, mockingly, in my ears. 'We specially asked for a double bed.'

'Will you be all right?' asked Felicity.

'The walk will do me good,' I replied.

'You'd better take this,' she said, sliding my jacket off her shoulders and handing it back to me. 'Thank you.'

'It looked better on you,' I told her, putting my jacket back on. Felicity giggled.

'Tell your parents I had to rush off before breakfast,' I suggested.

'I'll tell them you've had to go and practise your toe scrunching.'

'When will I see you?' I asked her.

'Pick me up at Le Lapin Fou. The address is in the telephone book. Every taxi driver knows it.'

'What time?'

'Come at six. I'll show you round,' she said. 'And now you'd better go.' She put her arms around my neck and kissed me. 'Are you sure you don't want me to ask the night porter to ring for a taxi?'

I shook my head. 'I'll be fine, thanks,' I told her. I still didn't go. 'I love you,' I whispered. We were still holding hands.

Tears appeared in Felicity's eyes.

'What's the matter?' I asked her, concerned. 'Have I said something wrong?'

She shook her head. 'I thought you'd never say it,' she whispered.

I waited.

'I love you too,' she whispered back.

I don't remember anything at all about the walk back to my apartment though it was presumably uneventful.

## ~ Chapter Thirty Eight ~

Despite not having got to bed until dawn (and being so excited that I had not slept at all) I got up at 8.30 and went downstairs to check my mailbox.

Rosemonde had promised that her cheque would be with me by now and when I found that my mail box contained nothing more exciting than a telephone bill and an advertisement for a company generously offering to fit new windows I thought it rather irritating of her to have failed to stick to her word. There wasn't even a note of apology.

I had cleaned out my bank account in order to make sure that Rosemonde had the money she needed to save her flat ,and her failure to send the cheque she had promised meant that I was now pretty well broke. Standing there in the hallway I emptied my pockets and found that I had 170 francs in my wallet, in notes, and about 15 francs in loose change. Hardly enough to get me through the day, and certainly not enough for me to take a taxi to Le Lapin Fou and buy a meal for two.

While I was downstairs I popped along to the baker's two doors away and bought a couple of croissants. I took these upstairs, brewed a pot of coffee and made myself breakfast while I tried to decide what to do next. As I sipped and chewed the old adage about being neither a borrower nor a lender kept popping into my head. I wished I'd remembered it earlier.

I really didn't like to telephone Rosemonde (it seemed so demeaning to have to chase up a debt) but in the end I plucked up the courage, picked up the telephone and dialled the number she had given me. There was no answer. I dialled again. No answer. I waited five minutes and then dialled the number again. There was still no answer.

At this point I began to feel a trifle concerned. I wasn't worried. But I was concerned. Even though there had been no response to the telephone I decided that I would go round to Rosemonde's flat and see if she was in. I washed up my breakfast things and put away the coffee, the butter and the jam. I then locked my front door, hurried downstairs and took a taxi to Rosemonde's flat. Despite my anxiety I honestly thought that two minutes after reaching Rosemonde's flat I would have a cheque in my hand for the sum I was owed. Little did I know just how big a surprise I had ahead of me. If I had even imagined what lay ahead I would have probably saved the Metro fare and walked.

The shock came when the concierge at the address Rosemonde had given me had never heard of her, and did not seem to recognise my description of her. I pressed him. I pushed. I raised my voice. I pleaded. But it was all in vain. For a while I wondered if she had simply given the concierge a healthy tip to develop amnesia in order to put off callers she didn't want to see. But this theory didn't last more than a minute or two. I eventually had to accept that Rosemonde had given me a false address. And it was at this moment that I really began to worry. I immediately realised that if she had given me a false address then there was a very good chance that I would never see my money again.

Outside I found a telephone kiosk and dialled Rosemonde's number once more. It seemed pretty pointless, but what else was there to try? The number just rang and rang. No one answered it.

I didn't know what to do so I took another taxi to the Fag and Ferret in the hope that I could get some useful advice from Albert. But Albert wasn't there. I walked from the Fag and Ferret to his hotel and found him still in bed. He wasn't asleep. On the contrary he was reading the paper (the one for which he wrote) and having breakfast.

'This newspaper is a disgrace,' he said, waving the paper in the air and then tossing it to one side. The crumpled pages separated and floated to the floor beside his bed. 'It is packed with miserable stories about miserable people. It makes me depressed to read it.' He stared at me over his half-moon spectacles, reminding me of an old school master.

'You look a bit under the weather,' he said, halting the progress of the tea spoon with which he had been about to decapitate an innocent looking boiled egg. 'What's up? Do you want a drink?' His hand reached towards the telephone, ready to call room service. I had known Albert long enough to know that he wasn't offering me a cup of tea. Albert regarded alcohol as the universal panacea. He prescribed it for all physical and mental ailments. I declined politely. It seemed an appropriate moment to keep my wits about me.

'I've been conned,' I told him, by now seriously agitated. 'All my money has been stolen.'

'Ah,' said Albert. 'That's not good.'

'It's terrible!' I cried, in despair. 'It was the money I was going to use for the magazine.'

'Who's stolen it?'

'A woman called Rosemonde.'

I told him the story.

# ~ Chapter Thirty Nine ~

'So,' said Albert when I had finished. 'You lent all your money to a woman?'

'Yes.'

'A woman you had met just the once?'

'Yes,' I said quietly. I didn't know whether to feel embarrassed or ashamed. I paused. 'Well, actually, it was twice,' I said, rather defensively.

'The once when you bought her lots of champagne and the once when you gave her all the money that you hadn't spent on champagne?'

'You make me sound really stupid,' I said, although he was simply telling the bald truth. It was hardly his fault if what I had done really was stupid.

Albert looked at me. 'You met her, by accident, while waiting outside a Metro station for a woman who never turned up.'

I sighed. I could hardly believe it myself. 'Yes,' I croaked. Even my voice seemed embarrassed. I made an effort to speak a little louder. 'She and her husband decided to get divorced and so she didn't want to have an affair with me.'

'OK. There's no need to shout. And this is the woman to whom you lent the money?'

247

'No. This was the woman I was supposed to be meeting.'

Albert scratched his head. He seemed puzzled. 'The woman who didn't turn up?'

'The woman who didn't turn up. The woman who didn't turn up was called Paulette. I don't know her other name. She didn't turn up because she and her husband had agreed to get divorced...'

'...so she didn't need to have an affair?'

'That's right.' I sighed. 'It didn't make much sense to me when she told me and it doesn't make much sense now.'

'No, no, that bit I understand,' said Albert. 'The French are like that. Why would a woman want to take a lover if she didn't have a husband?' He thought for a moment, struggling to get the facts assembled in order. 'But she definitely wasn't the woman to whom you lent the money?'

'No. The woman who didn't turn up because she and her husband were getting a divorce was called Paulette. The woman to whom I lent the money was called Rosemonde.'

'Rosemonde was the woman you met outside the Metro?'

'Yes.'

'By accident?'

'Yes.'

'And to whom you subsequently gave every penny you had saved?'

'That's right.'

'Over a lifetime of hard work?'

I nodded.

'The money you had got from selling your house?'

'Yes.'

'And your redundancy money?'

'Yes.'

'And whatever else you had managed to put on one side for a rainy day?'

'Yes.' I sighed, cross with myself rather than with him. 'Do you really have to rub this in quite so much?'

'I'm sorry. I'm just trying to get it straight in my mind,' said Albert. He paused for a while, playing with the stem of his wine glass. He looked at me, held his head slightly to one side and smiled before asking the next question. 'This was the money you were going to invest in our magazine?'

'Yes,' I croaked. My throat felt very dry. I looked down at my hands and examined the nail at the end of my left index finger. I felt worse about letting Albert down than I did about losing all my money. Gradually, I became aware of a strange sort of spluttering sound. I didn't like to look up. I had a feeling that Albert was crying. There wasn't a lot more to look at on or around the nail on my left index finger so I turned my attention to the nail at the end of my left middle finger. It looked about as interesting as the nail at the end of my left index finger. In fact, I was already tiring of the subject. If I had been asked I would have been happy to confirm that fingernails were, as a subject for investigation, of strictly limited entertainment value: down there alongside stand up comediennes and presenters on early morning television. The spluttering seemed to be growing in volume. I was now certain that Albert was crying. I could understand it. His magazine, his dream, seemed doomed. He no longer had a job as a columnist and now he didn't have his magazine either. I could hardly blame myself for him not having his job as a columnist but it was certainly my fault that there would not now be a magazine. I felt worse, far worse, about letting Albert down than I did about being conned and losing my money. The spluttering was getting louder. I tried hard – but in vain – to think of something comforting to say. I wanted to sink into the woodwork and disappear.

When I eventually found the courage to look up I could hardly believe my eyes. Tears were rolling down his cheeks but Albert wasn't crying, he was laughing. He was holding one hand across his mouth, gripping his abdomen with his other and rocking backwards and forwards.

'Are you OK?' I asked, thinking that perhaps he had had some sort of nervous breakdown.

Albert looked across at me and nodded. His eyes were red and his cheeks were wet with tears. He removed his hand from his mouth, looked at me, struggled for a moment to control himself, failed and started to laugh out loud. 'I'm sorry,' he said. He took a handkerchief out of the breast pocket of his jacket and stuffed it into his mouth in an attempt to stop himself laughing. 'I'm sorry.'

I don't know why but watching Albert laugh made me feel a good deal better. The money had gone and it wasn't coming back but it wasn't the end of the world. I smiled at him and nodded. 'I suppose it is a bit funny,' I admitted. I started to laugh. I wasn't really sure what I was laughing at. Losing all your money to a confidence trickster isn't necessarily the funniest thing that can happen. But I felt like laughing and laughing made me feel better so I laughed.

Albert looked at me, as though trying to decide whether or not I was offended by his laughter. He seemed relieved to note that I was not offended. 'I'm sorry,' he mumbled. He spat out the handkerchief. 'A bit funny?' he said. His laughter got louder and more out of control. 'A bit funny?' he said again. 'It is, without a shadow of a doubt, the daftest thing I've ever heard of. I've met a lot of crazy people but you...! What can I say? You may have lost a busload of money but you've acquired a priceless anecdote. I wish I was still writing a column.'

We both laughed for several minutes.

'You are,' I said, when I eventually managed to stop laughing enough to speak.

'I are what?' demanded Albert. For some unknown reason this triggered another bout of laughter. We had both reached the point at which virtually anything, with the obvious exception of anything prepared or produced by anyone describing themselves as an 'alternative comedian', would have appeared funny.

'You are still writing a column,' I told him, when I could control my breathing, my tongue and my lips long enough to speak.

This news seemed to startle Albert. It had the bizarre effect of sobering him up almost instantaneously. 'Am I?'

'I think so,' I said. 'Didn't you say that you had to write your column until the end of the month?'

'Absolutely,' said Albert. 'Up until the end of the month.' He nodded, remembering. 'If I don't write until the end of the week I'll be in breach of contract and they'll sue me for every penny I haven't got.' He looked at me. 'When is the end of the week? Hasn't the week ended yet? The weeks seem interminable these days. I blame the government.'

I looked at my watch. 'Tomorrow.'

'Streuth!' said Albert. 'It's still this week then. What time is it?'

I looked at my watch again. 'Half past twelve.'

'In the afternoon?'

'In the afternoon. What time do you have to get your column in by?'

'Now will do fine,' said Albert, who had taken out his mobile telephone and dialled the number of the features desk at the newspaper for which he worked.

I listened, in awe, as he proceeded to tell my story – the one I had just finished telling him – in a neat and precise 800 words. At the end he finished with a few paragraphs explaining that he and I had been about to go into business together, starting a new magazine about Paris. And in his final sentence he said goodbye to the readers whom he had amused

251

for so many years. When he had finished dictating he suggested to the sub editor who had taken down his copy that they called the piece "A Real Champagne Charlie."

I felt a complete idiot. But I felt curiously proud to have provided Albert with the material for his final newspaper column.

# ~ Chapter Forty ~

When he had finished writing his column Albert rang down for room service and had a drink (to celebrate his last hour's work for the newspaper he had begun to loathe and the editor he hated). He then picked up his telephone again, dialled a number he did not need to look up, apologised for ringing so early, blew a kiss, asked a question, listened carefully to the reply, wrote something down in his diary, blew another kiss, said goodbye, severed the connection, redialled and managed to get hold of a detective whom he knew by name.

'I'm impressed,' I told him, when he had made an appointment for us to see a policeman at a local police station. 'How do you come to know policemen?' Albert was not the sort of man who I could imagine hanging out in cafés and bars frequented by members of the Parisian gendarmerie.

'He's a contact of Lucie's,' Albert explained, with a careless shrug. 'She knows all sorts of strange people,' he added, with a bit of a grin.

When Albert had got dressed we emptied a bottle of wine in the hotel bar ('No responsible citizen can possibly be expected to walk into a police station without at least a couple of drinks inside him,' Albert explained, somehow managing to make this claim seem eminently reasonable) and then

tottered around the corner to the local police station. Although
he must have been greatly disappointed that the funding for
his magazine had disappeared in such a stupid way he ut-
tered not one word of criticism. All I got from him was sympathy and understanding; the sign of a true friendship.

The outside of the building where the local gendarmes
drank coffee and hung out when not speeding around the
city in beaten up Citroen motor cars was bland, uninterest-
ing 1970s concrete but the inside of the building looked like
a set from an old Maigret movie.

On the other side of a counter which marked the limits
of the reception area where we had been told to meet Lucie's
friend, two middle-aged detectives were sitting at old-fashioned 'sit up and beg' typewriters, hammering keys with just
two nicotine-stained fingers each. Both were puffing away at
Gauloise cigarettes and the air was thick with blue cigarette
smoke. Both men wore hats perched on the backs of their
heads. I hadn't seen a man in Paris wearing a hat of any kind
and these two detectives must have stood out in the street as
much as if they had been wearing pink tutus.

One of the men stopped clattering at his typewriter for
a moment, looked up and raised an eyebrow. Albert gave his
name and then gave the name of the detective he had arranged to meet. The two fingered typist nodded, picked up
an old-fashioned black Bakelite telephone, dialled a short
number, muttered something in incomprehensible provincial
French and then let the receiver clatter noisily back down
onto the rest before turning back to his typewriter and continuing to clatter away. He did all this without removing the
cigarette from his lips, simply moving it along to one corner
of his mouth and speaking out of the other corner.

I sat on a cheap plastic stacking chair while Albert
strolled around examining posters and 'Wanted' notices. The
biggest poster carried the simple words 'Défense de Fumer'.

I watched the policeman who had passed on our message. Judging by the fact that he kept stopping, cursing, using the backspace lever, and crossing something out with the 'x' key before continuing I got the impression that he was either a very poor typist or a perfectionist whose literary style required constant fine tuning. I don't know why, I am perhaps being unfair, but I figured that he was probably just a poor typist. When his cigarette had burnt down to a useless butt he tossed it into a metal waste bin, pulled a replacement with his lips from an opened pack, lit it, and carried on. He did this so automatically, so effortlessly, that I imagined that it was something he did constantly throughout the day. I tried to work out how many cigarettes he smoked a day but gave up.

After two and a half cigarettes Lucie's contact appeared. He was full of apologies and seemed genuinely contrite for having kept us waiting. He was about sixty, medium height but well-built, with rather long grey curly hair. Like Felicity's father he smoked a pipe. He bore an unnerving resemblance to the way I had always imagined that Simenon's hero Chief Inspector Maigret would have looked.

He led us down a maze of corridors to a small windowless office which contained a desk, piled high with papers, two filing cabinets, three cheap chairs and very little else. There were piles of papers and files on top of the filing cabinets, on two of the three chairs and around the edges of the room. The room was thick with tobacco smoke. The Maigret look-alike carelessly tipped the files from the two chairs and motioned for us to sit down.

Feeling increasingly embarrassed I explained what had happened. By now even I was finding it difficult to believe that I had been conned out of my money so easily. To my relief the detective was sympathetic and hid any contempt he may have felt for my unworldliness. I gave him all the information Rosemonde had given me about her. There wasn't much and I didn't have much faith that any of it would be accurate. I suspected that the name she had given me would probably turn out to be as real as the alleged address and telephone number. I also gave him a fairly complete description. I wasn't even confident that this would prove useful. I had begun to doubt everything about her and if the policeman had told me that 'she' was a 76 year old bald, male Russian sailor in drag I would not have been surprised.

When I had finished giving him information the detective picked up his telephone (like his colleague in the outer office he too had an old-fashioned black Bakelite instrument) and murmured some instructions to another police officer somewhere else in the building.

I was impressed. It took them less than five minutes to discover that the telephone number Rosemonde had given me belonged to an empty flat in the Marais. The flat belonged to a German businessman who used it for no more than three or four weeks a year. They confirmed that the address she had given me was also false. It took them another five minutes to identify Rosemonde as an Australian citizen who was also known as Kitty Lucas. In a strange way I was relieved to discover that I had been conned by a well-respected professional. Kitty had apparently used the name Rosemonde on numerous occasions in the past.

The detective Albert knew told me that enquiries through Interpol had confirmed that Kitty/Rosemonde was known to the police in several countries as a very successful confidence trickster. She always worked alone and her marks were always single men.

'She usually gets engaged to them first,' the detective told us.

'We didn't get that far,' I said. 'She didn't need that much time.' I thought about it for a moment. I really did feel terribly stupid. 'I just trusted her,' I said. It was my only excuse, my only explanation. 'I felt sorry for her. And I trusted her.'

'Your only fault is that you are too generous, too sympathetic,' said the policeman, kindly.

I did not find that I obtained much consolation from what I learned about Kitty/Rosemonde.

I found no consolation in the news that she invariably took money from vulnerable, middle aged men who were besotted by her charms. And I was not cheered when the police told me that there was very little chance of their ever catching her.

'I'm afraid we're not going to recover your money,' said the winner of the Chief Inspector Maigret lookalike competition. 'Even if we catch her she'll have spent it all on gigolos and champagne.'

He reported that the bank in Monaco had told him that the account to which my money had gone had been closed the following day – after someone had sent a fax transferring every franc it had contained to a bank in Gibraltar.

The detective then led Albert and I back along the maze of corridors to the reception area. The two policemen were still typing and smoking.

Throughout this unhappy (and I have to admit, deeply embarrassing episode) I had never given up hope that my money would be recovered. Now, in a mixture of halting French and indignant English I thanked Lucie's friend and told him that I hoped that the gigolos gave Rosemonde (or whatever name she was using at the time) a series of unpleasant infections which resulted in lots of unsightly rashes and a good deal of itching. I added that I hoped that the champagne gave her heartburn and chronic indigestion.

The policemen received my acidic comments with more sympathy than I had expected. I left the police station to a spontaneous round of applause. It was the first time I had ever been applauded by policemen and although the joy of the moment did not entirely compensate for the financial loss I had endured I nevertheless walked out into the drizzle with something approaching a spring in my step.

For two hundred yards I managed to convince myself that the loss was inconsequential. It was, after all, only money. I had met Felicity and I had been around long enough to know that when fate deals you one good card she usually tosses in a couple of duds — just to keep you on your toes.

Then, suddenly, as I walked past a newspaper kiosk, the real horror of my plight broke through and my thin veneer of complacency cracked wide open. The sight of row upon row of colourful magazines hanging on racks outside the kiosk reminded me that I now didn't have enough money to buy a copy of a magazine — let alone start a new one.

I realised that if I was to stay in Paris I needed to find a job or to find some other way to make some money.

I didn't even have enough money to take a taxi to Felicity's club in Montmartre. I wanted to sit down on the kerb and cry. But that wouldn't have helped anyone.

I knew that if I had asked Albert to lend me some money he would have happily given me his wallet. But I couldn't bring myself to ask. I thanked him for his understanding, his practical support and his help and told him that I had a date with Felicity.

'Are you OK?' asked Albert. He put a hand on my arm.

'I'm fine,' I lied, as convincingly as I could. 'Just a bit bruised. I feel such a fool.' I swallowed hard to stop myself crying. 'I'm sorry about the magazine,' I said. 'I was really looking forward to working with you on it.'

'What's with the pessimism?' demanded Albert, remarkably upbeat. 'Something will turn up. We'll do that magazine together. Just you wait and see.'

I didn't believe him. And I don't think he believed himself either. But I grinned at him. 'Sure!' I said.

'Do you need some cash?' he asked.

'No, no,' I lied. 'I'm fine.'

And then we hugged one another. I don't know who initiated it. But it seemed perfectly natural. And good. Although when we broke from our impromptu clinch we both looked around rather nervously, said goodbye formally and headed off in our different directions: Albert towards the Fag and Ferret and me towards Montmartre. It is normal for Frenchmen to hug one another in the street. They do it all the time. But it's not the sort of thing Englishmen do.

I reckoned that if I walked quickly I should just be able to get to Felicity's club on time. I had a spare Metro ticket in my wallet but I thought it might be a good idea to keep it there. A Metro ticket may not sound like much in worldly wealth terms but when it's nearly all you've got you don't want to squander it.

When Albert had disappeared around a corner I took out a small map which I had picked up from the hotel I'd stayed at when I had first arrived in Paris.

When I had worked out the best route to Montmartre I started walking.

# ~ Chapter Forty One ~

The walk to Montmartre took me just over an hour. I walked quickly and didn't stop to admire the architecture, the parks or the shops I strode past on the way.

I walked across the Pont Royal, through the Jardin des Tuileries, across the Place Vendôme (past The Ritz Hotel from which were emerging gaggles of American and Japanese tourists of such excruciating bad taste that I swore to myself that if I ever became inordinately rich and wanted somewhere to toss my money aside it would certainly not be there), past the original Paris Opera House and on past Galeries Lafayette (to shoppers what the Musée d'Orsay is to genuine art lovers).

I marched up the street next to the church of Ste Trinité and up on ever northwards towards the Boulevard de Clichy and the southernmost edges of Montmartre, dominated, as indeed is Paris herself, by the absurdly, unreal majestic wedding cake white Basilique Sacré-Coeur.

My shoes had begun to pinch, my legs were aching and demanded a respite but I neither slowed nor rested. I was nervous and excited and walking, dodging the other, slower, pedestrians, the tables and chairs on the pavement, the motorists (even on the pavement one was not safe from them for they parked and abandoned their vehicles with two wheels on the pavement whenever they could) and the dogs kept me occupied and stopped me thinking too much and becoming even more apprehensive. Part of me was in a hurry to get there and part of me wanted the journey to never end.

Le Lapin Fou was buried on the slopes of the famous hill of Montmartre and as I got closer the questions and anxieties which had beset me before, and which had been suppressed by the effort of walking so far and so fast, began to reassemble and queue up for attention.

Would Felicity be working? Would she be in her costume? How would I cope with seeing her wearing two spangles and a bunch of feathers? Did she wear a costume at all? Maybe she would consider herself overdressed in two spangles and a bunch of feathers. I still couldn't really imagine her as a stripper, a lap dancer or a hostess but I had forced myself to accept reality and, rather to my surprise, I knew that I really didn't give a damn what she did for a living. I had fallen head over heels in love and nothing else mattered.

At night Montmartre is one of the most exciting places in the world, packed with clubs catering for every imaginable taste (and a good many tastes which are pretty well unimaginable).

'Have you got the time?' a woman asked, both ambiguously and provocatively. She was standing, looking a trifle unsteady, in the middle of the pavement. I wasn't sure whether the unsteadiness was a result of something she had drunk (or sniffed or injected) or of the fact that she was struggling to balance on absurdly long stiletto-heeled shoes.

To get round this human obstacle I would have to step into the gutter, and that was full of water, so I stopped a yard and a half away from her. The road was narrow and busy and the traffic was fast, furious and dangerous. I didn't want to step into the road unless I had to. The woman was wearing a black blouse which was unbuttoned to the waist and her huge breasts were bulging out of an inadequate black bra. Below the waist she was wearing a short black leather skirt with a zip at the side. The zip was open up to her waist so that I could see the expanse of white blotchy thigh between the top of a fishnet stocking and the black and red suspender belt which held it up.

My initial guess was that she was somewhere in her mid forties and that if anything she could have been even older than this. But when I looked a little closer I realised that this was probably a wild over-estimate. She could have been in her thirties or even her twenties. She was wearing far too much make-up but the make-up could not hide the fact that her eyes were dark and she looked tired and rather distant. Her black shoulder-length wig needed combing and the fact that it was slightly askew gave her a pathetic, slightly comical look.

She had a cigarette in her left hand and without warning she lifted it to her mouth, took a drag and blew a lung full of smoke straight at me.

Slightly startled I stepped back half a step. She winked at me, smiled and then raised an eyebrow.

'I'm afraid not,' I answered, equally ambiguously. I hesitated and then spoke. 'I'm trying to find a club called Le Lapin Fou.' I found it difficult to know where to look. In order to avoid staring at the areas of skin on display I tried to look straight into the woman's eyes but she seemed to take this as a sign that I was interested in her.

'It isn't open yet,' said the woman. 'You've got a couple of hours. Come with me and I'll keep you entertained.'

'That's very kind of you,' I said. 'But I'm meeting a friend who works there.'

In an instant the woman changed. 'Why didn't you say so?' she demanded. 'Who's your friend?'

'Felicity,' I replied. 'Felicity Dingle.'

'I know Felicity!' said the streetwalker, with a big smile. 'Lovely girl! You come with me sweetie-pie. I'll take you to Le Lapin Fou. It's only round the corner.' She took hold of my elbow and, using me as a support, clip clopped her way along the pavements of Montmartre.

Less than five minutes later we were standing on the pavement outside an unimpressive building which was painted entirely in maroon.

There was a porch and doorway in the middle of the building but there were no windows at all. On both sides of the porch three glass fronted display cabinets had been fixed to the wall. The display cabinets all contained photographs of beautiful girls wearing very little and posing in blatantly provocative poses. Each cabinet contained the name 'Le Lapin Fou'. The same words appeared in gold lettering on a sign above the front door.

'I used to look like that a few years ago,' said the streetwalker, as I looked at the pictures on display. I was hunting to see if I could see Felicity's picture.

'You still look just as good as any of these,' I lied, gallantly. I thought she had sounded rather wistful at the sight of so many photographs of slender and nubile young women.

'No I don't,' replied the woman immediately. 'But you're an absolute doll to say so.' She looked down and pulled the two sides of her blouse together, as though suddenly realising for the first time just how much of her body she was displaying.

'I'd better get back,' she said, suddenly seeming embarrassed. 'There are always new girls around on the streets these days. They come in from the provinces by every train and if you move away from your pitch for too long one of them will move in.'

As she started to move away I walked after her, reached

into my back pocket and pulled out my wallet. 'Wait a moment, please,' I said. I took a note out of the wallet and held it out to her.

'No thank you,' she said, holding up a hand. 'That's not necessary.'

'Please,' I said. 'I'd like you to take it.' I closed the wallet quickly and slipped it back into my trouser pocket before she could see that it was now empty.

'OK then,' said my guide, speaking quietly. 'Thank you love,' she added, taking the note from my hand. She slipped it skilfully into the top of her stocking.

I noticed, for the first time, that it was not the first note to be stored there, though if her stocking top served as her purse she wasn't a good deal better off than I was.

She nodded towards the front door of Le Lapin Fou. 'Just knock on the door,' she said. 'And then stand back a little so that they can see you properly.'

I waited until she had gone. Clip clopping away on the pavement. Audible long after she had disappeared from sight.

Then I knocked on the door and, as she had advised, stepped back so that I would be clearly visible to anyone inside.

# ~ Chapter Forty Two ~

I had expected to have to stand on the pavement outside Le Lapin Fou for some time, but Felicity had clearly warned the doorman that I was arriving. She must have given him my description for I had hardly had time to step back from the door after knocking before I heard bolts being drawn back. Then the heavy door swung silently inwards and the doorman, a huge fellow with a bald head, tattoos on the backs of both hands and huge gold loops in his ears stood to one side so that I could enter. He wore black track suit bottoms, a black T-shirt and black shoes and looked like a pirate, only much more frightening.

He was well over six feet tall and probably weighed well in excess of three hundred pounds. He had a bad complexion, tiny pale eyes (he squinted when he opened the door and let in what was left of the daylight) with about as many laugh lines as an egg, and a sour mouth, downturned at the edges. I wouldn't have liked to have him looking down at me if I had been sitting in the dentist's chair but he was a good choice for a doorman; not the sort of fellow you would choose to tangle unless you were drunk or carrying an Uzi machine gun. I nodded and murmured my thanks as I edged past and hoped that I didn't look as nervous as I felt.

The inside of Le Lapin Fou had clearly been decorated with night time visitors in mind. Black was the colour of choice. The floor, the walls and the ceiling were all black. The floor was covered with what looked like black linoleum and the walls and the ceiling had been painted black. The only light came from rather dim lights fitted at ankle level along both sides of the corridor.

On the left, just inside the main door, a hatchway and doorway led into a cloakroom. A plump woman in a flowered smock was being very busy in there with a vacuum cleaner. She had her hair tied in a ponytail and the cigarette between her lips had about an inch of ash on the end of it. Apart from her, and the doorman, there was no one else around.

'Where can I find Miss Felicity Dingle?' I asked, in hesitant, halting French.

'Go straight down zee corridor, take zee second left and go down zee stairs,' the doorman replied in the sort of English favoured by German soldiers in World War II movies. 'Zen take see first turning on zee right. Go up two flights of stairs and zen turn left. Take zee second corridor on zee right.'

When he'd finished I waited for a moment, hoping that he would click his heels together. He didn't so I repeated the instructions to myself, under my breath, in the vain hope that I would remember them. I then set off down the corridor.

Inevitably, I got lost.

Other men who got lost in French night clubs, famous for shows in which buxom young women remove all their clothes to entertain the customers, probably find themselves in the artistes' dressing room – surrounded by semi-naked dancers, snake charmers, fire eaters and singers.

But after wandering around for what seemed like an hour or so (but what was probably no more than five minutes) I found myself in a cul-de-sac. In front of me there was a fire door. I turned round, retraced my steps and knocked quietly on every door I passed. The fourth knock produced a response. A tiny woman, as round as she was tall, opened the door, stared up at me and demanded to know what I wanted. She had very short black hair and a face as round as her body. She had a mouthful of pins and these rather hindered her ability to speak clearly. Behind her, crammed together in a gloomy little room, there were racks and racks of stage outfits. The outfits were predictably skimpy but the feathers adorning them had clearly been ordered by the ton. You get a lot of feathers in a ton.

I apologised and explained that I was looking for Felicity Dingle. This produced an immediate response. The woman opened her mouth and grinned broadly. To my surprise the pins stayed where they were.

'I will show you to her,' the little woman said.

She closed her door behind her and started off down the corridor at a pace that would have been impressive if she'd been built rather more athletically. Given her shape and size her speed was remarkable. From behind, in the dim light, it looked as though she was simply rolling along the corridor like a big beachball. We went down one flight of stairs and up two and her speed never slowed.

'Here is Mademoiselle Dingle,' said the rotund dressmaker a few minutes later, standing outside a door which looked exactly like all the other doors we had passed.

I thanked her, we exchanged smiles and then she disappeared.

For a moment or two I watched as she disappeared back down the corridor. And then I turned my attention back to Felicity's door.

All my fears and anxieties had now returned.

What, I wondered, would she be wearing when she opened the door? Would I be able to look her in the eye without showing my embarrassment if she was wearing one of those skimpy little outfits adorned with feathers? Would I be able to look her in the eye at all.

I dragged together all my courage and knocked on the door.

The door opened.

And it is absolutely no exaggeration to say that when I saw Felicity I had the shock of my life.

Since I had first heard that Felicity worked in a strip club I had frequently wondered about what she did there.

Did she take off all her clothes? Did she work on a stage or did she wander among the customers, talking to them and allowing them to fondle her? Did she go home with them? Did she sleep with them?

While walking through the streets of Paris towards Le Lapin Fou I had toyed with many different possibilities and many different images.

But my imagination had not prepared me for what I saw.

# ~ Chapter Forty Three ~

'Hello,' said Felicity. 'You found me OK then?'

'Yes,' I replied, almost but not quite struck dumb.

She stood back and opened the door wide. I entered. She closed the door. There was no one else in the room.

'The club isn't all that easy to find,' she said. 'Particularly in the daytime. At night, when all the decorative lights are on, you can see the club from both ends of the street. But in the daytime it rather merges in with the other buildings.' She paused. 'This isn't the prettiest part of Paris.'

'It wasn't too difficult to find,' I assured her. 'Even in daytime.' I reached out, gently held her shoulder and pulled her towards me. She did not resist. I lowered my head and kissed her. She kissed me back. I kissed her again.

'Most of the taxi drivers know where the club is,' said Felicity at last, during a slight pause in the kissing.

'I didn't get a taxi. I walked.'

'All the way from the apartment?'

'Yes.'

'Gosh. That's a long way.'

There was a pause, during which we simply looked at one another. Then we kissed again.

'You're looking well,' said Felicity, pulling away from me.

'It's all the exercise and fresh air.'

'Is the air in Paris fresh?'

'Oh, I think so.'

'Did you find your way around the club without getting lost?'

'No, I'm afraid not. I had to ask for directions.'

'Who did you ask?'

'I don't know her name. A small, round lady with pins in her mouth. I think she's probably some sort of dressmaker.'

'Danielle. Our costumier. She does all the stage costumes. She's wonderful.'

'She was very sweet.'

'She has a reputation for being something of a dragon sometimes. She obviously took to you.'

'Actually she seemed to take a liking to me when I told her that I was coming to see you.'

Felicity blushed. 'Did she?' She paused. 'She's a good friend. I've told her about you. About us. She probably guessed who you are.'

'What did you tell her?'

Felicity blushed still deeper. 'Never you mind.'

'Was it good?'

'Yes.'

'OK. That's all right then.'

We held hands and gazed into one another's eyes for a month or two. I thought yet again that she was without doubt the most beautiful woman I'd ever seen. I pulled her to me and put my arms around her. She put her arms around my neck. Her eyes sparkled and her hair shone. I couldn't help wondering what on earth she saw in me. A middle-aged, balding, slightly overweight guy in his fifties. There was one thing about being poor: she certainly wasn't after my money. She was radiant.

She was also fully clothed. She was wearing a grey knee

length tailored skirt with a matching jacket, a white silk blouse and black, low-heeled shoes.

'Would you like to sit down?' she asked.

'No thank you. I'd rather stand so that I can hold you.'

'I'm sorry about the office.'

'Why?'

'It's a bit dull.'

I looked around. There was a large desk, upon which sat a computer monitor and keyboard. The rest of the desk was covered in papers. Behind the desk there was an executive style chair in black leather. The only other chair had a pile of files on it. There were three filing cabinets in the room and they were all piled high with papers.

'It looks great to me,' I said.

'And I don't usually dress like this,' she said, indicating her grey jacket and skirt.

'I think you look wonderful.'

'You're just being sweet.'

'No, I'm not. I think you look terrific. Actually, to be honest I'm just relieved to see you wearing clothes!'

As soon as I'd said this I wished I hadn't.

For a moment Felicity looked puzzled. 'Why? What do you mean?' She frowned. Why are you relieved to see me wearing clothes?'

'Well, you know...working in a club...this sort of club...a place where women well, you know...'

'You thought I was one of the strippers?' asked Felicity incredulously.

'I wasn't sure,' I admitted. 'It sort of vaguely crossed my mind. As a possibility. Just a remote possibility.' I felt myself starting to blush. 'Not really a possibility. More a, well a, silly thought. Just a notion.' By now I was, I felt sure, bright red.

Felicity stared at me. For a moment, despite my flush, I

went cold. And then, much to my relief, she started to laugh.

'You're not cross with me are you?' I asked, anxiously.

'Not in the slightest,' she said, when she had managed to control the giggling long enough to talk. 'Actually I'm very flattered. I'm much too short and far too old and my boobs are too small for me to get a job as a stripper.'

'I think you'd make a marvellous stripper,' I insisted. And then I realised what I'd said. 'Well, from what I've seen of you. Although I can imagine the rest. Only sort of, of course. In theory. But in theory I think you'd make a wonderful stripper.'

She held her head to one side. 'You wouldn't have minded?'

'Minded?'

'If I'd been a stripper?'

'It was only a vague sort of thought.'

'You wouldn't have minded?'

'No.'

'Not at all?'

'No. Not really.' I hesitated. 'I love you,' I said. 'I was jealous. But I wouldn't have really minded. It wouldn't have made any difference.'

Felicity put her arms around me and kissed me. 'You are the sweetest man I've ever met,' she said quietly. 'And I love you.' She kissed me again. 'You would have been jealous?'

'Yes.'

'Good. I'm glad about that.'

'You want me to be jealous?'

'Oh yes. I would be jealous if you were a stripper.'

The idea was so ludicrous that I couldn't help laughing. We held one another for a while, kissed some more and looked into one another's eyes a good deal. I sat on the edge of her desk and pulled her to me.

'So, what exactly do you do here?' I asked her at last.

'I'm the business manager,' said Felicity. 'I trained as an accountant and then took a business management degree.' She took one hand from around my neck and waved it around the office. 'I look after the books and the accounts. I suppose some people would say I'm the boring bit of the club.'

'But the bit that makes sure it makes a profit.'

'Yes, that's true,' smiled Felicity. 'I make sure that the owner doesn't spend more than we're making. And it's a lot more fun than working in a bank.'

'Talking about money reminds me that there's something I have to tell you,' I said.

'What's that?'

'I don't have any.'

'Money?'

'Money.'

'It doesn't matter.' She shrugged. 'We don't need much money. And I have quite a good salary.'

'No,' I said. 'You don't understand. I've lost all my money. Every penny. I wasn't rich before. But I had some money. I had enough to be fairly independent. And now I'm poor. I'm pretty well as poor as anyone can get. I don't have any debts at the moment but if I eat tonight I will have.' I paused, trying to think of some way to explain just how poor I had become. 'I didn't walk here because I wanted the exercise. I walked because I couldn't afford a taxi.'

Felicity looked concerned. 'Why? What on earth has happened? Have you been robbed?'

'It's a rather long story.'

'So, tell me,' she insisted. 'I don't care how long it is. I want to know what happened.'

I told her.

I was embarrassed about it. I felt a complete idiot. But I told her. I told her everything. I told her about Rosemonde.

I told her how I'd been conned into parting with my money.

And at the end I told her that I could no longer afford to back Albert's magazine and that it looked as though I would have to go back to England and try to find myself a job.

# ~ Chapter Forty Four ~

'You can't just give in,' said Felicity, when I had finished my
sorry tale. 'You can't just abandon the magazine.'

'I don't want to give in,' I assured her. 'But I don't see
that we've got much option. Albert doesn't have a job so the
bank won't lend him any money. And my money has all disappeared with Rosemonde.' I felt embarrassed, ashamed and
rather sorry for myself.

'You are a big softy,' she said quietly. It was her only
critical comment then or ever after. If there had been any
doubt before it was her uncritical acceptance of what had
happened which sealed my love for her. I hadn't known her
long but I already felt that I knew her better than anyone else
I'd ever met before.

'Soft?' I said. 'Stupid more likely.'

'No,' insisted Felicity. 'You thought she was in trouble.
So you helped her. What you did was kind and honourable.
What she did was unforgivable. She took advantage of an-
other human being's generous nature.'

'That's what all confidence tricksters do.'

'No, it's not. Most of them take advantage of people's
greed. And in a way that's fair enough. People who are greedy
are fair game. But you weren't being greedy. You were being

275

kind.' She looked at me for a while. 'I hope you'd do the same thing again,' she said.

We both sat and looked at each for a while.

'The police say there's absolutely no chance of recovering the money?'

'Not a hope.'

'I wish I could help you and Albert,' said Felicity. 'If I had the money I'd lend it to you.'

'You're sweet,' I said. 'But I wouldn't let you.'

'That's silly.'

'No, it isn't.'

'It's irrelevant anyway,' she said. 'Because I haven't got it.'

We sat in silence for a moment or two.

'I know!' said Felicity suddenly. 'What about my father?'

'What about him?'

'I could ask him. He's always looking for new investment opportunities.'

'No,' I said flatly. 'No. No. No. I'm definitely not borrowing money from your father.'

'But he'd be pleased to help. He'd make money out of it.'

'No,' I said. 'Definitely not. Besides your father thinks I'm a professional golfer. He's going to get very confused if we tell him that I want to start a magazine.'

'It would be a good way to explain the fact that you've given up golf,' said Felicity. 'We could say that you've got an injury and that you can't play professional golf any more.'

'No,' I said, shaking my head. 'It's very sweet of you but I can't possibly borrow money off your father.'

'You're very stubborn aren't you?' said Felicity, with a sigh.

'When it comes to borrowing money from my future father-in-law I'm immoveable,' I told her. 'No. No. No. It's very nice of you to suggest it. But no.'

I folded my arms and did my best impression of a defiant man. I meant what I had said. We sat in silence.

'What did you say a few moments ago?' asked Felicity suddenly.

'When?'

'The last thing you said. Say it again.'

'I said that I wasn't going to borrow money from your father.'

'No you didn't.'

'Yes I did.'

'No, you phrased it differently.'

'Did I?'

'Yes. And you know very well you did,' said Felicity, half laughing. 'What did you say?'

I thought about what I'd said. 'You mean that bit about my refusing to borrow money from my future father-in-law?' I said. I had spoken from the heart, without thinking, and now I felt bad about it. I wished I hadn't said it. But I couldn't take it back.

'That's the bit.' Felicity blushed and lowered her eyes. 'If my father is going to be your father-in-law then...' she blushed still deeper and seemed to have abandoned the sentence. 'You and I would be...' she tried again but didn't get much further. I knew what she was talking about, of course, and realised that she wanted me to say the word first. So I had to say it.

'If your father became my father-in-law then it would obviously mean that we were married.'

'Yes,' said Felicity. She stroked my hair. 'Is that a proposal?'

I hesitated. I simply didn't know what to say. The thought had slipped out, had become words, without my thinking things through properly. I now had cold feet not because I didn't want to marry Felicity but because I knew that I couldn't feed and clothe myself, let alone a wife. Offering marriage to a woman I knew I could not look after seemed grossly dishonourable. I had spoken without thinking, spoken from the heart. I wanted to marry her but I couldn't.

Felicity sensed my embarrassment and my reluctance to say what I realised she wanted to hear. I desperately wanted to ask her to marry me and I was overjoyed by the thought that she seemed ready to accept. But I simply couldn't ask the woman I loved to marry me when I knew I was totally broke and homeless.

'I'm sorry,' said Felicity, backing away from me. She looked as though she was about to cry. 'I obviously misunderstood. I'm sorry. I shouldn't have embarrassed you like that.'

'I want to marry you,' I said. 'But I can't. I'm broke. How can I marry you with things as they are?'

'What's money got to do with love?' asked Felicity. And suddenly she turned and headed for the door.

She had opened the door, left the room and started to run down the corridor before I'd moved. I got up from the desk, rushed to the door and looked out. The corridor was empty. Felicity had disappeared.

'Felicity!' I called. 'I'm sorry. Where are you?'

The corridor remained empty and silent.

# ~ Chapter Forty Five ~

It took me an hour to find Felicity. And I doubt if I would ever have found her if it hadn't been for the help of the tiny dressmaker and the huge doorman.

I met the dressmaker by accident.

Hurrying along a corridor, completely and utterly lost, I bumped into her as she came around a corner. She was carrying a huge armful of costumes for the club's dancers and she, and the costumes, ended up on the floor.

'Where are you going in such a hurry?' she demanded, after I had apologised and had helped her to her feet.

I tried to explain. 'Felicity and I have had a misunderstanding. I don't know where she is.' I started picking up the costumes.

The dressmaker looked at me quizzically. 'A lover's tiff?'

'Yes. I suppose so.' A feather came off one of the costumes I was holding. I tried to stick it back on.

She raised an eyebrow, questioningly.

'I sort of mentioned marriage and she sort of accepted and then I didn't actually ask her...,' I confessed, the words tumbling out in something of a rush.

'You did that and she did not kill you?' asked the dressmaker incredulously.

'I was stupid, I guess,' I admitted. I was having no luck at all with the feather which seemed to have a mind of its own.

'Stupid?' said the dressmaker. 'No. Stupid is understandable. Stupid is the man who drinks too much or bets on the horses. You are not simply stupid. You are an imbecile! An absolute imbecile!' She slapped my wrist. 'Put down that silly feather. You are making things worse.'

I stared at her, not knowing what else she expected me to say.

The dressmaker helped me out. 'And you want to marry her?'

'I don't know...'

'What is there not to know?' sighed the diminutive dressmaker. 'Do you love her?'

'Yes.'

'You have no doubts?'

'No doubts.'

'Then there is no problem. She loves you. That I know for certain because this she has told me.'

'Has she really?'

'Yes. And so?'

'You don't think it matters that I don't have any money?'

'Money? Pfui to money. You are in love. What for do you need money?'

'Well, food, somewhere to live, clothes, heat – that sort of stuff.'

The dressmaker waved an arm around dismissively. 'If you are not going to ask her to marry you I am not going to help you find her!' she told me bluntly.

'I love Felicity,' I said softly.

'And so you want to marry her?'

'Yes. I want to marry her.'

'And do you think she wants to marry you?'

'Yes. I think so.'

'I think so too. She has talked of no one else but you for weeks. So. Are you going to ask her to marry you or shall I go back to my room and finish repairing these silly costumes for the silly girls who wear them and cause all the feathers to moult?'

'I'm going to ask her to marry me,' I said.

'Good,' said the dressmaker, with a big grin. She stood on tip toes, reached up and planted a big kiss on my chin. 'And so let us leave these costumes here and I will help you find her.'

We put the costumes down in a rather untidy pile on the floor and I followed the dressmaker on a high speed tour of the club. When, after ten minutes or so, we had still not found Felicity the dressmaker headed for the front door.

'Have you seen Felicity?' she asked the doorman.

'She vent out,' said the doorman.

'Where did she go?' demanded the dressmaker.

'I vas told not to tell,' said the doorman, holding himself very straight and trying to look both fierce and dignified. 'I cannot betray zee confidence.'

'Where is she, Thomas?' demanded the dressmaker, her tone making it clear that she was not in a mood to be trifled with.

'She is in zee café,' said the doorman.

'Which one?' I demanded.

'Ze von across zee road,' said the doorman. He opened the front door. Looking across the road I could see Felicity sitting at a table in the window.

I thanked the dressmaker and the doorman, dodged between a taxi and a delivery van, and ran across the road.

## ~ Chapter Forty Six ~

Felicity admitted later (much later) that she had seen me the moment I came out of Le Lapin Fou.

'I was embarrassed, disappointed and angry. But far angrier with myself more than with you,' she eventually told me. 'When you described my father as your potential father-in-law my heart leapt. And then when you started talking about having no money and not being able to marry me I thought you were just making excuses. I thought you had realised that you'd made a mistake. I thought that perhaps referring to my father as your potential father-in-law was just a slip of the tongue. I ran out of the club hoping that you would run after me and find me. I didn't hide very well, after all. When I saw you coming out of the club, with Danielle and Thomas my heart leapt. But I forced myself to try to stay calm. I didn't want to rush to any false conclusions again.'

But it was later when she told me this.

When I walked into the café opposite Le Lapin Fou Felicity pretended not to see me. She was drinking an expresso and reading a copy of Le Figaro which she had taken from a rack near the door.

I walked straight over to her table. I knew she was pretending not to see me because even when I stood over her, no more than two or three feet away from her, she continued to pretend to read the newspaper.

'I'm sorry,' I said quietly. I knew that I had to handle things carefully. If I just walked in and asked her to marry me she would probably say 'no'. I've never been very good at this sort of thing. I really didn't know what to say or how to say it.

'You have nothing to apologise for,' said Felicity, still not looking up. She sounded very matter-of-fact, as though she was talking to a colleague with whom she had had a minor disagreement.

'May I sit down?'

She didn't say anything but when I pulled out a chair and sat down she did not object. She looked up at me for a brief instant, and then looked back down at her newspaper again. I hoped that the fact that she had not told me to go away might be a good sign. It was the only small piece of hope I had so I accepted it gratefully.

'I was brought up in an era when it was thought that a man contemplating marriage must be able to look after his wife,' I told her, leaning forwards slightly and speaking in little more than a whisper. 'In the days before feminism and political correctness a gentleman would not dream of proposing marriage if he couldn't support his future partner. Heaven knows I'm not claiming to be a gentleman. But that was one of the rules and although I've done a lot of things I wish I hadn't done, and I've done a lot of things I shouldn't have done, I've always tried to play by the rules. Just because you fail doesn't mean you shouldn't keep trying.'

A waiter had appeared and was hovering beside my chair. He asked what I wanted. I looked up at him, almost surprised to see him there, and was, for a moment, confused. When I realised what he wanted I ordered a coffee. Recognising the delicacy of the moment the waiter murmured something which I did not catch, nodded and scurried away.

'When I discovered that I had lost all my money I felt a great mixture of emotions,' I went on. 'I felt angry – though the anger was directed more at myself than at Rosemonde. I felt embarrassed because I realised I'd been very stupid and had allowed myself to be conned. I felt frightened because I realised that without money the world can be an even scarier place than it is normally – and I have to admit that to me the world always seems pretty scary. I felt ashamed because I felt that I had let Albert down very badly. I like Albert very much. I haven't known him all that long but he's the best friend I've got and he's probably the best friend I've ever had. Starting a magazine with him would fulfil every dream I've ever had. And I felt sad because I thought I would probably have to go back to England, with my tail between my legs, and try to start again. I love Paris. I love my life here.'

Felicity had picked up her newspaper and was now completely hidden behind it, as though she was hiding from me. I didn't feel hurt or offended. In my heart I felt she was justified in ignoring me. I had hurt her badly. I didn't know what to do to put things right so I simply carried on telling her the truth. The truth was the only hope I had.

The waiter brought my coffee, put it down on the table in front of me and disappeared again without saying a word.

'Most of all I love you,' I continued. 'I don't know when I first realised that I had fallen in love with you. It started some time ago and it has slowly grown and blossomed. At first I didn't think there could possibly be any chance for me. You're beautiful, you seem so confident and you're much younger than I am.'

Felicity did not say anything and the newspaper didn't move. I didn't seem to be getting anywhere. But I persevered.

'I first thought about asking you to marry me that evening when we walked by the river, after I'd met your parents. I asked you. But you said 'no'. And I didn't dare ask again. We hadn't known each other long. And although I knew I was in love with you I didn't really know how you felt about me. So I didn't say anything more, though I told you how I felt. But although I didn't say anything more about marriage I didn't stop thinking about it.'

'I had just about plucked up the courage to ask you to marry me when I discovered that I had lost every penny I had. When the rent is due on my apartment I will have to leave. I can't even afford to buy food. I have nothing. I lent Rosemonde every centime I had because I felt sorry for her and I trusted her. Heaven knows, I wasn't rich before that happened. But I had enough to live on. I had a little security. And I had enough to look after you.'

I stopped. Felicity still hadn't spoken. I realised that I might have said the wrong things, sighed in exasperation, took a sip of my coffee and blundered on.

'I'm not suggesting that you need looking after. I know you have a good job,' I went on, trying to repair any damage which I might have done. 'I know you can look after yourself very well.' I paused, and thought for a while. I was learning a good deal about myself as I talked. 'I suppose that what I'm talking about here isn't your need but my feeling of responsibility. And my need. And the sense of guilt that always goes with a sense of responsibility.'

I sipped some more coffee, took a deep breath and carried on. I'd gone too far to stop, too far to retrace my steps. My only hope was to continue onwards and hope that eventually I might begin to make sense to at least one of us. 'I'm a bit old-fashioned,' I said, with a sigh. 'I know all this probably makes me sound like something out of the stone age but it's the way I feel.'

'Today when I referred to your father as my father-in-law I suddenly felt overwhelmed with a sense of guilt. I desperately wanted to carry on and to ask you to marry me. But I didn't because I felt that I didn't have that right. I love you but I can't look after you properly. Where would we live? How on earth would we eat? I've always believed that a woman has a right to expect her husband to look after her. I felt...oh hell I've said it all and I'm starting to repeat myself. I don't know what to say except that I do love you. I love you with all my heart. And if, knowing everything else you still...'

Slowly, across the table from me, Felicity lowered her newspaper and put it down on an adjacent table. I was astonished to see that she was crying and had clearly been crying for some time. She reached across the table and took my hand.

'I love you,' she whispered. The words were almost inaudible and I moved still closer to her to make sure that I heard her properly. She squeezed my fingers. 'You are a fool,' she said softly and although tears were rolling down her cheeks her eyes were smiling.

'Will you...' I began, my own voice croaking.

'Ssshhh!' said Felicity, reaching up with her free hand and placing her index finger across my lips.

I felt hollow as I suspected that she didn't want to hurt me by refusing me.

'Will you marry me?' she asked me.

I looked at her. I hadn't expected it.

'This way you don't have to feel guilty,' she said. There was a long pause. 'Unless you say 'no', of course,' she added.

'I'm not going to say 'no'.'

'So say it.'

'Yes, please.'

'Now kiss me.'

I leant across the table, put my arm around her, pulled her towards me and kissed her. She put her arm around my neck and kissed me back.

As I did so I heard cheering from outside the café. We

pulled apart and both looked out of the window. Standing on the pavement, separated from us by nothing more than a sheet of plate glass, were Danielle the dressmaker, Thomas the doorman and half a dozen girls I did not recognise. They were all grinning and waving at us.

My leg felt damp. I looked down and discovered that I had knocked over the remains of my coffee. There was a dark, spreading stain on my trouser leg.

A wise man once said that in every day of glorious sunshine there is always at least one small cloud. I was so happy basking in the sunshine that I didn't care about the cloud in the slightest.

## ~ Chapter Forty Seven ~

'What on earth have you got there?' I asked Albert, when Felicity and I walked into the Fag and Ferret a few hours later. Albert, looked at me, raised an eyebrow and lifted an envelope from the bar counter in front of him. He examined the envelope carefully, holding it up to the light and checking both sides. 'I think it's an envelope,' he said at last. 'It may have a letter inside it.'

'OK. It was a pretty stupid question,' I said. 'But where have they all come from?' Several hundred letters were piled on the bar counter. And at the base of Albert's stool there was a mail sack – filled almost to the brim with more letters.

'They're from readers,' explained Albert. 'The paper sent them to me. They came in after my last column.' He flicked at the pile of the letters on the counter in front of him.

'There are heaps more back at the hotel,' said Lucie, who was sitting beside Albert. 'The people in London had to send the sacks over by a special courier.'

'What on earth do all those people want?'

'Dunno,' said Albert, with a shrug. 'I haven't started opening them yet.'

'Maybe they've all written to say how sorry they are that you're leaving the paper?' I suggested.

'That's what the editor thinks,' said Albert. 'He wants me to stay. No one can remember the paper getting so much mail about anything before.'

'That's brilliant!' said Felicity.

'Have you accepted?' I asked him, selfishly thinking that this would mean that we would be able to go ahead with the magazine after all.

'We're negotiating,' said Albert, with a smile. 'They've already agreed that I don't have to work in London.'

'Now Albert is negotiating a pay rise,' said Lucie. 'I'm very proud of him. As Margaret Thatcher once said: "Pennies do not come here from heaven. They have to be earned here on earth".'

'How on earth are you going to answer all these letters?' Felicity asked him.

'I don't have the faintest idea,' confessed Albert, with a shrug. 'I usually get no more than a dozen letters a week. I dump the ones from the nutters and scribble postcards to the rest.'

'How many are there?' I asked him.

'I've just been trying to work it out,' said Albert. 'I reckon there are three thousand in this sack. And there are four more sacks back in my room. That's fifteen thousand. And they're still coming in.'

'Wow!' said Felicity. 'And I thought my mother got a lot of Christmas cards!'

'It will cost a fortune to buy postcards and stamps for fifteen thousand people,' said Lucie quietly.

Albert put his head in his hands. 'Perhaps we could just lose them,' he said.

'How are you going to lose so many letters?' asked Lucie.

'I'm always losing things,' said Albert. 'They fall out of my pocket. I leave them in cafés and in taxis.'

'I think someone would notice and come running after

you if you left fifteen thousand letters in a taxi,' I pointed out.

'Anyway, it will be more than fifteen thousand,' said Albert, with a sigh. 'The features editor in London told me that they're still pouring in.'

'Maybe you should start opening them,' suggested Felicity.

'I can't open all these!' said Albert. 'It'll take me for ever.' He rifled a hand through the letters.

'We'll all help you,' said Lucie. 'Aristotle said that a friend is a single soul dwelling in two bodies. Here we are one soul in four bodies.' She picked up a handful of letters and gave them to Felicity. Then she gave a handful to me and took a handful herself. She called the barman over. 'Do you have four knives we can borrow?'

The barman produced four knives from the cutlery box. Lucie handed them around. Albert looked at the knife she handed him, pulled a face and asked her what it was for.

'To use as a letter opener,' Lucie explained.

'Thank god for that,' he said, with feigned relief. 'I thought you were suggesting that we all commit ritual suicide.'

We started slitting open envelopes.

'There's a cheque in with this letter,' said Felicity.

'What for?' asked Albert, looking up.

'Twenty pounds,' replied Felicity.

'No, not how much, what's the cheque for?'

'I don't know yet,' said Felicity. 'I haven't read the letter.'

'Mine too contains a cheque,' said Lucie, in astonishment.

'How much?' asked Albert.

'Ten pounds,' replied Lucie.

'Good heavens!' said Albert. 'The readers must really love me.' Not surprisingly, he seemed pleased.

'Well, they do,' said Felicity, who had been busy reading two pages of tiny scrawl. 'But this one hasn't sent you
money just because she likes you.'

'So why has she sent me money then? Is she worried
that I might be starving to death – thrown out into the street
by an ungrateful editor?'

'She says she's sent you money because she was so sad
to read about Tony losing his money,' said Felicity, reading
on. 'She wants to invest in the new magazine you were planning to launch together.'

'So does this one!' said Lucie, holding up the letter which
had accompanied the cheque for £10. She skimmed through
the neatly typed letter. 'He says he'll send more when he can.'

'Good heavens!' said Albert, who had by now finished
opening the envelope he had taken from the pile he'd been
given. 'This woman has sent us a cheque for £50!'

'I've got a rather crumpled and worse for wear five
pound note,' I said, pleased to be able to contribute to the
fund and holding the note aloft.

'Splendid stuff!' said Albert. 'There's a change bureau
round the corner. We can swap that for francs and buy a
round of drinks with it.'

'You will not do any such thing!' said Lucie, sternly.
'These people aren't sending you money so that you can buy
drinks.'

'No? Everyone has to drink!'

'This is amazing,' said Felicity, who had been busy rip-
ping open envelopes. 'I've just opened three envelopes and
two of them have got cheques in!'

'If all these envelopes contain cheques or cash there
must be a fortune here!' said Albert.

'I hate to be really boring about this,' I said. 'But what
are we going to do? Do we have to send all this money back?
Can we keep it?'

'They all seem to be sending the money because they want to help with the new magazine,' said Lucie. 'I think you can use it!'

'I don't know,' I said. 'It doesn't seem right somehow.'

'I'm not very happy with it, either,' said Albert, gloomily. 'I feel like a bloody beggar.'

'There is another way to look at it,' said Felicity who, unlike the rest of us, had put the contents of the envelopes she had opened into a neat pile on the bar counter. We all looked at her and waited for her alternative view. 'We could consider all these donations as investments.'

'Investments?' said Albert.

'In what?' I asked.

'In the magazine, of course!' explained Felicity. 'You already have a company don't you?'

We agreed that we had.

'We could give people shares according to how much money they sent.'

'That sounds very complicated, 'said Albert.

'It isn't really,' said Felicity.

'But how do we decide how much the shares are worth?'

'We have to talk to the accountant who set up the company,' said Felicity. 'But, for example, if you and Tony want to keep 51% of the company you can decide to sell the other 49% of the shares to outside investors. It will involve a lot of paperwork and the administrative costs will be high, but if just half of these envelopes contain money – and judging by the envelopes we've opened the proportion is likely to be much higher than that – we could easily be talking about something in the region of £100,000. That's a million francs.'

Lucie whistled.

'That's serious money,' said Albert.

'Could we start a magazine with that much?' I asked him.

'We certainly could!' he said. 'We could start a very nice magazine with a million francs. But we need someone to organise it all. Who do we know who could set up a company and allot shares? It sounds like technical stuff to me. The closest I've ever been to corporate finance was buying shares when British Gas was privatised.'

'We've got Felicity!' I said. 'She's an accountant.'

Albert looked at me and then at her. 'Would you do it?'

'Set up a company for you?'

'And run it for us?'

Before Felicity could answer I put down the knife I was holding and reached across and took her hand. 'You don't have to say 'yes',' I told her.

'I'd love to help,' said Felicity. She looked at me and squeezed my hand. 'You're going to be busy,' she told me, with a smile. 'I'd like to be busy with you.'

'I want to help too,' said Lucie.

'You can,' Albert told her. 'We need a section dealing with Paris night life. Why don't you help Tony put it together?'

Lucie seemed delighted with that. 'But I want to do more,' she said. 'I want to invest!'

'But we've got all this money!' said Albert, waving his knife at the mail.

'You need more,' said Lucie. 'You need a little office somewhere. And you will have to pay for printing and for photographs. And then there is the telephone and the taxes on the office, and the distribution and the advertising to let people know that the magazine exists. And you will have to pay the contributors and the editor.'

We all looked at her. We knew she was right. A million francs sounded a lot of money. But the more money we had to start with the more we would be likely to succeed.

'First of all why don't we finish opening these envelopes?' said Lucie. 'Then we will talk!'

'Do you mind if I ask you something?' Albert said to me, as we all got back to slitting open envelopes.

'Of course not. Ask away.'

'When you came in this evening you looked like a cat who has just drunk a pint of cream.'

I looked at Felicity and smiled. 'Did I?'

'What's happened?' asked Albert.

'What makes you think that something's happened.'

'I know something has happened,' insisted Albert. He turned to Lucie. 'Didn't you notice it?'

'Certainly!' said Lucie. 'They both look very happy. I have never seen Felicity looking so beautiful and so radiant.'

I put down my knife and the envelope I was holding and took Felicity's hand. 'Shall I tell them?'

'I don't see why not,' she replied, blushing.

'Tell us what?' demanded Albert, laughing.

'We're getting married.'

Albert and Lucie, clearly surprised, exchanged glances and then responded with whoops of joy. Lucie kissed Felicity and then kissed me. Albert kissed Felicity and tried to kiss me. And then I borrowed 500 francs from Albert and bought two bottles of champagne.

The impromptu celebrations slowed things down considerably. It was a couple of hours before we started opening envelopes again.

# ~ Chapter Forty Eight ~

It took us several days to open and sort all the mail. We had opened all the envelopes by the end of the second evening but by then there were another four sacks of mail waiting to be opened. For a while the mail was coming in faster than we could open it. Fortunately, at the end of a week, the flow of mail slowed down considerably.

In the end Felicity's guess about the amount of money Albert's readers would send in proved to be over optimistic. It wasn't her fault. The first few envelopes we slit open had nearly all contained cheques but as we continued opening envelopes we found that only one in every seven or eight letters contained cheques, postal orders or money. Most of the rest contained simple good wishes. One or two, no more than half a dozen in total and all anonymous, were mildly uncomplimentary or downright rude, telling Albert that he was boring and opinionated and that they were glad he had gone. What they meant by this, of course, was that he had expressed opinions which did not match their own. Whenever possible we didn't show these to Albert. Far, far more readers, a thousand times more, thanked Albert for the pleasure he had given them over the years. I was touched by the comments I read and so, I know, was Albert. I don't think anyone had realised just how many hearts he had touched with his column. His simple honest style, his mischievous sense of humour and his ability to bare his soul and share his passions had won the hearts and minds of thousands of people whom he had never met.

By the time we'd finished opening and sorting the mail we had collected £29,746 in cheques, postal orders and cash. At Felicity's insistence Albert paid the cheques and the cash into a new bank account opened in the name of the company he had set up and which he and I jointly owned. The postal orders were sent back to England to be paid into a bank account there and then moved by electronic transfer to Paris, to the company's new account. Sending letters of acknowledgement to all the readers who had sent good wishes would have taken up all the money that had come in so Albert, who had by this time, successfully renegotiated his contract with the newspaper, wrote a piece for his column in which he thanked all the readers who had written to him.

He also explained that the people who had sent cheques or cash would be given shares in our new magazine. (In due course this brought a new flurry of mail from readers who wanted to invest in the magazine. When we'd counted their cheques we found that we had an additional £7,528 – mostly in contributions which varied between £20 and £50.)

'It's a great start,' said Felicity, speaking in her new role as unpaid Company Secretary. 'But even if we do everything on a shoestring £30,000 – roughly 300,000 French francs – isn't anywhere near enough capital with which to start a magazine.'

'I went to see my bank manager yesterday,' said Albert. 'On the strength of my new contract with the paper he'll lend me £10,000 to invest in the magazine.' He looked pleased with himself, like a conjuror who has just pulled off a difficult trick.

When I looked at Felicity I knew that in her heart she knew that this still wasn't enough money. I cursed Rosemonde, who had stolen my savings, and silently damned her for wrecking our dream. With my savings, Albert's loan and the funds which the readers had contributed we would have been very well-placed for our new venture.

'I want to invest too,' said Lucie, before there was time for any depression to set in. 'It's about time I retired from the business, and as Tennessee Williams wrote: "You can be young without money but you can't be old without it". I need somewhere sound to invest my savings.'

'You're going to retire?' said Albert, who seemed surprised but also pleased.

'I am.'

'That's wonderful!' said Albert. He put his arm around his girlfriend. I had long known how much he loved Lucie and I knew that although he had pretended that he didn't mind in the slightest it must have been difficult for him to deal with the job she did. There were tears in his eyes.

'And I mentioned the idea of the magazine to a few friends of mine,' Lucie continued. 'They're all keen to invest too – if you'd let them.'

'I don't mind in the slightest,' said Albert. He rubbed at his eyes, rather roughly. 'Do you mind?' he asked me.

'I certainly don't object,' I said, in turn, looking at Felicity, knowing that she wouldn't mind either, but for Lucie's sake, and Albert's sake, wanting her to say so.

'As Company Secretary I certainly don't object,' laughed Felicity. 'The more money we can raise the greater our chance of success.'

'You're going to retire completely?' Albert asked Lucie. He was clearly more interested in the fact that she was planning to give up her work than in the fact that she wanted to invest in our magazine. 'No more clients?' He loved her too much to have ever asked her to give up her work but he loved her enough for what she did to hurt.

'That's right,' said Lucie, with a smile. 'No more clients at all.'

'How...er...much are we talking about?' asked Felicity. 'How much do you want to invest?'

'I would like to invest 500,000 francs,' said Lucie. 'And four of my friends would each like to invest 100,000 francs. Is that acceptable?'

I was stunned. I hadn't realised that Lucie had saved so much money. 'We can't possibly let you invest that much,' said Felicity, shocked. 'It's far too risky. I'd feel terrible if the magazine failed and you lost all your money, especially now that you're planning to retire from business.'

Albert, smiling, put his arm around Lucie and gave her a kiss.

'The magazine isn't going to fail,' said Lucie. 'As the great Virgil almost said: "We can because we think we can.".' She smiled. 'Besides,' she added, 'as Lord Dewar said: "The road to success is filled with women pushing their husbands along.".' She kissed Albert and he blushed. 'And I'm not retiring from the world of business,' Lucie continued. 'I'm just exchanging one business for another. It's kind of you to be concerned about me but please don't worry – I'm not putting all my eggs into the one basket. The rest of my money I will leave invested in very boring bonds and blue chips. My bank manager has always been trying to persuade me to be a little more adventurous with my money. Now he will have his way at last. And when the magazine is a great success we will all become very, very rich.'

I pulled a piece of paper and a pencil stub out of my jacket pocket and started to do sums, trying to work out how much money we had for the magazine.

Felicity did the sums before me. 'With the money from

Albert's readers, the loan he has negotiated from his bank and with the money invested by Lucie and her friends we will have well over a million francs,' she said.

'Do you think that is enough to start a magazine?' I asked her.

'Absolutely,' said Felicity. 'Last night I spoke to a friend of mine who works for a French publisher. She says her company allocates between five and ten million francs for a new project.' She smiled and shrugged, as if this was quite absurd. 'But she admitted to me that with a little care a magazine could be launched with a million francs.'

'How on earth can we do it for a tenth of what they would spend?' I asked, a little worried.

'They have huge overheads,' explained Felicity. 'They pay top salaries and they have lots of men in suits who sit around in meetings trying to come up with marketing plans. Most of their money is spent on things we don't have to bother with. For example, we don't have to have posh offices in an expensive building just off the Champs Elysee.'

Albert and Lucie had been whispering together. Suddenly they kissed and then Albert cleared his throat and asked the barman to bring a bottle of chilled champagne and to put another on ice.

'I have an announcement to make,' he said. He paused dramatically, extending the suspense, then looked at Lucie and kissed her. 'Lucie and I are getting married,' he announced with great pride and joy.

Felicity and I looked at one another and then at the two of them. Felicity kissed Lucie and I put my arm around Albert and gave him a hug. Albert asked me to be his best man. I accepted on condition that he agreed to be mine.

'Do you fancy a double wedding?' Albert asked Felicity. 'It would, of course, produce a considerable saving in the costs of the reception.'

# ~ Chapter Forty Nine ~

Albert and Lucie and Felicity and I all got married exactly four weeks later.

We had by then found cheap offices to rent and plans for our new magazine were coming along very quickly. A friend of Lucie's had introduced us to the marketing director of a large French media conglomerate. We explained the magazine to him and he was immediately full of enthusiasm. He offered us an excellent distribution deal.

Publicly I said that I wanted to marry before things became too busy for us to take time off for honeymoons. But the truth, which I confessed to my fiancée, was that I simply didn't want to wait. I told Felicity that I wanted to marry her before she had time to come to her senses.

Felicity's parents were very good when we explained about Omar. I had been worried about their reaction but I think they were both too excited about their daughter getting married to have any hard feelings about the deception. They flew over to Paris four days before the double wedding.

'You had me fooled,' said Felicity's father. We were sitting in a café on one of the grand boulevards, while his wife and daughter spent the afternoon trying on dresses and then searching for handbags, shoes and hats to match them. Felicity still hadn't found her wedding dress. 'But I must admit that you gave me good advice.'

I looked at him, surprised and puzzled. I couldn't remember ever giving him any advice.

He leant closer, looked around, and whispered. 'I tried that golf tip you gave me,' he told me. He looked around to make sure that no one could overhear. 'It helped me take five shots off my handicap.'

'I'm p-p-p-pleased,' I managed to stutter.

'We must have a game sometime,' he said. 'I didn't like to suggest it before. But now that I know you aren't a professional...'

'That would be nice,' I agreed. 'In a while perhaps,' I added quickly.

'Why wait?' Gilbert asked. He was full of enthusiasm. 'I brought my clubs with me. Never travel without them. I've got a new three wood I'd rather like to show you. Titanium shaft but a genuine wooden head. Remarkable piece of work. Very expensive. Where do you play?'

I took a deep breath and confessed. 'I don't play golf at all I'm afraid.'

'Not at all?' I doubt if Gilbert could have been more startled if I'd told him that I didn't sleep.

'Not unless you count a game of crazy golf. But that was when I was 14.'

Gilbert ignored this. 'I think you'll find that with your new business responsibilities the ability to play golf would be a great asset,' he said, very seriously. 'I've done a lot of good deals out on the golf course.'

'Oh yes. Absolutely.'

'Get a chap relaxed, chit chat about this and that and by the time you're on the fifteenth green you can bring up the business.'

I nodded, wisely.

'We should get you kitted out with some clubs,' said Gilbert, taking out his wallet and putting a note on the table. He stood up. 'Where's the nearest golf shop?'

I thought for a moment. We were in the middle of Paris at the time. 'I think La Samaritaine has a pretty good golf department,' I told him, referring to one of the city's largest department stores.

'What if your wife and Felicity come back?' I asked him. 'Shouldn't we wait here for them? We said we would...'

Gilbert looked at his watch. 'Believe me,' he said, with the experience of a man who knew what he was talking about, 'they won't be back here for at least three hours.'

He was right. Felicity and her mother didn't get back to the café for another four hours.

By that time Gilbert had bought me a huge golf bag, fourteen clubs, two boxes of golf balls, a pair of golf shoes (with three sets of interchangeable spikes for different conditions), a huge, multicoloured golf umbrella, a waterproof jacket, a pair of waterproof trousers, a woolly hat for wet weather, a peaked cap for sunny weather, a pair of sunglasses for very sunny weather, a pair of checked trousers, a jumper with a small logo of a golfer on the right breast, a box of assorted wooden tees, a golf glove for my left hand, a device for repairing pitch marks should my ball ever land on the green, a lightweight, easily folded golf trolley, a sponge for wiping my balls, a special towel for wiping my hands and clubs, a card holder with a small pencil attached and an extendable ball retriever for picking balls out of ditches and streams.

The two of us had to carry this mass of equipment through the middle of Paris (the owner of the one empty taxi we had found had taken one look at our parcels and then sped off in alarm).

'I'm sorry I'm late, darling,' said Felicity, when she and

her mother finally appeared. Even before they had sat down Gilbert had ordered two pots of tea and half a dozen croissants. Felicity was empty handed. Her mother was carrying one small carrier bag.

'Did you find anything?' I asked.

'Mum bought some gloves,' said Felicity. 'But I didn't see anything I liked. We're going to have another look tomorrow.' She looked around us, at the golf bag, the golf clubs, the trolley and the huge pile of parcels. 'Have you been shopping?' she asked me.

'I'm going to learn to play golf,' I told her.

'That's lovely darling,' she replied, squeezing my hand in a very affectionate way. 'Can I come and watch you practise?' She thought of something. 'Hey, wouldn't it be funny if you got so good that you really did turn professional?'

'I don't think that's very likely,' I warned her. 'I'm a bit too old. And, besides, I've never been any good at ball games.'

'But you never know!' insisted Felicity. 'That would be marvellous wouldn't it? You could play on the professional circuit as 'Omar' couldn't you?'

'I really don't think it's very likely,' I pointed out again. 'Could you really not find a dress you like?'

I was getting worried. We were getting married in three days and Felicity still hadn't found a dress.

'Oh don't worry about it,' she said, remarkably offhand about the whole thing. 'I'm sure I'll eventually find something I like.'

# ~ Chapter Fifty ~

Felicity fooled me right up until the end.

The day before we were due to get married she asked me if I had a jumper she could borrow.

'What sort of jumper?' I asked her, surprised.

'Oh, I don't mind,' she replied. 'Something long enough to be decent.'

'Why on earth do you want to borrow a jumper?' I asked, genuinely puzzled.

'I thought it would make a nice wedding outfit,' she replied, keeping a straight face so well that I was quite convinced that she was serious. 'It would be something unusual. If you have an old, blue jumper that would be even better. Something old, something borrowed and something blue. I'll wear new underwear.'

I was frantic. 'You can't wear one of my old jumpers!' I told her. 'Lucie will be wearing an amazing dress. Albert told me that she had it made by a friend who works as a dressmaker. You'll be upset if you turn up in an old jumper and she's wearing a beautiful dress.'

For myself I didn't care what Felicity wore. As far as I was concerned she would be the most beautiful woman in the world if she'd turned up wearing blue dungarees, a woolly hat and a pair of oversized muddy Wellington boots. But the little I knew about women convinced me that she would care very much about looking her best.

She put her arm around me and kissed me. 'You are sweet to worry about me,' she said quietly. 'Please don't worry. Everything is going to be absolutely fine.'

'Honest?'

'Honest.' She smiled.

'OK.'

I tried to sound content but in my heart I still wasn't entirely satisfied.

Part of the problem was that I didn't have any money to give Felicity for a dress. At Albert's insistence I was now receiving a small salary from the magazine so I wasn't broke. But I had insisted on taking only enough to pay my basic living costs. If the magazine succeeded my share of the company would ensure that I became rich. Meanwhile I wanted to make sure that the magazine had the very best chance of succeeding. And I knew that the best way to do that was to make sure that as much money as possible was spent on making the magazine look good and on getting it seen by as many people as possible.

Our rather straightened circumstances would improve after the wedding when I moved out of my tiny apartment and into Felicity's (which was considerably larger than mine and which had no plumbing problems and, therefore, no need for a plumber).

But in the meantime, although Felicity was reasonably well paid, we weren't exactly flush with money. It had, therefore, been with some relief that I had accepted Felicity's parents offer to pay for the wedding, including the costs of our share of the reception.

Actually, it wasn't so much of an offer as an insistence. 'The bride's father traditionally pays for the wedding,' Gilbert had told me in a manner which dared me to defy him. 'And I'm a very traditional sort of fellow.' I knew that Gilbert's offer to pay for our wedding had included the cost of a dress (he had even insisted on paying for the cost of my hiring a morning suit) so I didn't really understand why Felicity hadn't found something expensive, made of a good deal of silk and lace.

In the end it turned out that I had, of course, worried quite unnecessarily.

I had forgotten that one of Felicity's best friends at Le Lapin Fou was Danielle, the dressmaker.

When Felicity and her mother had pretended to be trying on dresses in Printemps and Galeries Lafayette they had been having a fitting with Danielle. And Danielle had designed and made the most beautiful wedding dress I'd ever seen.

The four of us got married in the best kept secret in Paris: the Basilique Ste-Clotilde.

As I stood in the church and watched Felicity walking up the aisle towards me, looking like a fairy Princess and escorted by a justifiably proud father, with the church packed with her friends from Le Lapin Fou and Lucie's friends from the Rue St Denis, I couldn't help thinking how much my life had changed in such a short time.

'He'll be back in six months,' Ethel had said to Jack at my garage sale. It's too late for him to start again.'

I sent Ethel a postcard to let her know that she was wrong.

It's never too late to start again.

*Other books by Vernon Coleman*

# The Bilbury Chronicles

A young doctor arrives to begin work in the small village of Bilbury. This picturesque hamlet is home to some memorable characters who have many a tale to tell, and Vernon Coleman weaves together a superb story full of humour and anecdotes. The Bilbury books will transport you back to the days of old-fashioned, traditional village life where you never needed to lock your door, and when a helping hand was only ever a moment away. The first novel in the series: other titles include *Bilbury Grange*, *The Bilbury Revels*, *Bilbury Country* and *Bilbury Pie*.

*"I am just putting pen to paper to say how very much I enjoyed The Bilbury Chronicles. I just can't wait to read the others."*
(Mrs K., Cambs)

*"...a real delight from cover to cover. As the first in a series it holds out the promise of entertaining things to come"*
(Daily Examiner)

*"The Bilbury novels are just what I've been looking for. They are a pleasure to read over and over again."*
(Mrs C., Lancs)

Price £12.95 (hardback)

Published by Chilton Designs
Order from Publishing House • Trinity Place • Barnstaple •
Devon EX32 9HJ • England
Telephone 01271 328892 • Fax 01271 328768

# The Village Cricket Tour

This superb novel tells the story of a team of amateur cricketers who spend two weeks of their summer holidays on tour in the West Country. It proves to be a most eventful fortnight full of mishaps and adventures as the cricketers play their way around the picturesque coastline of Devon and Cornwall.

*"The only word to describe (this book) is hilarious. It is the funniest book about cricket that I have ever read. In fact it is the funniest book I have read since Three Men in a Boat."*
(Chronicle & Echo)

*"I enjoyed it immensely. He has succeeded in writing a book that will entertain, a book that will amuse and warm the cockles of tired old hearts."* (Peter Tinniswood, Punch)

*"His powers of observation combine with his penchant for brilliant word pictures to create a most delightful book ... a first class example of humorous adventures in the West Country"*
(Sunday Independent)

'*The Village Cricket Tour has provided me with much amusement and a great deal of pleasure.*'
(Mr A., Canada)

Price £12.95 (hardback)

Published by Chilton Designs
Order from Publishing House • Trinity Place • Barnstaple •
Devon EX32 9HJ • England
Telephone 01271 328892 • Fax 01271 328768

*Other books by Vernon Coleman*

# The Man Who Inherited a Golf Course

Trevor Dukinfield, the hero of this novel, wakes up one morning to discover that he is the owner of his very own golf club – fairways, bunkers, clubhouse and all.

This unexpected present lands in Trevor's lap as a result of a distant uncle's will which he discovers, to his dismay, contains several surprising clauses. To keep the club he must win an important match – and he's never played a round of golf in his life!

*"This scenario is tailor made for Vernon Coleman's light and amusing anecdotes about country life and pursuits.*
*His fans will lap it up."*
(Sunday Independent)

*"Hugely enjoyable, in the best tradition of British comic writing."*
(Evening Chrinicle)

*"Light hearted entertainment ... very readable."*
(Golf World)

Price £12.95 (hardback)

Published by Chilton Designs
Order from Publishing House • Trinity Place • Barnstaple •
Devon EX32 9HJ • England
Telephone 01271 328892 • Fax 01271 328768

# Mrs Caldicot's Cabbage War

Thelma Caldicot was married to her husband for thirty dull and boring years. The marriage could not have been described as fulfilling in any way, shape of form, but she stuck it out in her usual uncomplaining and subservient way. Then, one afternoon two police officers knocked on her door to bring her some news that was to radically change her life.

Mrs Caldicot's Cabbage War is the poignant, warm and often funny story of an ordinary woman who, after being pushed around by other people for most of her life, finally decides to stand up for herself.

*"Thank you so much for Mrs Caldicot's Cabbage War.
All your books are great."*
(Mrs N., Surrey)

*"... quite hilarious and my sort of reading."*
(Mrs C., Darwen)

*"A splendid relaxing read."*
(Sunday Independent)

Price £12.95 (hardback)

Published by Chilton Designs
Order from Publishing House • Trinity Place • Barnstaple •
Devon EX32 9HJ • England
Telephone 01271 328892 • Fax 01271 328768

For a catalogue of Vernon Coleman's books
please write to:

Publishing House
Trinity Place
Barnstaple
Devon EX32 9HJ
England

| | |
|---|---|
| Telephone | 01271 328892 |
| Fax | 01271 328768 |

*Outside the UK:*

| | |
|---|---|
| Telephone | +44 1271 328892 |
| Fax | +44 1271 328768 |

*Or visit our websites:*

www.vernoncoleman.com
www.lookingforapresent.com
www.makeyourselfbetter.net